THE CRIES OF INNOCENTS

Steven Allen Fleischmann

This is a work of fiction. All of the characters, organizations, and events portrayed are either products of the author's imagination or are used fictitiously.

Printed in the United States of America
ISBN 10: 1494337290
ISBN 13: 9781494337292 (Paperback)
LCCN: 2013922289
CreateSpace Independent Publishing Platform
North Charleston, South Carolina

This book is dedicated to
my sister, who was pure of heart and died too soon;
my father, whom to this day I have no memory of;
my mother, who lived a hard life and always did her best;
my son, who has made me smile every day
since the day he was born;
and most of all,
to my wife, who has always had
more confidence in me
than I've ever had in myself;
and who makes my life worth living.

ACKNOWLEDGMENTS

After eight years of what can only be referred to as the most creatively exhilarating time of my life, *The Cries of Innocents* is done. I would like to thank my family and friends, for whom there are no words expressive enough to convey my everlasting appreciation of their support throughout this multi-year process.

Also, a special thanks needs to go out to my longtime friend and graphic designer, Greg Bishop, who, with his incredible talent and patience, took the cover design which I indelibly had etched in my mind, and brought it to life on the computer screen, and then, onto the printed page.

AUTHOR'S INVITATION

Darkness to some brings a peaceful night of pleasant dreams. To others, darkness represents the omnipresent danger of delving into areas best left repressed.

There are many forms of darkness.
The **darkness of night**—the absence of light, obscuring the hideous deeds that evil men do.
Darkness of the soul—the unfathomable depths to which some men will succumb to feed their own desires and ambitions.
The **darkness of emptiness**—an abyss filled with void memories, too painful to remember, best left in the cold obscurity of blackness.
The **darkness of shame and guilt**—an internal parasite that eats away at the goodness within, and renders its victims hopeless of redemption.
And last, but not least,
the **darkness of undesired, yet uncontrollable urges**—feelings and acts that would repulse you on any day of your life, except today.

You are cordially invited to venture into the dark hallways of Ryan Cain's mind, as the tormented son of a holocaust survivor struggles with his father's physical and mental deterioration, and the possibility that he himself might, unknowingly, be a serial killer.
Tread carefully however,
for in the darkness lurk atrocities . . . real or imagined,
that have driven many a soul to the brink of insanity.

June 10, 1956
Beach Street

INVISIBLE AS THE air they breathe.

Nobody knows these five boys. If they disappeared from the face of the earth, their absence would go unnoticed. Emotionally malnourished nine-year-olds are like discarded seedlings unable to take root without proper nurturing or cultivation. Each strives to attain the necessary nutrients to sustain his own life, while cautiously sharing what is left with the others in his garden.

The castaways have bickered for years, never knowing, or caring to ask, each other's names. They fight like siblings, over nothing and everything, and then forgive each other by day's end for whatever is said.

As they sit on the warm carpet of their private beach, silky grains of sand funnel between their toes providing a calming therapy for their harsh lives. They liken themselves to the breaking waves, smashing into immovable walls of jagged rock, always returning for more.

If one is wounded, they all bleed. They've become insepa-rable, these blood brothers. Each able to finish the other's sen-tences, read the other's thoughts, and even pass for one another, if the light shines dim enough.

"Sometimes, I feel like doing bad things to him."

"Cut him some slack. He's been through a lotta bad stuff."

"So, does he have to share it with us? Doesn't he have any grown-ups he can talk to?"

"It's sad. I can't even look at him."

"Take a look at us. We're losers and he made us this way. Who invited him into our private place? I don't feel sorry for him. I hate him. I wish he'd die already. Hey idiot, are you writ-ing this stuff down?"

"Of course dumb ass, that's what I do."

"Are you crazy? You can't put what we're saying on paper. Gimme that."

An ominous voice breaches their solace. "Bring me Ryan. I must speak to my son. Bring Ryan to me. Now."

"Fuck, not again. Leave the kid alone, you big bully."

"Yeah," chime the others in unison.

No sooner does the leader of the group stand in acknowl-edgment of the voice, than he vanishes.

"Where is he? Where'd he go? Is he coming back?"

"How should we know?"

"Maybe he's in trouble. Let's go find him."

"If we're gonna look for him, we'll need to call him some-thing. He needs a name."

The boys sit in silence, stumped by the challenge.

"A name? We never needed names before."

One of the boys jumps to his feet.

"Lazarus . . . returner from the dead, that's what we'll call him. If anyone can come back, it's him. I mean, Lazarus."

"Maybe we should all have names. Names that describe us."

"Okay, you guys can be Dipshit, Asshole and Douche Bag. I'll be Sir."

"Shut up, you jerk. This is serious. If he doesn't come back we'll probably end up killing each other. He's the only one of us we all like."

Again, the disturbing voice interrupts their petty nonsense. "Blood, torture, dismemberment, Nazis, they're coming." The boys cover their ears, trying to drown out the words of the unseen source. They know the voice only too well, its tone, its inflection. It has always brought fear to their hearts, but now it has crossed the fine line separating bad judgment from abuse. No matter how hard they try to deflect the words, they worm inward, through their ear canals, taking root in their souls.

A chilling gust douses the foursome with a heavy spray of the ocean's salty mist. The inevitable storm has begun. Nothing will ever be the same for the newly baptized Loner, Watcher, Writer and Optimist.

"Hello. Can anyone hear me? Where am I?" Lazarus cries. "I've been taken. I don't know where I am, but it's cold. Really, really cold. And dark. I don't like it here. I don't see any way out. Please answer if you can hear me. I'm scared."

***

Twelve years later . . .

Morning:

His cell is dark. Not peaceful dark. Disturbing, claustrophobic dark. The kind of dark that threatens to swallow you whole.

There are no windows, no pictures. No distractions from the endless hours of loneliness. Visitors are forbidden.

The screams in his head grow louder. Lazarus spreads his fingers wide, applying pressure to both sides of his skull, attempting to prevent its detonation into a million pieces. *How do you erase nightmares? Silence the cries?*

He stares into the nothingness that surrounds him. *What's happened to my life? I was once a boy enjoying a child's simple pleasures. I had friends. Or was that someone else? I'm not sure anymore.*

"Talk to me, you son-of-a-bitch," he cries out, knowing there will be no response. "Why have I been taken prisoner? Why can't I get these terrible images out of my head? What is it you want? I know you can hear me. Show yourself. Confront me, you coward."

In the silence, he closes his eyes, reliving his days on the pristine sands of Beach Street with his four 'brothers.' *What's happened to them? Can they possibly still be searching for me? Will I ever see them again? And, the boy named Ryan, I'm afraid to think of what's become of him.*

PART I
THE DARKNESS

"Monsters are real, and ghosts are real too.
They live inside us and sometimes, they win."
—Stephen King—

CHAPTER 1
April 17, 1968
Upper Manhattan

THE SELF-ANOINTED "Lord" of Fort Tryon Park stood poised atop the hillside. His mid-length, reddish-brown hair blew in the wind, exposing his chiseled features. Piercing green eyes and an auburn five o'clock-shadow provided a ruggedness that made girls weak in the knees. Derek Vespers, age twenty-two, loomed ominous at six-foot-two with the body of an athlete, the stature of a Greek god, and the guile of a con man.

A three-inch scar, his only physical imperfection, ran through his left eyebrow and extended halfway down his cheek. Somehow, as the gods would have it, the blemish seemed to intensify his animal magnetism. He carried the look of a conquering Viking displaced in time.

Vespers ran his fingertips along the full length of his scar, a self-conscious habit he'd developed since sustaining the blemish three years earlier. He thought it a sign of weakness that read:

Hey, look at me; I got my ass kicked by some loser. Vulnerability contradicted the invincible persona Vespers worked so hard to portray. For months he'd schemed, *when the right moment presents itself, that son-of-a-bitch will pay for what he's done.*

When the opportunity arose, a revenge-driven Vespers blindsided his perceived nemesis with a baseball bat. Both, the loser's skull, and dreams, lay fractured in a dark alleyway.

Whenever the scar started to itch, Vespers thought of his once-vital adversary, hospitalized and in a coma. The itch always went away.

CHAPTER 2
April 17, 1968

Morning:

THE EXPLOSION INSIDE the Loner's skull radiated like a cannon firing upon his soul, his head ready to burst at any moment. The sight of '*his angel*' embraced by the arms of '*the Devil*' ignited more pain than he could bear.

"No, no, no, no. Please, no," he prayed to a god he didn't really know he believed in.

Haunted by his childhood, the Loner considered himself a mere shadow of who he once hoped to be. All he aspired to now was to be left alone. No expectations. No one to disappoint.

He stood motionless, hands buried deep within his pockets, wondering, *what kind of God would allow this to happen?* Vespers left arm hung over the shoulders of the most beautiful girl the Loner had ever seen, his fingertips lingering inches from her perfect breasts. From afar, the Loner had often admired the *now-endangered angel*, knowing full-well he would never actually meet her. If, by chance, she'd ever look in his direction, he'd quickly turn away, too insecure to maintain eye contact for even an instant.

The Loner lived up to his moniker—present yet invisible, unskilled in social graces, destined to roam the streets, a mere observer of other peoples' lives. He cursed his own cowardice for not having the courage to warn his *angel* of Vespers' true nature.

She was olive complexioned; a vision of beauty the Loner often fantasized about. He thought her name was Robin but wasn't certain. It didn't matter. To him she would be Robin. He cherished the moments when he'd catch a glimpse of her during his daily outings. A kind word from her would have been enough to occupy his dreams for a lifetime.

A few strands of Robin's shiny, long, black hair blew across her face, hiding in part her enormous, caring brown eyes and perfect white smile. She appeared so innocent, so beautiful, the mere sight of her made the Loner lightheaded. Kindness emanated from her eyes, and her smile made him smile too. Whenever she'd shrug her right shoulder ever so slightly toward her head, her eyes fluttering, the Loner thought he'd died and gone to heaven.

In his right hand, Vespers held a tightly rolled joint. If you wanted drugs, Vespers was the man. He took a pensive hit and repositioned the joint to the lips of the angel and then each of the other beauties surrounding him. For every one hit Vespers inhaled he initiated several long-drawn hits for each of the girls.

He took special care in the seamless positioning of the joint to their awaiting lips. He liked being in control of out-of-control females.

Why can't you see him for the lowlife predator he really is? the Loner thought, hoping to telepathically deliver his message into the angel's mind. *He's going to hurt you. Please, walk away. Why can't you see I'm the one who . . ., who . . .*

He couldn't bring himself to complete the thought.

What if she really can hear me?

Fear and self-loathing ripped at his heart.

I'm an idiot. She'd never have anything to do with a loser like me.

The Loner shriveled, his head bent in sorrow. With a tortured sense of despair he walked away.

***

Late afternoon:

Fools, all of them. The Writer jotted down notes as he spied Vespers' return to his lair. *The evil in him is so clear, and yet, these foolish girls don't see it until it's too late. Haven't they heard about the fifteen year old girl, Willow, who Vespers got pregnant four years ago and how, in her despair, she hung herself?*

The Writer shared two commonalities with the Loner. They both despised Derek Vespers, and both went by a unique moniker. The Writer's friends, all three of them, dubbed him "the

Writer," because he chronicled the existence of a select few individuals for a book he was working on. Not the most creative nickname he'd ever heard, nonetheless, to the point.

Among his peer group, the Writer seemed the most approachable, possessing patience, and insight. And, while not forthcoming in sharing much about himself, he displayed a sincere desire to listen to others.

It's time to leave, the Writer decided, sensing the oncoming presence of the Watcher, an angry soul whose company he found annoying. "We should do something about these neighborhood assholes," the Watcher had voiced to him on a previous occasion. Then, he'd mimicked shooting a gun with his thumb and forefinger, saying, "One pop between the eyes, and problem solved."

To the best of the Writer's knowledge the Watcher was all talk, and while prone to violent thoughts, the Writer didn't believe the Watcher would ever act upon his emotions.

Then again, what do I know, maybe today's the day?

***

Evening:

Impure thoughts of the evening's planned activities had Vespers eager with anticipation. He'd arranged for the Loner's *angel* to meet him back at his place for a night she'd not soon forget. His hand-picked lair provided the remote privacy he required.

Two years earlier, Vespers had approached the immigrant superintendent of 19026 Fort Washington Avenue, and painted a disturbing picture of just how dangerous this country could be for the super's two, young stepdaughters. "Of course, if I lived nearby, they'd be much safer. I could keep an eye on them for you," he said, feigning sincerity. "Why, only a year or two ago, a young girl was found hanged in one of the neighborhood basements. Suicide, they said. Young girls are so vulnerable." Vespers could be very persuasive.

The superintendent, Otto Sussman, had waited a long time to secure his highly-sought-after job. Trouble was the last thing he wanted. So, despite what his clenched fists were telling him, Sussman acquiesced to the not-so-subtle threat and allowed Vespers to move into the vacant sub-level apartment.

People came and went in perceived safety at all hours. Still, few tenants chose to venture the poorly lit basements at night, which allowed Vespers to enjoy uninterrupted privacy while entertaining whomever, and however he pleased.

At seven thirty, Vespers approached his den of visceral pleasures, full of himself, thinking about the drug-and-sex-filled evening he was about to embark upon. The star performer was due to arrive at eight thirty. Just enough time for Vespers to shower and prepare for the deviant sexual surprises he had planned. This beautiful, but naïve, girl would never succumb to his fantasies under normal conditions, but Vespers' drugs were laced with hallucinogens, and in no time at all she would become a puppet to his every depravity, as the others before her.

The cold, damp basement flashed like a disco with fluorescent lighting that flickered on and off. Twelve-inch overhead steel pipes ran in every direction. A grungy boiler room, dirty laundry cubicle, and several tenant storage facilities lined the walls. In the rear, concealed by a blockade of worthless old newspapers, was a small two-bedroom apartment, initially intended as the building superintendent's residence. However, in recent years, supers warranted more elegant living facilities and occupied premises on tenant apartment levels.

Vespers reached into his pocket to remove his keys, unaware of the figure standing in the shadows. The eight-inch hedge-trimmer blades pierced his flesh at the base of his skull. His head wrenched backward, eyes shut, mouth gaping wide. Blood oozed down his chin as his gurgled plea fell upon deaf ears. "Help me. Please, help me."

The assassin stared into his prey's eyes, twisting the blades deeper. *Good night, M'Lord.* Fully inserted, he gave the handles a vicious tug. Vespers' skull split like a walnut, pieces of bone flying in every direction. The smiling merchant of death took one long, final look before exiting.

CHAPTER 3
March 1961
Washington Heights

DEATH IS A game changer. While it frees its victim and releases the horrors of the deceased's tormented mind, it often relocates unaddressed issues to vulnerable family members.

Ryan Cain's life began its downward-spiral five years earlier, at the time of his father's passing. Physicians attributed Ryan's social, physical, and psychological deterioration to his father's demise. One doctor indelicately stated, "Childhood experiences sculpt each of us into whom we become, and Ryan Cain is a piece of clay dropped one too many times."

Overnight, the nine-year-old child was forced to transform from a timid boy into an anxiety-ridden man-child, trying to help his mother survive in a world ready to gobble her and her family up. Memories of the first nine years of his life had been taken hostage and held somewhere, deep within his mind. Only one partial memory, desperately seeking to find its way back to consciousness, had averted captivity. Something his father had told him over and over again. Incoherent words scrambling about, like individual links of a disassembled chain trying to reconnect.

The alarm clock rattled its annoying cry. Ryan awoke from his troubled sleep, curled under his blanket, clutching at his worn pillow. "Stop, let me go," he shouted, flailing his arms to ward off the demons of his nightmare.

Calmed back to reality, Ryan jumped out of bed and removed his pajamas. He avoided looking in the full-length mirror which hung on the back side of the bathroom door. He hated the sight of the psoriatic patches that ravished his arms and legs, *the creeping crud*, as the kids at school referred to it. He threw on yesterday's underwear, jeans, and long-sleeve flannel shirt, laced his high tops and was ready to go. Lesions covered, only his flake-filled hair remained for the other kids to taunt him about. *Not so bad. I can live with that.*

No shower, no brushing his hair or teeth. A cold splash of water on his face, and Ryan readied himself for another day that couldn't end soon enough. He grabbed the bag-lunch from the refrigerator that his mom always prepared the night before.

Exiting the doorway, Ryan heard his mother, Regine, call out, reminding him to come straight home from school. Gunther Heber, the building superintendent, was coming over at three thirty to fix the windows that stuck, the ceiling that leaked, and the toilet that wouldn't flush.

"Thank God for Gunther," Regine would often say. It seemed to Ryan, that Gunther spent more time in their apartment than they did, always fixing one thing or another.

Passing Gunther on his way out of the building Ryan confirmed that he'd see him later.

It had become routine. "Nobody's-dog" poked his scruffy head from the alleyway. His tail slapped the air at the sight of the boy. Ryan knelt, ruffled the tufts of the down-on-his-luck pooch's head and fed him half of his sandwich. "Here ya go boy, peanut butter." Both their favorites. Once the pup finished lapping up the sticky residue from his benefactor's hands, Ryan kissed the terrier's head and readied himself to meet his dreaded new day in hell. "Gotta go now. See ya tomorrow."

CHAPTER 4

January 1962

RYAN HAD NEVER killed anyone. At least, not that he knew of.

Why are these bloody images taking over my dreams? First it was once a month, then once a week, and now, almost every night. I don't want these nightmares, or the cries that accompany them, entering my mind anymore. What's happening to me? What did I do to create these horrors? I wish I could remember.

As his dreams became more vivid, more graphic, and more violent; Ryan prayed no one would ever make him angry enough to find out what he was capable of.

***

Ryan turned fifteen. He was slight of build and one of the shortest kids in school. Bullies found him easy prey, and insensitive kids still taunted him. When his few friends started dating and going to parties, Ryan felt more alone than ever.

"Hey loser, get off of our block. We don't allow freaks on our street," Derek Vespers, the leader of the neighborhood 'cool guys' shouted. Ryan kept walking. *What a bunch of assholes.*

***

Ryan clung to his one joy in life . . . baseball. Baseball provided a reason for living. It was the crutch that held him up, while the rest of life tried to pull him down.

A third-baseman requires three things: fast reflexes, the ability to backhand balls hit down the line, and, "no fear" of hard-hit line drives. Those were Ryan's gifts, and he played them for all they were worth. The small parcel known as third base, or "the-hot-corner," was Ryan's "heaven on earth."

Ryan came into the world with a congenital deformity, leaving the bones in his left forearm anatomically reversed. In lay terms, that meant he couldn't rotate his left hand palm side up, the way everyone else did. What he could do though, was rotate his arm in a backhand position better than anyone else alive.

While doctors called Ryan's unusual bone configuration a deformity, anyone who watched him play third base called it friggin' cool.

Already situated at his position, Ryan shouted, "Let's get started. I got third." *Here, I'm just one of the guys.*

"Hey batta, batta, batta," Ryan taunted his opponents, trying to lure them into hitting his way. When playing third base, Ryan was referred to as a human vacuum. When people said, "Ryan sucks," it was in praise of his ability to ensnare any ball hit his way. Off the field—well, the phrase wasn't quite so complimentary.

Ryan could hear the players in the opposing team's dugout.

"Holy shit, did you see the play that kid just made? How'd he do that?"

"Luck," another player responded.

Ryan looked over, smiling. *Hit my way and watch me get lucky a few more times.*

They did. And he did.

"Hey, great game kid," one of the opposing players called out.

Such a small gesture, yet it would make Ryan feel good about himself for days.

"Thanks, you too," he responded in a hushed whisper, unused to compliments.

Nine innings always went by too quickly, but like a starving sparrow, Ryan learned to relish whatever crumbs life would feed him.

His esteemed status at third-base had taught him a valuable lesson. *A negative really can be turned into a positive.* He often reflected on that thought, as he had more than his fair share of negatives to convert.

On his way home he replayed the words still fresh in his mind. "Hey, great game kid." *Maybe tonight I'll be able to dream about my day on the field?*

CHAPTER 5

January 1921 – March 25, 1933
Hitler's "Hanussen Years"

THROUGHOUT THE EARLY TWENTIES, Adolf Hitler took lessons in public speaking and mass psychology from a man named Erik Jan Hanussen. During the early stages of Hitler's movement, Hanussen's visions foresaw the possibility of Hitler becoming the great leader who would reunite a crumbling Germany.

In response to his overwhelming success in the public speaking and psychological arenas, greatly attributable to Hanussen's tutelage, Hitler opened his mind to Hanussen's astrological and fortune telling beliefs. Over time, Hanussen became renowned as Hitler's clairvoyant, "the Prophet of the Third Reich." Hitler wouldn't make any important decisions without first confirming the ultimate success of his tactics with Hanussen.

In March 1932, Hanussen decreed, "I see victory for you. You cannot be stopped. You will become Reich Chancellor of Germany within one year's time."

Hitler proclaimed Hanussen *the oracle of the ages*, the most revered clairvoyant since Nostradamus. Over the next year, Hitler consulted with Hanussen daily. Hitler was an addict and Hanussen's prophecies his drug of choice.

On February 26, 1933 Hanussen stated that in his vision he'd seen "a great house" in flames. Hours later, the Reichstag burned to the ground. German communists took the blame for the fire, paving the path for the suspension of all civil liberties, while the consolidation of power fell to Adolf Hitler.

***

On March 25, 1933, as on so many occasions before, Hitler summoned Erik Jan Hanussen.

Son-of-a-bitch, how could he do this to me? I gave the man respect. What will others think if they find out? Without saying a word, after Hanussen entered the room, Hitler drew his revolver, pointed his weapon, and placed one clean shot through Hanussen's heart.

For good measure, he fired one more round into his head.

A most charitable gesture, Hitler mused, given the fact he'd just learned of Hanussen's Jewish heritage. The most renowned oracle since Nostradamus lay dead at Hitler's feet, blood spreading like a huge ink blot across his chest.

Hitler bent over his former mentor, retrieving his possessions. Inside the left-breast pocket of Hanussen's jacket, drenched in blood, resided an indecipherable, folded piece of parchment containing six quatrains, entitled "The Fate of . . .

Hitler's mind raced. He stood frozen, for what seemed like hours. Lifting Hanussen's torso by his lapels, he shouted, "Wake up, you Jew bastard. What does this say?"

Fists clenched, white knuckles throbbing, Hitler threw his one-time friend to the ground, kicking him over and over. Hanussen was never seen again. His lifeless body lay rotting in a field on the outskirts of Berlin.

CHAPTER 6

April 1933

THE DEAD MAN wouldn't shut up. Speaking in whispers he exacted his revenge. "The Fate of...

Hitler awoke in a pool of sweat. "Speak up you bastard. I can't hear you," he commanded his apparition. The life-like vision taunted his every dream. To no avail he closed his eyes, trying to return to Erik Jan Hanussen's recitation of the blemished parchment quatrains.

Consumed by a need to replace his former mentor, Hitler had sought the help of a group called the Munich Astrologers, its members well-renowned for the accuracy of their uncanny prophecies. He hoped to use their predictions and premonitions to his full advantage, as he had Hanussen's. Still, they weren't Hanussen. *Damn him for being a Jew.*

Asleep again, Hitler heard Hanussen's anguished cries mutate into deranged laughter.

CHAPTER 7
May 12, 1965
Columbia Presbyterian Hospital

Morning:

ABDO BETARÉ STOOD a smidgen under six feet tall at a trim 165 pounds. His jet black hair, cropped close, and thin mustache enhanced his suave, tanned Mediterranean look. The expression in his deep set, mocha-brown eyes was a dead give-away to his compassionate heart. His relaxed demeanor put people at ease. It served him well in his profession as a child psychiatrist.

Abdo reflected back eighteen years. He recalled sitting in the very same hospital on a cold winter's day with Ryan's dad, awaiting Ryan's arrival. It was December 1946, when Sandor and Regine Cain celebrated the happiest moment of their lives, their son's birth. Truly a miracle, given that irreparable damage sustained years earlier all but eliminated the possibility of Sandor fathering a child.

It proved to be the first of two such miracles for the Cains. They would leave all the grief and horror of their earlier years behind, and relish in their bright new future. Abdo shared in their euphoria. *Those* were very happy days.

Today, as Abdo entered the Columbia Presbyterian Hospital intensive care unit, those moments seemed a million years ago.

Regine wept by Ryan's bedside. She'd known so much tragedy. *Why has God forsaken me? First Sandor. Then Willow. Now this.*

"Why did you let this happen?" she cried, raising her eyes to the heavens. "He's such a good boy. Hasn't he suffered enough?"

Ryan gave Regine's life meaning. Now he lay in a coma, the victim of an assault with a baseball bat. The irony did not go unnoticed by Abdo. The same instrument from which Ryan derived so much pleasure, had been used to obliterate his life.

He looked so fragile lying there; his face bruised, head bandaged, intravenous lines in both arms, and a breathing tube inserted down his throat. Regine was beyond consoling, but Abdo knew she would endure. Ever since he'd first met Regine, twenty-six years earlier, she'd proven herself an anchor that could hold steady throughout any storm.

Afternoon:

Abdo gazed down upon Ryan's motionless body. Life support monitors beeped, serving as metronomes in the concert of life and death. Images of Ryan's tragic childhood flashed through

Abdo's mind. He hoped beyond reason. *Perhaps, Ryan can once again beat the odds?*

Returning to his office, the daunting task of updating Ryan's case history awaited him. Abdo knew Ryan's medical resume by heart. An abbreviated synopsis stapled to the front of the constructed chart read.

Property of Dr. Abdo Betaré
"Patient: Ryan Cain"

1946: Doctors anticipate Ryan will have limited use of left hand and arm due to congenital birth defect.

Update 1952: Ryan proves physicians wrong. Has overcome almost all limitations.

1956: Ryan's father dies. Ryan loses childhood memories prior to time of funeral. Patient's singular memory is that his father told him something very important before dying.

1957: Ryan develops severe case of psoriasis. Specialists suggest memory loss and skin malady are attributable to trauma of his father's passing.

1957: Ryan demonstrates unpredictable mood swings. Passive, other times aggressive, often angry. *Need to follow-up.*

1961: Age fourteen, Ryan hit in eye with baseball. Tear in right pupil. Irreparable damage to retina. Diagnosis: *permanent blindness in right eye. No chance for sight recovery.*

Update: January 1962: Again, Ryan proves doctors wrong. Patient awakens to vision of light. Doctors reexamine. No medical explanation.

February 1962: Sight restored.

July 1962: "Ryan's Miracle." Ryan relates story of riding his new bicycle in Bennett Park. Swears he was about to die, heading full speed toward spiked fence. Patient indicates he closed his eyes, and after reopening them, found himself two blocks from where he'd started, going in a different direction, unscathed. I have suggested the possibility of a dream, or, that he simply turned and avoided collision without recollection. Nothing will convince Ryan this was not a miracle. Patient's mindset improved. Now believes he has purpose in life. Sees hope that he will survive whatever life throws at him.

1964: Ryan's younger sister, Willow, age fifteen, commits suicide by hanging. Willow three months pregnant. Ryan finds sister's body. Ryan deeply depressed. Harbors strong feelings of guilt. Seems to have secrets he won't talk about.

Abdo entered Ryan's current condition to the chart. *Is this to be Ryan's epitaph?*

CHAPTER 8
February 19, 1967
Hospice Center Coma Ward

NEAR THE DOOR of the hospice ward Regine sped past an elderly woman being comforted by the embrace of a young priest. They stood next to a body, covered with a sheet, awaiting transport to the morgue. Regine couldn't let her mind go to that dark place.

The coma ward consisted of two rows of eight beds, separated by draw-curtains. For twenty-one long months Regine sat by her son's side at every available moment, praying beyond hope for a miracle that would most likely never come.

No. Ryan's strong, and he needs me to be strong. He will survive. He always survives, she kept reminding herself.

Her eyes scanned the room. The silence was deafening. Visitors rarely, if ever, spoke to one another. What was there to say?

After rendering comfort to the grieving widow, the youthful priest approached Regine.

Regine tried to will the priest in another direction. *No. Walk away. Don't stop here. My Ryan is alive. You can't have him. Keep walking.* She thought it bad luck to have a clergyman visit Ryan's bedside.

Confronted by the man in black, she rose.

"I'm so sorry. I don't mean to disturb you," said the priest, sporting heavy stubble on his face. "I'm Father Patrick Flint."

Regine found Father Patrick's demeanor endearing, but she couldn't get the picture of the man on the gurney out of her head.

"I'm Regine Cain," she said, extending her hand to shake. "And this is my son, Ryan."

She noticed that Father Flint displayed difficulty extending his arm in response. "I'm sorry; are you hurt?" she inquired.

"No, no, please, don't concern yourself; it's nothing, merely a fateful reminder from my violent youth. Actually, it helps me to focus on where I've been, and where I'm going."

It appeared clear to Regine that the young, ruggedly handsome priest wanted nothing more than to ease the burden of her troubled soul.

"I wanted to let you know, I've seen you here many times before, and I've been saying a prayer for you, and your son, every night. I'm a few years older than Ryan. We met briefly several years ago. He's a fine young man, Mrs. Cain. In a strange way, your son gave me pause to reexamine my own misguided life, and helped turn it around. It wouldn't be an exaggeration to say that your son helped make me the man I am today. Please let me know if there is anything I can do for you, or your son."

Before Regine could ask what he meant by his unusual comments, Father Patrick Flint left the room.

Regine gently stroked Ryan's limp hand, wondering: What did he mean when he said *you* had influenced his life?

Trying to put Father Flint's visit out of her mind, Regine reached for the radio on the nightstand, searching for the Giants-Mets baseball game.

Ryan loved baseball. In particular, he loved the Giants, prior to their move from New York to San Francisco in 1957. Ryan couldn't get enough of Willie Mays, the "Say Hey" kid. He used to say, "Willie Mays could kick Mickey Mantle's butt."

Regine knew nothing about sports, so she would often wonder, who is Mickey Mantle, and why would Willie Mays want to kick his butt?

After the Giants moved away from New York, Ryan became a devoted Mets fan. Regine didn't know which team he would root for in this game, and then realized, that in his current state, it didn't make a difference.

Although she didn't think Ryan could hear anything, she fine-tuned the radio dial, just in case. Ryan would savor nothing more than a double-header, except for a double-header that went into extra innings. He could never get enough baseball.

Regine smiled, imagining her sweet boy enjoying the game in his mind. Removing two overworked knitting needles and a half-completed sweater, Regine continued her bedside vigil.

The cycle of rushing from home to work, and then to Ryan's bedside consumed her life.

As evening approached, the ballgames and post-game programs came to a close. Regine gathered her things for the sad trip home. She took her son's hand into her own, bent over, and kissed him on the forehead.

Walking away, Regine looked at Ryan and said, "I love you."

To her amazement, Ryan's lips moved ever so slightly. "I love you, too."

CHAPTER 9

February 20, 1967
Hospice Center Recovery Ward

THE ELEVATOR DOORS opened. Abdo had visited Ryan on several occasions over the past two years, but never before on a visit of hope or joy. When Regine called, he couldn't believe his ears. "He's awake, Abdo. He's awake." The words played over and over again in his head. His heart raced as he made his way toward Ryan's bedside. Once again Ryan had overcome insurmountable odds.

Following his visit, Abdo paused at another room. He'd made this same stop on many occasions. A symphony of beeps, pumps, and slurps beckoned his attention. A shrunken, gray, skeleton-of-a-man laid immobile, tubes attached to every limb. Life-support equipment lined the walls of his living tomb. A portrait of agony and torment, the man's ashen face bore a heavy keloid scar in the form of a "Star of David" etched into his forehead.

Nurses entered and exited the near-corpses' room with timed precision. They moved in and out within a matter of seconds. Upon prior observances, Abdo had never witnessed any attempt to make physical contact or verbal communication with the patient. This day was different.

He might not have noticed *her* either, except for the fact that the nurse holding the patient's hand, while whispering in his ear, appeared so hideously unattractive.

Abdo scolded himself for his petty observation. It wasn't like him to be judgmental. However, this woman's features— her squinty eyes, upturned nostrils and rotund-body, poised on short legs, gave her the appearance of a human "pig."

He couldn't put his finger on it. Something about this nurse, other than her demeanor, made his skin crawl. *She's a total stranger, yet she frightens me.* The last time he felt this kind of disturbing knot in the pit of his stomach was during the war, in 1939, when he was forced to flee for his life.

The hushed voice of a woman standing behind Abdo caught him off-guard as she summoned the unattractive nurse. "Gunda, was machst du? Mach schnell."

Turning her face from view, Nurse Gunda Schloss, as her name tag identified her, rose, straightened her uniform, and bulldozed her way past Abdo, nearly knocking him over. Her name tag fell to the floor. As the two women scurried off, he'd have sworn he heard her snort.

A morbid curiosity overcame Abdo. Picking up the lengthy chart, he read of the patient's unusual circumstances. A detailed

THE CRIES OF INNOCENTS

accounting disclosed Jewish descent. Abraham Lerner had possessed the foresight, and means, to flee Europe and escape Hitler's terror regime by emigrating and transferring his wealth to the United States in 1932, just months before Hitler's rise to power.

Reading on, Abdo realized that, coincidentally, it was in Washington Heights that Abraham Lerner was beaten and left for dead. Before fleeing the scene, his assailants took the time to carve a deep "Star of David" into his forehead, which in turn formed a star-shaped keloid defining his ancestry's plight.

Police follow-up stated . . . *Witness viewed incident from distance. Reported group of young men running away.*

In the end, authorities suspected that a hate group had ventured into the densely populated Jewish community, and Lerner found himself in the wrong place, at the wrong time.

The case remained unsolved.

***

People referred to Abraham Lerner as lucky, having fled Europe when he did. Doctors felt him lucky to have survived the night of his beating. Now, twenty-one years later, and still in a vegetative state, no one referred to Abraham Lerner as lucky anymore.

No friends or family could be found. He'd left no written instructions for such a situation, and possessed what appeared to be an endless flow of funds to provide for the ongoing support he required.

After being moved from facility to facility, the Jewish Federation heard of his condition and made arrangements for his care, until the eventual time of his death. No one ever expected he would last the night, let alone these many long years.

Looking at Abraham Lerner, Abdo could feel the pain of a thousand deaths reverberating inside this man's skull. His dark, staring eyes cried for death that wouldn't come. Abdo couldn't understand God's justification for letting one man suffer this much, but he knew it was not for him to make that kind of judgment. He was thankful no such fate awaited young Ryan Cain.

Leaving the hospital, Abdo retrieved the strange woman's name tag from his pocket.

He hoped to never see "Nurse Gunda Schloss" again.

CHAPTER 10
January 1968

RYAN HAD BEEN seeing Abdo for close to a year, trying to get a grip on where his life had been, and where it might be headed.

Upon awakening from his coma, Ryan weighed a scant hundred pounds. His coloring appeared anemic, yet to Abdo's surprise, Ryan's psoriatic lesions had gone into remission. Not one lesion occupied his body, not a single fleck on his scalp. Ryan's recuperative capabilities remained an enigma. It bode well for the possibility of a full recovery.

Months in rehab, relearning to walk, gaining weight, and exercising to strengthen atrophied muscles brought Ryan to his current state. On a superficial level Ryan was progressing at an incredible pace. Physically, Ryan was in the best shape of his life. Emotionally, Abdo still harbored concerns—the same concerns that troubled him prior to the assault.

Abdo sat at his desk, mulling over Ryan's updated case history. For the hundredth time, he scrutinized the most recent entries.

> May 12, 1965: Ryan assaulted with blunt object—possibly a baseball bat. Skull fractured. Multiple bones broken. Admitted to Columbia Presbyterian Hospital. In coma. Prognosis: Unfavorable.
>
> February 19, 1967: Ryan awakens from coma.

Reflecting on the overwhelming carnage inflicted upon the Cain family, Abdo vowed to do everything in his power to help them recover. Raising his pen, he began to write.

> January 23, 1968: Ryan's progress continues to amaze. He is six feet tall, a hundred and seventy pounds, and in excellent physical condition. My concerns lie within his psychological profile. He displays signs of depression and secrecy. I believe he harbors guilt over his sister's suicide. There are things he's not willing, or able, to talk about.
>
> Significant mood swings.
>
> He's sometimes sullen and passive, other times angry and aggressive. Hostility in his tone and use of profanity concern me. These changes not unexpected, given his history.

There is more here than meets the eye. I need to find out what's going on inside this poor boy's head.

CHAPTER 11

May 1968

THE WRITER STOOD at a crossroads.

What are you afraid of? Put up, or shut up. You've been taking notes for years. Do something with them. Are the others right about you? They think you're a loser and live in a fantasy world, like the Loner.

I'm not like the others. I'm going to be somebody. I'm going to make a difference.

Talk, talk, talk, I've heard it all before. If you don't do it now, you'll be a loser forever.

I'll show you. For better or worse, my book starts today.

Determined to prove himself, he started writing. His hand wouldn't stop. His mind worked quicker than the pen could dispense ink. Words describing the backdrop of his long-conceived novel poured onto the page.

Prologue

Turn on any local news station and you'll hear someone say, "I never would have thought he would do something like that," or, "He was always so quiet, so polite."

Every neighborhood, rich or poor, black or white, or anywhere in-between, shares one thing in common—a diversity of people. Kind people, generous people, depraved people, selfish people, religious people, introverts, extroverts, and yes, miscreants.

Thing is, it only takes one asshole to turn everyone's world upside-down.

Washington Heights is a beautiful, cultural, and seemingly safe place to live. It is a melting pot of nationalities that migrated to plant roots in a new country and live a healthy, wholesome lifestyle.

Primarily residential, the neighborhood hosts strips of commercial activity along 181st and 187th Streets, garnishing a full range of shops including groceries, restaurants, bakeries, drug stores, florists, and a full spectrum of specialty shops.

Life is good in Washington Heights. Most residents are oblivious to what they don't want to see. "See no evil, hear no evil, and therefore no evil exists," is the mantra of the times. It is the decade of peace and love.

In reality, though, evil and temptation exist everywhere. And where evil exists, there inevitably develops a need for an avenger. Someone to right the wrongs, to protect those who can't protect themselves, to punish those whom the police don't deem bad enough to warrant their attention. In these most unsettling months of 1968, through a strange and ironic twist of fate, destiny has anointed a most unlikely candidate to take on that role.

The Writer sat reading, and rereading, his creation. He'd never felt so proud of anything in his life, although it saddened him to think a neighborhood killer spurred his motivation to begin his new journey. *I can do this. I'm going to write a book.*

The Writer slept without disruption, dreaming up a title for his upcoming masterpiece.

CHAPTER 12
June 13, 1968

AT NIGHT, WHEN there are no noises to mercifully distract his ravaged mind, the Watcher sits in the darkness and contemplates the emptiness of his life. He has often considered the option of death, but has sworn to never succumb to its temptation.

He checks the time. *Not yet.*

The claustrophobic, six-by-eight room he occupies is a testimony to his pathetic existence. The chipped walls are barren and in need of a paint job. The mousetrap sitting on the cracked linoleum is vacant for the moment—but surely not for long.

An annoying rattle from the radiator invades his silence. The building's superintendent has been over several times to try and remedy the problem, but the endless beat goes on.

He checks the time again. *Is that fuckin' clock working?*

He and his mother share space and time, nothing else. He knows she loves him, but they live in their own separate worlds. No conversations, no newspapers, no books. There is nothing to stimulate thought in the vacuum he calls home. Speech and opinions had never been encouraged.

The Watcher shrivels in his matchbox of safety and solitude. He thinks, and waits. Soon it will be time to go out for his evening adventure. His palms are sweaty as he again peers toward the clock. *Almost time.*

Darkness has become his friend. As the clock's dial quivers toward nine p.m. the Watcher dons his black-hooded sweatshirt, looking forward to another evening with his unknown family of strangers.

Every building has an alleyway. Many afford gates or fences to discourage entry, while others portend easy access through side doors best left unopened. The Watcher knows them all. He's climbed every fence, scaled every wall and ventured through every doorway a hundred times. He's seen and heard things never intended for anyone on the other side of both, open and closed, doors and windows.

The Watcher harbors a plethora of information on both normal and dysfunctional human life forms. Families, lovers, wife-beaters, sadists . . . they all perform on his private stage. Time goes by too quickly as he prowls the neighborhood. He often thinks *he* should write a book. But then again, he doesn't have to. One of his brothers-in-survival is already doing that.

Where do the hours go? It's already time to head back. It's almost eleven, and he only has five minutes to return and meet with the others.

The "Quad," as they refer to themselves, meets at eleven o'clock every evening, and he's never late. These get-togethers are what keep him and his three compatriots sane.

The Watcher moves about the backstreets and alleyways like an Olympian on a track, in perfect stride.

He is the gold medalist in the darkest of events. He'll be there on time.

CHAPTER 13
June 14, 1968

THE WATCHER PACED. The Writer scribbled. *The Loner* daydreamed. And, *The Optimist* was late.

"Where's the damn Optimist?" grunted the Watcher with his usual impatience. "It's already after midnight."

"Don't worry, he'll be here," reassured the Writer.

"If he doesn't show up soon we'll start without him," the Watcher said in an authoritative tone.

"We can't do that," said the Loner with trepidation. "It takes all of us to have a meeting of the Quad. Those are the rules."

Four boys, four strangers, four friends . . . bonding in camaraderie to help each other survive and unravel their questionable fates. They'd selected the name 'Quad' because the circular entry to Fort Tryon Park was called the quad. *That quad* offered a teenage sanctuary where *they* appeared out of place. They relished the irony of naming themselves "*the Quad*," a group of four, where *everyone else* would be out of place. An aberrant ensemble of unique personalities, these outcasts shared a common hatred of neighborhood bullies. Their feelings toward each other were more complex.

The Watcher, the cynic of the group, refused to believe nice guys finished first. Still, he tolerated the Optimist. He thought him an unrealistic schmuck who wouldn't harm a fly. As for the Writer, the Watcher wished he'd stop asking so many questions. He felt sorry for the Loner. Nothing would ever distract him from his dream world. *Robin this, Robin that. Get it into your head, Robin ain't happening.*

The Writer loved all of these guys. Where else could he find such unique characters to profile for his book? They were so real. The Watcher, while annoying to be around, provided the angst and passion needed for his more brooding, darker character. The Loner provided the persona of the sympathetic hopeful. And, the Optimist provided the implausible reasoning for why all things would work out in the end.

The Optimist was reborn. He awoke one sunny morning with a new sense of purpose, believing he had something wonderful to accomplish, even though he did not yet know what it was. He held an unwavering faith that the Watcher would overcome his intense anger; the Writer would one day complete his novel; and the Loner would be united with the love of his life and live-happily-ever-after. The Watcher almost puked the first time the Optimist shared his insights.

The Loner remained a zombie. Sad, insecure, dejected.

"Sorry, I'm late," the Optimist apologized.

"Halleluiah, Captain Sunshine is here, let's get started," the Watcher muttered.

The Quad had been meeting every night for almost two months. As usual, it provided an outlet for venting frustrations. Knowing full-well nothing would ever come of their plans, they plotted against neighborhood villains. They ended each meeting with a hearty, "*Vengeance is ours!*"

To their surprise, days after venting about Derek Vespers and planning his demise, someone went and killed the son-of-a-bitch. For real.

"Thank God no one overheard us, plotting our *make-believe* revenge. People might think one, or all of us, killed him," the Loner said with nervous trepidation. The others concurred.

Tonight's featured lowlife: Billy "the Cockroach" Sane.

They all knew him. They all hated him. And they all took part in planning his due justice. In theory only, of course.

Vespers' killer listened with great interest. He despised the Quad. *You're all talkers, not doers. I don't belong in a room with talkers. Don't sit there complaining. Come up with a plan to kill the fucker and execute it. Vengeance is ours!*

The Loner went to bed dreaming about Robin. The Watcher replayed his evening's 'alleyway viewings' in his mind and drifted into a deep and disturbing sleep. The Writer passed out, visualizing and constructing another chapter of his book.

The Optimist, knowing everything would work out in the end, dozed off into a peaceful night's slumber.

Meanwhile, the assassin stayed up all night planning on how to kill the Cockroach.

CHAPTER 14

June 21, 1968

A tsunami raged within the Writer's head. Swells of inspiration unleashed a tidal wave of blue ink. Words devoured the page before him.

Chapter 1

Fort Tryon Park is a gift from God. Entering it is like stepping into a Monet. Lavish gardens adorn the lead-in pathway, while hundreds of flower varieties, all of different colors, shapes and sizes, form a pastel pallet of indescribable beauty.

Lush, rolling lawns arch downward, overlooking the Hudson River and Jersey skyline. Benches and gazebos house playful children while parents lovingly look on.

People come from miles around to walk the myriad of pathways that weave under arched stone-tunnels, through forests, culminating at a medieval monastery rising from the towering cliffs known as the Cloisters.

Fort Tryon Park is indeed the jewel of Washington Heights. However, as is the case with any jewel, if you look close enough you'll find imperfections.

In that very same park, day or night, behind many of nature's regal, hundred-year-old elm and birch trees, you can find a fifteen-year-old drug dealer selling nickel bags of Acapulco gold, or packets of Quaaludes. Muggers lurk behind trees, and deviants hide in the bushes, masturbating while they watch lovers on the lawns.

Not all is as it seems behind the well-fabricated veneer of this prestigious neighborhood.

As with people, a beautiful facade can only mask its underlying ugliness for so long.

CHAPTER 15

June 24, 1968

EARLY RISERS CONGREGATED along the building's sidewalk, babbling their endless stories. According to one older gentleman, a few weeks ago a very nice young man had been killed in the basement with a pair of hedge trimmers.

"It was a terrible thing. He once held the door open for me and helped me with some packages," one said to the other.

"Quite the tragedy," the other agreed.

Perched upon a parked car, Derek Vespers' assassin never felt so alive, listening to the tenants sharing their meaningless bullshit. He smiled, closed his eyes, and imagined shooting all of them. *Perhaps today I'll kill again? Perhaps not? I make those life and death decisions—me, and me alone. You people are sheep, and I run the slaughterhouse. So take heed, you stupid fuckers. You best stay on my good side.*

The more his neighbors talked, the more he relished sitting there, being the only one who knew what came next.

You pathetic morons. You'd lock your doors and shit your pants if you knew what I know. The party's just beginning. I'm just starting to have fun.

The Writer shook his head with concern. From his vantage point, the murder in the basement was a mere prelude of what was to come. He could feel it in his bones.

His final note of the day read, "As I become more in touch with the darker side of humanity, I find myself afraid and praying for the existence of God. I believe the good residents of Washington Heights will soon be joining me in prayer."

CHAPTER 16

1949

HAVING GIVEN UP hope of conceiving a child, Rosa and Arturo Sane adopted Billy at age one. He was to be the final piece that completed their picture-perfect puzzle.

Three years later, the Sanes were blessed with the miracle of conception. Nine months after that they were the proud parents of a beautiful baby girl, Lucinda.

"Funny," they thought, "the way things don't always turn out the way you plan."

***

Seventeen years later . . .

Billy had been molesting his sister for over a year. He threatened to kill her if she ever told anyone. On a sad, fateful day in October 1966, as Lucinda prepared the family's ironing; eighteen-year-old Billy had the urge. He didn't hear the key unlock the front door.

Arturo stood in the doorway, frozen. Lucinda's torn panties strewn aside, Billy pinned his sister's shoulders with his knees, while with two fingers he violated the sanctity of her most private domain.

Arturo seethed, the veins in his forehead pulsed. He clutched his son by the throat, lifted him off the ground and slammed him against the wall. While the fingers of his right hand tightened around Billy's neck, his left fist clenched, ready to explode in his son's face.

"I can't breathe," Billy garbled.

Arturo turned for an instant, looking back into his battered daughter's angelic eyes.

A mild-mannered man by nature, Arturo loosened his grip. Instead of beating his son senseless, he'd call the police. *Billy belongs somewhere where he can never hurt anyone ever again.*

As his father reached for the phone, Billy grabbed the still-hot iron. Over and over again he struck, blood and gray matter spattering from Arturo's head.

Billy ran to his room. Within seconds, he returned with two tabs of LSD which he kept for his own recreational use. The remaining tabs he flushed down the toilet, just to be safe. *The cops will wanna search the house.* Proceeding to shove the pills down his father's throat he shouted. "You had to come home early. Do you know how much this shit costs, you fuckin' asshole?" *I'd better wait an hour before calling the police.*

Lucinda sat paralyzed in the corner of the room, knees drawn to chest, her hands clutched behind her head, tears running down her cheeks. With the stare of a crazed animal, Billy turned and gave his sister an all-telling look. She got the message. *He killed Papa. Now what will I do? I have no one who can protect me. Billy will never stop. If I tell, he'll kill me. Or Mama? Oh my God. Mama.*

***

When the police arrived, Billy appeared overwhelmed. He played the victim well, and spoke with a nervous quiver. "Dad came home early. I don't know why. I was helping my sister with her homework. He seemed weird, kinda like he was on something. Then, for no reason, he started wailing on me, saying 'he was going to kill me.' He must've thought I'd done something terrible, but I don't know what. Like I said, I don't think he was thinking clearly."

Billy paused. *If that bitch squeals, I'll kill her.* Nervously, he put his hand in his pocket, making certain the torn panties were still there. Regaining his composure, he continued to play the role of a grief-stricken son and brother.

"I could see my sister was scared, too. I grabbed whatever I could and swung for my life. It was terrible. I don't know what made Dad go off like that. Honest, I swear, I had no choice. Ask my sister."

Lucinda sat huddled on the floor, in a catatonic state, offering no contradictory account of what had occurred.

CHAPTER 17
June 27, 1968

Morning:

AT TWENTY YEARS of age, Billy, a.k.a. "The Cockroach," harbored a festering rage that caused one to pause and question his gene pool. He stood five-feet-six, weighing in at, maybe, a hundred twenty pounds. He was an annoying little parasite with slicked-back brown hair, brown eyes, and skin that looked like he'd slept in a grease pan. His teeth were yellowed, his breath foul, and his conscience non-existent. Billy genuinely did resemble a cockroach.

Noon:

Other than his family, no one called him Billy. "The Cockroach" had no friends. Everyone knew about his father's death, and no one believed Billy's story. "That's the kid who killed his father," they'd say. Billy laughed at the cowards who pointed fingers when they thought he couldn't see.

He readied himself to go out and do what he did best. Make enemies. Before leaving, Billy relieved himself, urinating half in the bowl, half on the floor. He hawked up some phlegm, and spit into the basin without rinsing it down the drain. Then he ventured to the kitchen.

Rosa busied herself cleaning dishes, never once looking away from the sink. She'd avoided eye contact with her son ever since her husband's death. Even though Lucinda never said anything, Rosa knew Billy had lied. *Her beloved Arturo was a good man. Not at all like Billy.*

Billy slithered-up behind his sister. He ran his hand across her breasts while his mother's back was turned. He placed his head next to hers, giving her a peck on the cheek. "You like that, don't you? See you later, Sis." The words reverberated in her ears.

Exiting the building, the Cockroach pressed all the apartment buzzers. *Fuck all of you.*

Intentionally tripping an elderly gentleman carrying groceries, Billy grabbed an apple from the fallen bag, took a bite, coughed up sputum, and spit on the floor next to the old-timer.

"Thanks, gramps."

This is gonna be a great day.

Evening:

The Cockroach reveled in his expectation of a good day. Intimidating the timid, attacking the unsuspecting, and stealing from the helpless made him smile. He stood by the lamppost, a sinister grin painted on his face, as he screened the cast for his next venue of entertainment.

Fort Tryon Park flourished in the summer, presenting a perfect setting for both lovers and dreamers. It also served as the Cockroach's personal X-rated theatre.

The Cockroach knew the park's sixty-seven acres of wooded hills and landscaping better than most. Among his many other qualities, he was a devout peeper, and as a dog marks its territory, so also, the Cockroach left his markings at hundreds of locations.

Spring and summer were the Cockroach's favorite times of the year. So many lovers, doing what lovers do. The crotch of his pants rose just thinking about it.

At eight thirty, the Watcher spotted the Cockroach. His thoughts flashed back to the Quad's meeting where between them they'd painted a compelling portrait of this narcissistic lowlife. He also recalled how they'd agreed the world would be a better place without the Cockroach in it. The intensity of the Watcher's anger dizzied him. He closed his eyes for an instant. Upon reopening, the Cockroach was gone.

His prey selected, the Cockroach moved closer. He'd watched them many times before. They were an attractive couple, in their mid-twenties, who often frolicked in a remote spot down by the northeast lawn, near the gazebo.

It would be forty-five minutes till the action got steamy enough for the Cockroach's viewing pleasure. He knew their lovemaking by rote. His underwear became sticky in anticipation.

By nine thirty the Cockroach had positioned himself behind an ornamental cherry tree offering an unobstructed view of the young lovers. His eyes focused like a laser beam. A light drizzle went unnoticed.

Watching the young woman bring her boyfriend to climax, the Cockroach worked at pleasuring himself. His heart raced, while his hand pumped like a high-roller at a craps table. On his toes, back-arched, the Cockroach reached a spasmodic frenzy. His legs wobbled as his load spurted in the wind.

From out of nowhere, a hand reached from behind and grabbed him. Paralyzed by fear, the Cockroach froze as 'the assassin' strangled his genitals, encircling them between the thumb and forefinger of his gloved right hand. His penis and testicles hung like a Thanksgiving turkey's neck before slaughter.

The hooded figure raised his left hand, preparing to take one vicious swipe with a razor-sharp, straight-edge. In the moonlight, the Cockroach saw the polished steel blade reflect the terror in his own eyes. It was the same terror he had seen so many times in the eyes of his prey.

The Cockroach let out an unearthly shrill, sending a chill down the assassin's spine, and the lovers running for their lives. By the time the terrified couple returned with a police officer, the assailant had disappeared into the night.

It didn't turn out to be such a great day for the Cockroach after all.

CHAPTER 18

June 29, 1968

THE MEETING OF the Quad came to order. No one was late.

The Loner, Watcher, Writer and Optimist sat, pondering their dilemma. The gruesome murder of the Cockroach had started them thinking. *Two killings in as many months. First Vespers, and now the Cockroach is dead too, both occurring only days after we talked about taking revenge on those assholes.* The same thought flashed through each of their minds. *An unsettling coincidence?*

A mutual feeling of uncertainty, if not distrust, overtook the foursome. Each wondered, "Is it possible that one or more of us is involved in the killings?"

An awkward silence filled the room. Finally, the Writer spoke, "Did anyone see the Cockroach in the past couple of days?"

The Watcher thought twice before responding. "I saw him the night he died, out in front of the park. One second he was there, and then he wasn't."

The Loner, who spoke only on the rarest of occasions, voiced his concern about how it would look if anyone found out about the Quad's meetings.

The Watcher became defensive. "Are you planning on telling anyone *dream boy*? I know, sure as hell, I'm not going to. Besides, we didn't have anything to do with it. There must be a hundred people out there who hated those guys just as much, if not more, than we did. I say 'fuck it.' Whoever killed them did the world a favor."

The Optimist couldn't believe his ears. "I know we all despised those guys, but I wouldn't start going around congratulating whoever killed them. It's still murder. I'm sure they'll catch whoever did it. You know, like on TV."

"Get real," said the Watcher. "You're living in a fantasy world. I'll bet there are lots more bodies to come before they catch the guy. If they catch him."

That prospect brought silence to the group.

Disappointed, the Watcher said, "I guess this means we're not gonna talk about what we'd like to do to that shithead Phil, tonight."

The continuing silence gave him his answer.

On that note the meeting adjourned.

The assassin listened with great interest. *Please, don't stop now. Tell me more about this shithead—Phil.*

CHAPTER 19
November 3, 1938
Berlin

ADOLF HITLER REMOVED the pouch containing the parchment from inside his shirt. He had kept the cryptic prophecy next to his heart for over five years, removing it often, gazing at it whenever he felt the urge to reassure himself of his place in history. The message, however, remained illegible, obscured by the blood of a traitor.

The Final Solution progressed, but not fast enough to please der Führer.

Lunacy, disguised by a politician's twisted tongue, was taking a run at ruling the world. Hitler's dream resided a mere few hundred million deaths from fulfillment. The creation of a master race, with Hitler its supreme leader, seemed his unflinching destiny. Nothing would stop him from becoming the omnipotent god he believed fate had ordained him to be. He would do everything in his power to expedite the fruition of his vision.

Still, he wished he could make out the words on that damned parchment.

CHAPTER 20
November 4, 1938
Berlin

TO THOSE WHO SURROUNDED HIM, Hitler seemed both infallible and invincible. To contradict him constituted an unforgivable act of sacrilege, punishable by death. Blind obedience became the new religion of the Third Reich. Death was considered a merciful punishment, afforded those whom Hitler had once liked and/or respected. Far worse fates awaited the others.

November 5, 1938
A message arrived, marked '*URGENT*.' The Munich Astrologers requested an audience with der Führer as soon as possible. It was of the utmost importance.

Hitler placed his hand to his chest, as he had done so many times before, wondering if this was to be the ultimate confirmation of what he believed the parchment prophecies foretold.

November 6, 1938

Hitler's mind was distracted. All he could think about was the upcoming meeting with the Munich Astrologers, and the events that led to this moment. After all these years, the words of Erik Jan Hanussen still forged his destiny. He couldn't stop obsessing.

CHAPTER 21

June 30, 1968

TOMMY QUINLAN SAT behind his desk, unbuttoned the top button of his pants, took a deep breath and exhaled a sigh of relief. *Oh yeah, that's better.* The salad and carrot sticks which his wife prepared for him sat atop a pile of case files. He stared at the rabbit food with contempt.

The smell of greasy burgers accompanied by the sound of the desk sergeant sucking air through the straw of his drained milk shake tipped the scale of Tommy's dilemma.

"Somebody, bring me one of those burgers," he shouted in the direction of the squad room. "That's an order."

Quinlan's words ricocheted throughout the precinct like a stray bullet.

No one responded. Nobody looked in the boss' direction. They knew better.

Chief of Detectives, Thomas Quinlan, a third-generation, Irish-American police officer, stood an intimidating six-foot-four, two hundred and fifty-five pounds. Nobody with a brain messed with Tommy. If some fool did, it only happened once.

Of late, Tommy seemed on edge. Like a thief in the night, his mid-life belly had snuck up and overtaken him. He cursed the culprit which currently remained in a choke hold, a prisoner within the firm grasp of his fists. In self-defense, his stomach gurgled a response which seemed to say, "Don't blame me; you're the guy with no self-control."

It was a constant battle of wills, and so far, temptation was winning. When he wasn't listening to his gut, he could feel his pants, bursting at their seams, begging for mercy.

Grudgingly, Tommy crunched down on a carrot stick. From the outer office he heard someone say, "Told you he wouldn't crack. Pay up."

Sporting wavy, dirty-blonde hair, full-flush cheeks, and a contagious smile, Tommy embodied the hybrid spirit of a starved grizzly and a sleepy koala—sometimes ferocious, other times, sweet and cuddly. Everyone liked Tommy Quinlan. For the time being, they stayed out of his way at mealtimes.

Nearly twenty-five years with the NYPD, all of them stationed at the Washington Heights Precinct, Quinlan owned the highest case-closure rate in the history of the borough of Manhattan. Not that you'd know it walking into his office. Decorated on numerous occasions, Quinlan's medals and commendations spoke for themselves. At least they would have, if you could find them, buried in the bottom drawer of his beat-up file cabinet. The old, bent-out-of-shape, protector of information represented the only object, animate or inanimate, that preceded Quinlan's tenure at the precinct. He refused to part with it. He related to it.

On the wall behind Quinlan's desk, family photos displayed a lifetime of joyful memories. Off to the side hung a cherished 30" x 40" silk-screened montage of his favorite detective of all time, Sherlock Holmes. Logic and reason defined both their careers. The difference was Tommy's was real, and the case he and his team were currently working would force him to expand his instincts beyond what he could understand.

In three months Quinlan could retire with full benefits, if he so desired.

Katie, Tommy's wife, so desired.

For almost a quarter century Katie had devoted herself to raising their two boys, and participated as a regular volunteer at community functions. She never once complained. She loved her family, and her life. But now, Katie wanted to see some of the beauty the world had to offer before they got too old to enjoy it. It would be a welcome change from the ugliness Tommy's job often thrust upon their lives.

Two boxes, piled beyond capacity with travelogues, sat on the floor beside Quinlan's desk. They reminded him of his trousers… bursting at the seams, unable to be closed. He promised Katie he'd take a look. That was a month ago. The odyssey of retirement would have to collect dust a while longer. The violent butchering of Derek Vespers and Billy Sane had sent Washington Heights into panic mode.

It was an election year and the prospect of a serial killer running loose in the city had become a political hot potato. Two murders in as many months had Quinlan taking heat from the Police Commissioner, who, in turn, was taking heat from the Mayor, who was being blasted by the newspapers, who were having a field day sensationalizing the crimes and pointing accusatory fingers.

Calls suggesting that the two crimes were perpetrated by one and the same killer propelled both the *New York Post* and *Daily News* to play the gruesome murders to the hilt. The *News* dubbed the serial-killer, "The Shadow Assassin." The name stuck.

Quinlan took it in stride. He didn't get frazzled. And he certainly wasn't surprised. The same bullshit happened every time the heat came down on some politician.

The buck always stopped at Quinlan's desk.

Throughout his years on the Force, Quinlan had witnessed much of man's inhumanity toward his fellow man; however he'd never encountered anything like the sadistic outpour displayed in the two crimes he'd been called upon to investigate over the last two months. The attacks demonstrated an uncontrolled rage Quinlan couldn't even begin to understand.

Quinlan readied himself for his meeting with Patrolman Vincent Scumaci. Scumaci had been lucky enough to be the street cop flagged down by the lovers three nights earlier, on the evening of Billy Sane's savage demise.

Scumaci stood five-foot-eight and weighed a hundred forty pounds—fully attired. He could run "the-hundred" in ten seconds flat. And, for what it was worth, boasted to being able to eat more pasta, in one sitting, than anyone else on the planet.

What Vinnie lacked in physical intimidation, he more than made up for in enthusiasm and good common sense. Except, maybe, for *the pasta thing.*

Scumaci wore his Italian heritage like a badge of honor. Even his cologne gave off a hint of garlic. At the ripe old age of twenty-six, he'd been on the force almost two years, never experiencing any real action to speak of. Street action, that is. Vinnie's somewhat quirky, yet endearing mannerisms made him quite a hit with the ladies.

The Cockroach's murder scene had Vinnie's juices flowing. His mind became a blender of facts and suppositions. Through no doing of his own, he now stood confronted with his first real crime . . . a bona fide homicide. *This is what I signed on for. Not traffic duty or crowd control.* He was ready to do whatever it took to get himself permanently assigned to the case.

Months earlier, Quinlan consulted on a case with Scumaci. A B&E (breaking and entering) that overlapped into Quinlan's jurisdiction somehow found its way to Scumaci's charge.

Quinlan took an instant liking to the kid. Scumaci displayed a sharp mind. He presented himself as meticulous, both in work ethic and appearance, and offered up a tasteful sense of humor.

Quinlan couldn't quite put his finger on it but there was definitely a peanut-butter-meets-jelly kind of chemistry forming between himself and the eager, young patrolman. Together, they closed the B&E in record time, boding well for both Scumaci's coming evaluation and for possible future assignments.

Noticing Scumaci's signature on the Responding Officer and Witness Statement forms Quinlan wasted no time logging a request for Scumaci's temporary reassignment.

Initially met with resistance, Quinlan persevered, convincing the captain that Scumaci would be an asset to the process. He argued that Scumaci's close proximity in age to the victims, and his natural ability to schmooze with the ladies, could prove invaluable.

In a few minutes, Quinlan would reunite with Officer Scumaci to review what little information they had collected on the two murders, and to form a plan of action.

CHAPTER 22

July 1, 1968

THEY PLANNED TO get off to an early start.

Quinlan arrived at the stationhouse first. "Initiate a search for similar crimes fitting our M.O.," he instructed the desk sergeant. "Have it ready by day's end."

Next, he assigned Detective Harvey Cohen, a ten-year vet on the force, to compile a comprehensive file on both of the victims. "DOB, schools attended, jobs, run-ins with the law, friends, enemies, and anything else—no matter how seemingly insignificant—that might connect the victims. You know the drill, Harvey." Cohen's thoroughness and attention to detail had helped solve many a case throughout the years, his bald head a crystal ball filled with many useful insights.

Scumaci showed up at seven a.m. on the button, bright eyed, impeccably uniformed, and raring to go.

"Mornin' Chief, your car or mine?" Raising a half-eaten cannoli with his right hand, he said, "I got a box of these babies in mine. You'll think you died and went to heaven."

The Chief rolled his eyes, placing both hands on his stomach. "We'll take yours. Grab a couple of *babies* for yourself and bring the rest in for the boys. None for me. Katie's been on my case about my weight. Besides, if I put on another ounce, I'm gonna need a whole new wardrobe."

"Whatever works for you, Chief."

Retrieving the pastries from the car, Scumaci stuffed a cannoli into his mouth, grabbed three more for the ride, and ran the rest into the lunchroom, careful not to get any of the powdered sugar on his freshly pressed blues. "Hey, Chief, I know of this great pasta place not too far from the crime scene."

Quinlan shook his head in disbelief. *This kid is killin' me.* "Move it, Scumaci."

Scumaci stared at the box of remaining cannoli as though it were a departed family member. With great hesitation he left his loved ones beside the coffee machine. Exiting the precinct behind Quinlan, Vinnie looked back one last time, mourning his loss.

***

They decided to approach the murders with clear minds and fresh eyes, hoping to pick up on something, anything, that might have been missed in the initial go-round. The first order of business would be a reexamination of both crime scenes.

They set out for the basement of the building where, two months earlier, Derek Vespers' skull had been skewered with a hedge trimmer, and cracked open.

"Won't any new evidence we find be compromised?" Scumaci asked.

"Absolutely," Quinlan confirmed. "But still, revisiting a crime scene can stimulate new trends of thought about both the criminal act, and its perpetrator. It's worth a look-see. In the meantime, I got the boys at the station checking out phone leads."

While leads from observant citizens played an instrumental role in a case, and indeed often helped to bring closure, the type of press these crimes tended to generate would fuel hundreds of well-meaning, but nonetheless useless, calls.

"Ya know, kid, good leads are like good blind date . . . one in a million. To find the good one, you gotta check 'em all out. Better prepare yourself for some long, sleepless nights.

Let the dating begin.

CHAPTER 23

July 1, 1968

QUINLAN CALLED AHEAD to make sure the superintendent of Vespers' apartment building, Otto Sussman, would be available.

At seven thirty, Quinlan and Scumaci pulled up in front of 19026 Fort Washington Avenue. The six-story building, adorned with well-tended shrubbery in its front courtyard, stood a half block from Fort Tryon Park.

The sun rose without a cloud in the sky. Tenants had already started congregating on the sidewalk. For them, the murder that took place in their basement seemed ancient history. For Quinlan and Scumaci, it was just beginning.

No stranger to the building, or its residents, Quinlan buzzed the superintendent's apartment and announced himself. Otto Sussman responded, "I'll be right down."

Sussman looked to be fifty-ish, a little on the unkempt side, but overall, in pretty good shape. He displayed a firm hand shake and a gruff physicality about him. The nature of his job kept him active—unlike most of the residents his age, who spent their time in chairs behind a desk.

Sussman introduced himself in a strong German accent, while leading the officers down the side alleyway to the basement door. Quinlan estimated about forty-percent of the people in Sussman's age demographic, living in Washington Heights, possessed German accents to some extent.

"We don't get too many people coming down here since the murder," Sussman said, appearing a little nervous. "I put the garbage cans outside now, so tenants don't have to go inside. They come down in groups to use the laundry machines too. Nothing like this has ever happened on this block before. It was a terrible thing that happened here. And, terrible to see. These good folks seem okay on the outside, but I can tell they're scared shitless."

Sussman had found the body at about eight p.m., and immediately called the police. By eight-fifteen the responding officers had arrived and cordoned off the area.

True to the preliminary report—the basement was poorly lit, and damp.

Sussman led the way through a maze of pipes suspended from the ceiling. A grungy boiler room, laundry room and secured storage area adorned the spidery path leading to Vespers' currently unoccupied apartment unit.

White chalk markings, indicating the position of the body, remained visible on the cold concrete floor. Fragments of yellow crime-scene-tape remained adhered to the chipping grey plaster.

After passing a wall of discarded newspapers, Sussman paused. He pointed to an unlit corner of the dungeon-like basement. "Over there, that's where I store my garden tools. The other police officers said the killer must have taken the hedge trimmer from my bin and then used it to kill Mr. Vespers."

Quinlan asked the same questions Sussman had already answered twenty times before, with no new enlightenment.

Sussman unlocked the door to Vespers' apartment and handed the key to Quinlan.

After assuring them ten times over, Sussman again insisted, "No one has been in the apartment since the murder was committed, and to the best of my knowledge nothing has been removed." Quinlan let Sussman leave to go about his business. "We'll call if we need you."

Quinlan and Scumaci spent the rest of the morning rummaging through Vespers' belongings, trying to get a feel for the victim and his lifestyle. The preliminary report indicated the responding officers observed an abundance of pot, hashish, a wide assortment of uppers and downers, and a wide variety of sex-toys. The drugs were confiscated at the time of the search while everything else remained undisturbed.

"I'd say, 'a wide variety of sex-toys' is quite the understatement," Quinlan said with a look of revulsion. "What's your take, Scumaci?"

Behind a draw-string curtain hung an assortment of sexual paraphernalia that would have brought tears to the eyes of the Marquis de Sade. Scumaci, considering himself well-schooled in the art of lovemaking shook his head in disbelief.

"Hey, Chief, I'm far from prudish and I don't know what most of this shit is, let alone what it's used for. You're an experienced man; what the hell is all of this stuff?"

"Not a clue, Vinnie. But I can tell you they're not cooking utensils."

"And what do you make of this thing?" Quinlan asked in disgust, as visual images formulated in his mind. An inverted-V-shaped bench, with wrist-restraints and ankle pulleys occupied the far corner of the room.

"I'm afraid to let my imagination go there, Chief. This place gives me the creeps," Scumaci offered, with a hint of regret for those unfortunate enough to have first-hand knowledge of its use.

"So tell me, Vinnie, you've interviewed some of your contemporaries in the park. What do they have to say? Was our dead guy a paramour, or a predator?"

"He was an asshole, Chief. If I had a daughter, I wouldn't have let her within a hundred yards of this guy."

The interviews with Vespers' contemporaries confirmed he'd been dealing drugs for quite some time. They also painted a disturbing portrait of the deviant person Vespers really was.

Of the young ladies enamored by Vespers charms in the daylight, and later afforded the dubious distinction of entering his lair at night, not one of them said she would ever go back a second time. Understandably, the girls appeared hesitant to give details.

It didn't seem possible, but the list of prospective suspects kept getting bigger. A lot of people were happy to see Vespers dead—whether they admitted it to the police or not.

Quinlan and Scumaci took one last visual scan of the crime scene as they exited the apartment. Quinlan locked up and started toward the basement exit when Scumaci called out. "One minute, Chief. You know me, I'm a neat freak."

Scumaci walked over to the huge stack of perfectly aligned newspapers and tugged on one that appeared uncharacteristically askew. Sliding it free with great care he called out, "I don't know if this means anything Chief, but you'd better come take a look."

The headline read, "METS VICTORY." The letters V, I, and O had been circled with a magic marker.

CHAPTER 24

November 7, 1938
Berlin

IS THIS TO be the moment I've waited for? Will there now be a confirmation and clarification of Hanussen's last prophecy?

Der Führer paced the hallway in an agitated gait. He was determined to get his master plan for an elite Aryan society moving at a more progressive pace. *These Astrologers had better have a damn good reason for dragging me to this meeting.*

Entering the chamber, Hitler heard whispers of Erik Jan Hanussen's name. He took a seat, attempting to hide his excitement. His heart rate accelerated to the point of hyperventilation. The meeting now took on a prominent status in Hitler's mind. He knew that whatever the Astrologers planned to tell him must be important. Possibly momentous. Even historic.

The consequences for wasting der Führer's time would be severe, and they all knew it.

Once again, Hitler placed his hand to his chest, coveting his most prized possession. Able to wait no longer, he raised his clenched fist, ready to call the meeting to order.

CHAPTER 25

November 7, 1938
The Meeting

THE ASTROLOGERS BABBLED amongst themselves, until Hitler slammed his fist on the table, commanding silence. The banter in the room came to an abrupt stop. "What is the purpose of this meeting?"

The leader of the group, a robed elder-statesman, proceeded with trepidation. "It has come to our attention, that there is in existence, a parchment documenting your fate. It is believed to be the very last writing of Erik Jan Hanussen."

Hitler couldn't believe his ears. *How can they know about the parchment? I've told no one, shown no one.* He touched his chest confirming the presence of the document.

"We thought it of the utmost importance to bring the existence of this document to your attention, Mein Führer. It is rumored, Hanussen created two originals of this very document.

We have been advised that one is said to be in the possession of a man who lives in Vienna."

Hitler's heart raced. Two parchments? *Can it be? An identical twin? At last I'll know Hanussen's final vision.*

"I must have it. Bring me this man from Vienna," der Führer demanded, spittle spraying from his lips.

"There is a problem," the elder confessed. The mounting fear in his worry-ridden face was apparent. "We do not know exactly who is in possession of this document. Only that it exists and is said to be in the possession of a Jew in Vienna."

Hitler lunged at the elder's throat.

Seven astrologers had walked into the meeting. Six walked out. The elder statesman's body remained behind.

CHAPTER 26
July 1, 1968; Afternoon

QUINLAN WATCHED SCUMACI stuff another cannoli into his mouth.

"How the hell do you stay so thin?"

Scumaci smiled, taking another bite.

"By the way, Scumaci, that was a nice catch back there. I don't know if it means anything, but we sure as hell don't have anything else to go on."

"Any ideas on what VIO could mean, Chief?"

"Not a clue, other than the obvious. Someone's initials? An acronym for some group? Or maybe, just someone's random doodling. I do it all the time. It probably has nothing to do with the case. But it was still a good catch. I totally missed it."

"Does that mean I get a raise?"

"Yeah, right. I'll tell you what, I'll buy lunch. I know a place that tosses a mean salad. Then, we'll go check out the buzz on this Cockroach kid."

Scumaci sat nervously silent, wondering if this was some kind of test. *A mean salad?*

By the time the sun set, both Quinlan and Scumaci learned more about Billy Sane than either of them could stomach. Detective Harvey Cohen called to fill them in on what he'd found on the Sane kid's juvenile record. It provided an a-la-carte menu of threats, assaults, accusations and complaints. He'd been accused of a wide gamut of offenses, including theft, assault, destruction of private property and the torturing and killing of a neighbor's cat. The list seemed endless. No charges ever stuck.

The most interesting file to attract Cohen's attention dated back to October 20, 1966 . . . a file documenting the death of Arturo Sane, Billy's father.

The notation by the responding officer stated Billy Sane had killed his father in self-defense. However, a footnote at the bottom of the page read, "*Self-defense possible, but I suspect otherwise. No one talking. Family and neighbors seem afraid of this kid.*"

Moving on to the most current report in 1968, following Billy's murder, Cohen highlighted one interesting observation made by the investigating officer. "*No signs of mourning at the Sane household. To the contrary, both mother and sister appear relieved by Billy's demise. Neighbors show no sense of sorrow, openly exchanging stories confirming the violent temperament of the kid they called 'Cockroach.' Friends of deceased cannot be located, if, indeed, any exist.*"

Quinlan looked at Scumaci, intent on making one thing clear. "Everyone hated this little prick. You'll get no argument from me. He proved himself to be a worthless piece of shit a hundred times over. But nobody gets away with murder."

CHAPTER 27

July 19, 1968

IT SEEMED JUST another Friday night, a carbon copy of every other. Regine arrived home late from work, exhausted after a trying week. Her tired and swollen feet pushed the limits of her stretched leather shoes. Every year, New York's hot, humid summer wore Regine down a little bit more than the previous year. She changed into a housedress and prepared dinner for Ryan and herself. As always, they ate in silence.

Regine and Ryan shared an unspoken bond. They resided in the vacuum of their lives, understanding each other in their solitude, both thankful for brief moments of relative normalcy in their struggle for survival.

Life had presented such a difficult path since Sandor passed away, but Regine never complained. She pushed forward like a bulldozer, plowing her way past and through all obstacles. She thanked God every day for giving her son back. Having Ryan home again was all the comfort she required.

After cleaning the dishes, they sat and watched television. Regine looked over, into Ryan's sad, accepting eyes. She couldn't remember the last time either of them had laughed.

At a little before nine, Regine kissed her son goodnight and retired to her bedroom. Every night before placing her head on her pillow, Regine prayed for a better tomorrow.

At eleven thirty, Regine awakened to loud voices. Donning her floral robe, she peeked out from behind her bedroom door.

Who could be talking so loud at this hour? Does Ryan have friends over this late at night? Maybe it's the television?

She walked down the unlit hallway, noticing there was no glow coming from the living room. *It's not the TV.*

Approaching Ryan's room, she listened. Several boys argued in heated discussion.

Regine raised her hand to knock, but waited and listened for several moments more. While deciding what to do, Regine was caught off guard. The voice now speaking sounded deeper and angrier than the others.

Regine's command of the English language left something to be desired, but she'd have sworn she heard someone ranting about killing a cockroach.

She swooshed the door open, nearly fainting from the shock of what she saw, and heard.

Regine's prayer for a better tomorrow would have to wait for another day.

CHAPTER 28

July 20, 1968

TWO A.M. The shrill ring of the phone made him jump.

Every evening before bed, Abdo dreaded the possibility of a middle-of-the-night call. It didn't happen often, but when it did, bad news always awaited on the other end of the line. Good news waited till morning.

"Hello," he whispered, half asleep, doing his best not to wake Sonya.

At first he didn't know what to make of the call. The woman spoke rapidly and in German. He couldn't make out a word she was saying. "Regine, is that you?" He sat up after confirming her voice. Regine reverted to German whenever she became upset or excited.

"Slow down, Regine. Tell me what's happened, as calmly as you can. And please—in English."

Regine proceeded to relate the events of the evening, leading up to her opening Ryan's door a little past midnight.

"I was certain there were three or four boys in the room. I didn't want to go in, but when they started using bad language and talked about hurting people, I opened the door. I wanted to know what was going on. Instead, I stood there, speechless. In shock. I didn't know what to do.

"Ryan was asleep in his bed. I looked around. There was no one else in the room. Just my Ryan, talking in his sleep. I don't understand, Abdo. There were three or four different voices coming out of his mouth. I had to sit down or faint. I watched Ryan toss and turn, still arguing with himself. Then, all of a sudden, he stopped. He's sleeping peacefully now. What's going on? What's happening to my boy?"

Abdo tried to pacify Regine, but she was inconsolable and wept. He waited.

After a few minutes, Regine was ready to continue.

"What were Ryan and these other voices talking about?" Abdo asked in a measured tone.

"One second he was calm, then excited, then angry, then calm, then excited . . ."

Abdo interrupted, knowing Regine would go back and forth describing the emotional changes rather than providing any content she might have picked up on. "What exactly did he say, Regine?"

Regine rambled, out of control. She retreated to speaking German again, but caught herself. Relaxing for a moment, she took a deep breath and continued.

"First he was talking about a girl, and that made me smile. Then he, or they, told him to stop living in a fantasy. Then there was something about killing a cockroach. And something about this boy Phil who they hated, and one day he'll get what he deserves. He was calm, then angry. He even said something like, 'Don't worry, everything will work out.' Now that sounded like my Ryan. I'm so scared, Abdo. I don't know what to do anymore. Please help us."

Abdo comforted Regine, telling her it would be best for both her and Ryan if she could remain calm, knowing full well she wouldn't. Or couldn't. He requested she bring Ryan to his office at ten a.m., not that morning, but the following morning. Abdo wanted to be present the next evening, so he himself might witness Ryan's manifestations before meeting with Ryan in his office.

After arranging a time, Abdo instructed Regine to call if anything else occurred that night. "If I don't hear from you, I'll see you tomorrow night at eight thirty. Now try not to worry Regine. I promise you, we'll figure this out." Abdo hoped he could make good on his promise.

Regine spent the remainder of the night by Ryan's bedside, watching the second hand of the old desk clock twitch its way towards morning. Focused on the hushed *tic, tic, tic . . .*, Regine dozed off, her head resting next to Ryan's.

CHAPTER 29

July 20, 1968; evening

ABDO STOPPED OFF at the bakery to pick up dessert. It would be best if his appearance presented itself as a casual visit. Bearing pastries, Abdo rang the Cains' doorbell at eight thirty. While awaiting a response, a stocky man exited the apartment next door. Abdo recognized the man as Gunther Heber, the building superintendent.

Two-and-a-half years earlier, when the elderly couple living next door to the Cains had died in a hit-and-run incident, Heber jumped at the opportunity to move into the vacated two-bedroom apartment. Prior to that, he'd lived off-site.

"Evening sir, how are you today?" Heber inquired.

Not in the mood for small talk, Abdo responded with an affirmative nod.

Heber continued on his way offering a slight wave of his hand. Abdo assumed he was off to administer to the demanding repairs of the run-down building. Heber busied himself day and night with projects from his endless to-do list. At an earlier encounter, he'd confided to Abdo, "Work keeps my mind off of things I'd rather forget." The number tattoo on his forearm posed a plausible hint as to what those things might be.

Regine opened the door, accepting the box of desserts. The expression on her face provided confirmation of her harried state of mind.

Once they were seated in the living room, Ryan entered, appearing withdrawn and dejected. When Regine bombarded Ryan with questions, Abdo intervened. Well-meaning or not, he didn't want Ryan to feel interrogated, and Regine never minced words. Realizing the awkward unpleasantness of the situation, Abdo defaulted to sports. Baseball always seemed to ignite a spark in Ryan's demeanor. Not tonight.

Abdo made small talk. "Ryan, have you worked on any new drawings lately? Are you looking forward to doing anything special this summer?" Nothing piqued Ryan's interest. The limited spectrum of responses (yes, no, okay, not much, and I don't know) displayed his desire to be elsewhere. Before long, Ryan excused himself, heading out for his ritual evening walk. Abdo now shared Regine's deep concern.

At ten thirty, the front door unlocked. "Is that you sweetheart?" Regine called out.

"Yeah Mom, it's me."

"The news will be coming on soon. Would you like to watch with us?"

"Nah, I'm tired, Mom. I'm gonna hang out in my room for a while, and then go to sleep." *Please, leave me alone.*

At five to eleven, Ryan called from his room. "Good night."

"Good night, sweetheart. I love you," Regine responded.

"I love you too." *But please, stop asking so many questions.*

At eleven thirty, certain Ryan would be asleep, Regine turned the doorknob with the delicate touch of a cat burglar. Nudging the door open ever so slightly, she and Abdo waited, hoping to steal a peek at Ryan's inner demons. Part of Regine prayed there would be nothing to observe. Another part prayed the voices would reappear so Abdo could observe, first hand, what she'd witnessed.

Abdo spent most of the next hour reflecting on his frequent visits to the Cain household during Ryan's childhood. *I'm so sorry, Regine. I should have seen the warning signs. Perhaps there was something I could have done? It's my . . .*

"Abdo, look." Regine tugged at his arm.

At twelve forty a.m., Ryan became agitated, mumbling under his breath. His body jerked. His facial expression distorted. His eye movement became rapid. His words became clear.

"You're late. Where the fuck have you been?"

"There's no need for that tone."

"I'll use whatever tone I want."

"Stop writing that shit down, asshole."

It was SHOWTIME.

CHAPTER 30

July 21, 1968

THE SHADOW ASSASSIN *needed* to kill again. His lust for vengeance approached mania. Chest pounding with anticipation, he tried to talk himself down. "Take your time. Don't be a fool. You don't want to make a mistake, not like last time." He'd learned the hard way that impulsive actions can have severe consequences. Killing Phil Vulchek would take planning.

At five-foot-nine, carrying a muscular frame, Phil swayed about like an orangutan, only not as graceful. His eyes were dark in color and demeanor. With a jutting jaw and droopy lower lip, his head appeared out of proportion to the rest of his body. On top of his head, he sported thick black hair, combed straight back, and he wore four-day stubble on his chin. Also prominent was his ever-present body odor.

Contrary to the slithery, back-stabbing style of the Cockroach, whose quarry consisted of weak and unsuspecting victims, Vulchek could take care of himself in a scuffle, and wouldn't hesitate to pick a fight with anyone. If not handled with care, he could pose a problem.

The Shadow Assassin watched from afar, familiarizing himself with Vulchek's habits and daily routine. Then, utilizing what he'd learned, formulated the perfect kill.

At ten thirty p.m., on the Assassin's designated evening, Vulchek walked the wooded path on the north side of Fort Tryon Park. Three nights of surveillance had revealed him to be a creature of habit. Each night he took the shortcut leading to Dyckman Street, where he crashed at his girlfriend's apartment. If the Assassin's plan continued 'on-script,' the walkway, illuminated by nothing but moonlight, would prove to be Vulchek's shortcut to the hereafter. The X-factor would be whether Vulchek reacted the way the Assassin anticipated.

Vulchek spotted the disheveled man. Approaching the hooded figure, whose wallet lay on the ground with cash scattered about, he edged closer with caution. *Why is this fool wearing sweats in the middle of summer?*

"Thank God you came along," whimpered the Shadow Assassin, kneeling in the dirt, reeling in his prey. "That guy might have killed me. He took off when he saw you coming. Thanks a lot, man."

"Don't thank me yet, dipshit. I'll take that money as a reward for saving your worthless ass. Now get the fuck outta here, before I kick the shit out of you myself." Pleased with his good fortune, Vulchek bent to collect his bounty. The hooded figure reached for a crowbar concealed by shrubbery, striking one good whack on the back of Vulchek's over-sized head, making certain not to hit him hard enough to kill him. *Don't wanna spoil the fun.*

The Shadow Assassin dragged the unconscious body fifty yards into the wooded area. The selected tree stood ready, its sinewy arms reaching out to embrace its unconscious visitor.

Once he had him bound, the Assassin woke Vulchek with smelling salts and, with the dexterity of a ninja, shoved what appeared to be leaves into his victim's mouth. Duct tape hanging from a low-lying branch blew in the breeze. The Assassin used the silvery strips to tape Vulchek's mouth shut.

Standing back, the Assassin admired his perfectly-planned execution. It had taken ten minutes to complete the masterpiece—ten glorious, adrenalin-rushed minutes. Before leaving, the Assassin again stepped forward; patting Vulchek's bloated cheeks with his gloved hands. Vulchek wrestled with his bonds to no avail, trying to break free, his face painted in a frozen expression of panic.

The Assassin wished he could stay to admire this *thing of beauty*, but realized he'd already indulged himself too long. To remain would present an unjustifiable risk. He took a mental picture. One he could bring back into focus whenever he needed cheering up.

"Gotta go now, Phil. You don't mind if I call you Phil, do you? I hope this isn't going to create hard feelings between us, but we all agreed, you're an asshole. If you need anything, give a yell. Vengeance is ours."

CHAPTER 31

November 9, 1938
Berlin

THE MINISTRY OF INTELLIGENCE narrowed the list of possibilities to nineteen. Hitler felt destiny's hand guiding him. The opportunity to round up the bearer of his precious document's twin had fallen into his lap.

On Monday, November 7th, Ernst vom Rath, the Third Secretary of the German Embassy in Paris, fell victim to a German Jew's sniper bullet. The shooter was apprehended, and vom Rath died of the inflicted wound two days later.

The floodgates opened. The assassination of vom Rath provided the perfect excuse for the German government's counter response against German Jews. Hitler's Nazi party had been recruited to organize and execute the planned retaliation.

Hitler reveled. He'd never been more certain of anything in his life. Once again, fate had stepped in to play its inevitable role. Soon he would rule the world.

CHAPTER 32
November 9, 1938; 1:55 am
Vienna, Austria

IT WAS THE night that would become known as Kristallnacht, *the night of broken glass*. Orders to burn all synagogues to the ground flooded the transmission lines of Gestapo headquarters throughout Europe. The windows of Jewish-owned shops and residences were to be shattered, and all Jewish males arrested for deportation to concentration camps.

Regine stood by her window, located above the bakery where she and Sandor lived. The image reflecting in her eyes filled her with fear and terror. She could see the bright orange lights glowing against the dark, ominous sky. Synagogues blazed, their flames reaching toward the heavens seeking God's mercy.

The air became thick with smoke. People ran aimlessly through the streets, their screams muffled by the endless sound of breaking glass.

The door thrust open, the Gestapo swarming like bees to honey. They smashed everything in sight. Sandor rushed to Regine's side, holding her close.

"You're to come with us, Jew," ordered the SS officer.

There would be no discussion. Sandor was grabbed from Regine's clutching arms. Still wearing his pajamas, he was thrown down the stairs, and hoisted onto a waiting Nazi transport truck.

The SS officer had received his orders from der Führer himself. "Sandor Cain is not to be sent to Dachau, Buchenwald, or to any of the other camps. He is to be singled out and transported to Gestapo headquarters for interrogation. Alive."

Sandor Cain held the dubious distinction of being one of the nineteen Jews suspected of possessing the Hanussen document.

CHAPTER 33

November 25, 1938; 3:35 am
Berlin

THE SMELL OF death filled the air. An enraged Hitler placed a hypodermic syringe, along with a sealed envelope, on an empty table before addressing No. 19's frustrated interrogator.

"If he dies before I get the information I want, you'll take his place on the rack. You'll envy him his death. Now do your job."

The Gestapo agent snapped to attention. "Yes, Mein Führer. Right away, Mein Führer."

"I return in two days," Hitler fumed. "Don't fail me."

The two guards standing sentry outside the cell door contained their pleasure at the interrogator's failure to extract information from the Jew. The Schtroeber brothers, with right arms extended in salute, clicked their heels as Hitler stormed from the cell. New to their posts, the twin brothers felt certain they could do a better job than the officer in charge. They held their tongues. They'd wait for the right moment to show off their skills.

Consumed by frustration, Hitler had forgotten to retrieve the syringe and accompanying letter he'd come in with.

For the nineteen suspected caretakers of the Hanussen prophecy, minutes seemed like hours, days like years. Two weeks and eighteen too-horrible-to-describe deaths later, Sandor Cain remained the sole survivor, the Gestapo confident that No. 19, as they referred to him, was their man. The other eighteen bodies lay discarded on a stack of corpses awaiting incineration.

The unrecognizable body of No. 19 lay naked, strapped to a wooden rack, torso stretched beyond human endurance. A bloodied mound of mangled flesh, his hands hung limp from leather restraints hoisted above his battered head, broken at the wrists. Incoherent thoughts churned through his mind like paper through a shredder . . . a result of the experimental truth drug injected into his brain via the base of his skull.

The Gestapo agent replayed Hitler's warning in his head. *If he dies before I get the information I want, you'll take his place on the rack.*

No. 19's swollen testicles hung through a hole in the rack bed. Determined to break No. 19, the agent retrieved a wooden paddle and backhanded the throbbing orbs. No. 19 writhed in pain. "That's my warm-up swing, Jew," the frustrated interrogator warned. "Trust me, you don't want to see my forehand. Now tell me where the damn parchment is. This can end right now. We'll take you home. You'll see your wife again. Talk!" the interrogator shouted, his own life now on the line.

The prisoner remained silent. No. 19's ability to endure pain brought fear to the heart and mind of his torturer. Frustrated, he decided to retire for the evening and start over in the morning.

Later that night, Sandor heard the guards outside his door. They sounded drunk and getting drunker, as they readied themselves for some fun at his expense.

CHAPTER 34
November 25, 1938; 4:15 am

AT TWENTY YEARS of age, the ambitious, blond-haired, blue-eyed fraternal twins with a twisted sense of morality personified the picture-perfect Nazi poster boys. The Schtroeber brothers had stood guard by the cell door of the high priority Jew for more than two weeks, ever since he'd first arrived—still recognizable.

Their rank, or lack thereof, didn't entitle them to information regarding the importance of the prisoner. However, they couldn't help but overhear that he possessed something that the Führer sought.

Through the barred peephole of the cell door the brothers viewed No. 19's torture, and the injection of unknown drugs through long hypodermic syringes. At times, Gerhardt couldn't bring himself to watch. Not that he felt queasy about torture. He just had a thing about needles.

Two hours had passed since Hitler's unannounced visit and rapid departure. Witnessing the Gestapo interrogator's humiliation, the brothers toyed with the window of opportunity before them.

"I'm telling you Gerhardt. I heard it with my own ears. There's some big meeting going on. The Führer's own reference to his return in two days confirms it. Activity in the compound will be at a standstill."

"You'd better be right."

The brothers decided there'd be no harm in some liquid refreshment to help pass the night's long dreary hours—a quart of vodka should do the trick.

At three forty-five a.m., intoxicated beyond rational thought, the Schtroeber brothers decided to enter No. 19's chamber and extract the information that no one else could get. "We'll be heroes. We'll be decorated by the Führer himself," Hans slurred, retching a small amount of puke onto his uniform.

Once inside, they smiled at the sight of the outstretched prisoner. "Look at those testicles—holy shit." Gerhardt fell over laughing.

Sandor Cain remained conscious, but barely so.

"Wake up Jew; we're going to have a little talk. Just you and us. You're going to tell us what we want to know. Understand?"

Through the slit of his one, half-opened eye, Sandor Cain watched the brothers lean over him, issuing threats. No. 19 teetered on the fine line between life and death. Unless he gave them what they wanted, he knew these faces would be the last vision he would ever see on this earth. Yet, he said nothing.

He had nothing to say.

CHAPTER 35

November 25, 1938; 4:40 am

HANS AND GERHARDT Schtroeber spent their adolescent years trying to outdo one another, inflicting pain on stray animals. They experimented with razor blades, broken glass, fire, and assorted blunt objects. Evolving at a rapid pace, they outgrew animal torture. It no longer satisfied their hunger. They needed new stimulation, but what?

Adolf Hitler provided the answer. He offered them a new species with which to entertain themselves—humans. More to the point—Jews. Not that they cared. Any race or religion would do. They owed Hitler more than they could ever repay. He'd given their lives new meaning.

On the morning of November twenty-fifth, the intoxicated Schtroeber brothers made a life-altering decision. The rack holding Sandor Cain pulled taut, his naked body stretched to its physical limit. The ties securing his wrists and ankles cut through to the bone. With his head tilted to the right, his beaten face painted a portrait of tortured surrender. One more turn of the wheel and his body parts would separate. His testicles dangled, swollen and throbbing.

Verbal abuse brought no response from No. 19. The brothers' threats fell on deaf ears, further angering them, and heightening their resolve to inflict more pain upon their prisoner.

"The fucking Jew is faking," Hans shouted, feeling cheated of his entertainment.

On the counter to their right rested vise grips, scalpels, hot irons, and an assortment of other bloodied instruments. A few feet further down lay a pile of emptied hypodermic syringes. The sight made Gerhardt gag. His phobia of needles and injections amused his brother, providing a constant source of taunting. Gerhardt turned away.

"Get over it asshole and come here," Hans shouted. "Look, there's one full syringe left. Grab it. We've don't have much time."

The table to their left sat bare, except for one lone hypodermic syringe lying atop a sealed envelope. The underside of the envelope, if they'd turned it over, would have told them to stay away from that particular syringe. Handwritten, the envelope read, *Urgent: Führer.* Inside, it contained a message from Dr. Karl Brandt, Hitler's personal physician.

"Hey, Jew, look over here, see what we've got for you." Hans held the loaded hypo inches from No. 19's face.

"Look at this fucking needle; it must be six inches long. Where would you like it? In the stomach, the neck, the thigh?

I have an idea, how about those oversized testicles? Does that sound good, Jew? What, no comment? I guess the testicles it is." Hans gloated with delight.

"Look Jew, my brother, the pathetic excuse for a soldier, can't watch. I give you one last chance. Tell me what I want to know, and I'll see you are returned to your family."

No. 19 offered no response other than an instinctive groan.

"Fucking Jew, you had your chance. Gerhardt, get the vise grip. Grab hold of his nuts."

CHAPTER 36

November 25, 1938; 5:10 am

GERHARDT CLUTCHED THE vise grip encasing No. 19's scrotum, then turned his head to avert watching the oncoming syringe.

"Watch what you're doing, and hold them in place, you idiot," Hans shouted. "After this, he'll tell us anything we want to know."

With a single thrust Hans penetrated No. 19's left testicle, pushing so hard he pierced through the sphere, driving the needle deep into No. 19's abdomen.

No. 19 convulsed, pulling on the ties that bound his wrists and ankles. His head writhed from side-to-side. Then, nothing. His body lay still.

"You've killed him, Hans. Now who's the idiot? The information is gone forever. The Führer isn't going to forgive this. He's killed comrades for less. We're good as dead. Now what are we going to do?"

'80 Proof' sweat poured from their brows.

Returning the empty syringe to where they'd found it, Hans flipped over the envelope. It read: "*Urgent: Führer.*" His mind raced as he fumbled with the seal.

"Shit! This medication was prepared for the Führer by his personal physician. It says it's imperative Hitler take this for his condition. It doesn't state the condition. The Führer forgot this when he stormed off earlier. We're fucked. We have to get out of here and disappear, for good. Hurry, the next shift comes on at 6:00 a.m. We have less than an hour to prepare."

The brothers manned the sole duty post of the night. Untying No. 19, they hoisted him atop the other bodies awaiting crema-tion. Next, they would need to secure a prisoner to take No. 19's place on the rack. Once selecting a replacement of similar hair color, height, and mutilation, they'd make certain to choke him so as not to kill him, but leave him unable to speak.

If they hurried, they could set this thing up, lock the cell door, and return to their posts before the next shift relieved them. Then they would make their escape.

CHAPTER 37

November 25, 1938; 6:00 am
Berlin

HE LAY AMONG the pile of human decay struggling to remain lucid. No. 19, revered by his peers for his brilliant mind, had been reduced to a flickering ember, holding on for life among the burnt ashes of depravity.

The pain in his groin and abdomen, where the fifteen-gage syringe pierced through his right testicle and lodged in his prostate, made him oblivious to his broken fingers, shattered teeth, and half-closed, swollen eyes.

He could hear the volcanic furnace spew its fiery breath as though bellowing for more human kindling. The stench of burnt flesh suffocated the airways keeping him alive. With blurred vision he looked into the hollow eye sockets of the head lain next to his own. A sea of blood ran everywhere. Crimson droplets trickled to the corners of his mouth. He didn't know if the blood he tasted was his own or that of the dripping corpses piled atop him. Motionless, he waited his turn to enter the flames of hell.

If he lost consciousness, he would never again be of this world. He couldn't move, could barely think. He struggled to remain conscious. To succumb would be to perish and he represented the last in his line. He closed his eyes and imagined the children he'd once hoped to father. Who would they have been? What would they have become?

He thought he heard voices. He couldn't be sure. The weeks of torture had turned his mind into a vault of screaming agony. Soon he would be gone. He pictured his wife's face as if to say goodbye.

"Over here. This one's still alive."

CHAPTER 38

November 27, 1938
Berlin

IN THE MONTHS preceding No. 19's capture, Adolf Hitler had been administered a regimen of treatments, in the hopes of reversing his sterility. A prisoner himself, to the progressive deterioration of Parkinson's disease, the Führer took measures to produce a son who would carry on his legacy. Hitler's personal physician, Karl Brandt, seemed hopeful. The last of a series of injections had been delivered, in person, to the Führer for administering the next day.

Hitler entered the cell. His face turned beet red. His flaming eyes pierced the sentry's soul. "Who the hell is this? Where is my prisoner? Where is No. 19?" Hitler shouted. White foam seeped from the corners of his mouth.

The guards who had replaced the Schtroebers stood dumb-founded, unaware of the prisoner switch. Hitler poised his re-volver under the taller guard's chin. "Where is No. 19?"

The guard stammered. Hitler cocked the hammer of his gun, looked into the eyes of the terrified guard, and pulled the trigger. It took only seconds for off-duty soldiers to rush to the scene. With his counterpart splayed on the floor, the remaining guard, a youth movement recruit, emptied his bladder. "Bind him to the rack," Hitler instructed, "and remove that uniform. Is this what my army has become, a sanctuary for bed-wetting cowards and buffoons?"

Arms and legs splayed, as the soldiers bound the young re-cruit to the rack, he pled for his life. "Mein Führer, I assure you, I played no part in No. 19's disappearance. Please, talk to the Schtroebers. They were on duty when..."

"Silence," Hitler shouted, pulling the rack taut, prompting the cry of a dying animal. With hands clasped behind his back, Hitler paced circles before his captive audience. *No one crosses me. Incompetence will be met with death.* Hitler gave the rack one final turn. A pitiful shriek filled the air. Then . . . nothing.

Sandor Cain was gone. Hitler's chance to find Hanussen's parchment . . . gone. The Schtroebers . . . gone. Hitler burst into a psychotic rage. "Nobody knows a damn thing. I'm sur-rounded by idiots." The tremors in Hitler's hands exaggerated. Facial muscles twitched around hate-filled eyes. Sweat poured from his forehead.

The soldiers recognized the signs. Without turning their heads they shifted their eyes from Hitler's stare. One unified thought filled the room. *Avoid the Führer's wrath at all cost, praise his every move.*

Without provocation, Hitler stepped into the corridor and again pulled his revolver from its holster. Gun emptied, six more lay dead—four prisoners, and two of Hitler's own men. Amid the carnage, in the far corner of No. 19's cell, the now insignificant syringe which had earlier housed the sterile Führer's aspirations for fathering a successor, lay empty on the floor—its contents working within the prostate of prisoner No. 19.

CHAPTER 39
July 22, 1968; 10:00 a.m.

RYAN SAT IN Abdo's waiting room, his knees bouncing with nervous anticipation. At Abdo's insistence, Regine remained home. Her presence in the waiting room would put unnecessary pressure on all parties involved. Calendar cleared, Abdo put no time limit on the session.

He had spent hours preparing. On the one hand, he worried perhaps he was too close to the case and should refer Ryan to a colleague. On the other, no one knew Ryan as well as he did, nor would they have his insight into Ryan's history and personality.

Abdo sat at his desk, mesmerized by the photo of his own wife and daughter. He again pondered the divergent paths upon which fate had thrust the two families. His life had been blessed with so much happiness, and the Cains' with so much despair.

Ryan's therapy would be an emotional exodus through painful memories. Abdo prayed for the strength to see Ryan through it.

The moment was at hand. It was time to address what he'd witnessed the previous evening. Time to talk about things everyone had been avoiding: Ryan and Sandor's relationship, Sandor's death, Willow's suicide, Ryan's low self-esteem, and the personalities sharing Ryan's mind.

This was to be the first step of a long, arduous journey. They would proceed with caution. There would be no turning back. He and Ryan were going to get to know each other a lot better than either had ever anticipated. Abdo rose and opened his office door.

"Come in, Ryan."

CHAPTER 40

July 22, 1968; 10:15 a.m.

REGINE NEARED THE limit of her endurance. While Ryan sat with Abdo, Regine ventured to the one place where she could try to sort out the new devastation in her life. A place which in the past afforded her peace and serenity.

When they'd moved to Washington Heights in 1946, she and Sandor took the first of many walks in Fort Tryon Park. Nature's splendor was refreshing and everything in life seemed as it should be. She recalled, as though it were yesterday, Sandor asking, "What are you looking for?" as her eyes wandered the landscape.

"It's not important. I'll know it when I see it. Let's keep walking, it's so beautiful here."

Without warning, Regine scampered off in another direction. By the time Sandor caught up, his question required no answer. As a child, Regine spent her most cherished moments with her mother, frolicking beneath the willows in Vienna.

There, in a remote section of the park, as if scripted, stood a solitary weeping willow tree.

It was at that very spot where Regine shared with Sandor the most wonderful news of their lives—she was pregnant. Names had long since been chosen in hope of such a miracle. If a girl, she would be named Willow; and if a boy, he would be Ryan Lazarus. Ryan being the first name of the man who'd risked his own life procuring departure visas for both Regine and Sandor in their escape from Austria.

"Sandor, this is it. This is our spot. This is where we'll picnic and bring our children to play." Regine kept true to her word. They spent many wonderful moments under the lone willow.

So many years later, tears running down her cheeks, Regine sat alone staring at the willow in all of its resilience. She could sense the willow weeping with her, as though somehow it too remembered and shared her pain.

Regine closed her eyes. She envisioned Ryan running about, throwing his ball up in the air and trying to catch it, while little Willow found her favorite spot under the canopy of her namesake, and played with her dolls. The massive tree always made them feel safe, as the wind whispered its song through the low-lying branches.

On one particular occasion, Willow came running to Regine with a very concerned look on her face.

"What's wrong sweetheart? Why do you look so sad?"

"Those ladies, over there. They said our tree is weeping. Why is our tree crying, Mama?"

Regine smiled, lifting Willow to her lap, just as her mother had done with her so many years ago. She explained that the tree was named a *weeping* willow because of its draping foliage, and that the weeping willow had proven itself the strongest of all trees. "While most trees crack and break, the willow survives by bending with the wind and singing a song."

Willow smiled, "I'm glad Mama, because we both love our willow, don't we?"

"Of course, sweetheart. But you know, you are my most precious Willow, don't you?"

"I love you, Mama," Willow said, giving her mother an endearing hug.

Regine's mind returned to the present. *How could things have gone from so wonderfully perfect to so horribly wrong? First Sandor, then Willow, and now Ryan.*

Getting up to leave, Regine pulled herself together. She'd be there for Ryan now that he needed her most. She held back her tears. She would emulate the tree that had been her faithful companion throughout life's difficult journey. She would become the willow . . . strong and enduring.

CHAPTER 41

July 22, 1968; evening

THE SHADOW ASSASSIN, both of him, sat in the room reveling in the spoils of their vengeance. It felt so good to be doing this. Each killing made them feel more alive. They'd waited so long to exact their hatred and revenge. Who would be on the agenda at the next evening's late-night discussion? Their adrenalin pumped in anticipation of the next kill.

"Vengeance is ours!"

Chapter 42
July 24, 1968; noon

REGINE ACCOMPANIED RYAN to this next appointment. After sixty long minutes, Abdo opened his office door and escorted Ryan back to the reception room. He took Regine's hand, and led her into his study. Seating her in a cushioned leather arm-chair, positioned across from his desk, Abdo thought about where to begin. He wanted to assure her they would work their way through this—together.

"Coffee?" Abdo offered.

Regine declined with a slight turn of her head. Her hands trembled on her lap.

After a few moments, Abdo looked into Regine's eyes. Then he began.

"Ryan has what is known as multiple personality disorder. He also suffers from repressed memory disorder. I suspect the repressed memories began at the moment of Sandor's passing.

For the past twelve years Ryan has had no recollection of his childhood experiences, prior to, and including the day of, his father's death.

"Now, while repressed memory disorder is almost always the result of abuse—that doesn't apply here—at least, not *physical* abuse. I feel certain that what transpired between Sandor and Ryan during the moments preceding Sandor's death holds the answers.

"While those memories are not cognitive . . ."

Abdo caught himself. He realized by the look on Regine's face, that she didn't understand the terminology. He started over.

"While Ryan's earliest childhood memory is of Sandor's funeral, that doesn't mean earlier memories are not stored in his mind. They most certainly are. Ryan's mind has chosen to bury them and avoid the unpleasantness they bring with them. I'm going to try to help restore Ryan's memories to his conscious mind."

Abdo awaited a response, doubting there would be one. Regine remained frozen, unable to speak. She would need time to absorb what she was hearing, and then ask questions.

Abdo continued. "Multiple personality disorder is usually the result of a single, or series of, traumatic events in a person's life. We are both aware of the traumatic events in Ryan's life. Multiple personality disorder occurs when the mind can no longer deal with everything that's thrown at it. The mind searches for an escape by creating alternate personalities to help deal with the stress. The original personality can no longer cope and becomes lost in alter ego personalities—losing more and more of its own identity as time goes on.

"I believe these conditions, in Ryan's case, are inseparably entangled. When we begin to unravel one condition, we will also address the other.

"Now, I want you to think of Ryan's mind as a puzzle—a labyrinth—a maze of hallways, if you will."

Abdo could tell by Regine's expression that his analogy had flown above her head, so he stopped and thought for a moment.

"Let's start again. I want you to think of Ryan's mind as a hotel. In the hotel, each of his emotions occupies a room. The keys to all of the rooms are held by the proprietor of the hotel, which in this case is the Ryan you have always known and loved.

"When Ryan gets angry he temporarily unlocks the door to his anger emotion and that allows him to vent his feelings. This is also the case for his other emotions. Each of these emotions is allowed out, from time to time. That is a normal process in every human being.

"However, what is happening in Ryan's case is that it is no longer Ryan controlling the emotions, but rather his emotions controlling him. In essence, the keys to the rooms which store Ryan's emotions are no longer in his possession. They keys are now possessed by the emotions inside the rooms. These emotions can now come out whenever they want, for as long as they want.

"Are you still with me?" Abdo asked.

Regine sat silent, then nodded.

"Okay then. Inside Ryan's mind, independent of the emotions that are now in control, is the original holder of all the keys.

"This is very important. I don't want to lose you here, so tell me if you don't understand.

"Earlier, I referred to the proprietor of the hotel as Ryan. We are not going to call the holder of the keys by the name Ryan anymore. Ryan is your son, the entire package of individualism you've always known as a complete person. We are now going to call the proprietor of the hotel *Lazarus*.

"You are well aware, when Ryan was born, Sandor insisted on Ryan's middle name—Lazarus. Sandor believed in the strength of the human body and spirit to survive, despite all odds. His own life was a testament to that.

"Sandor came to understand that Lazarus is representative of the survivor in all of us, which allows us to overcome insurmountable odds. He named your son Ryan Lazarus Cain, so he would never forget that he is a survivor in a long line of survivors."

Abdo paused for a few moments to let what he had said sink in. He stood up, walked to the corner of this office, and poured coffee for both himself and Regine. She looked like she needed it. When he thought she was ready, he continued his evaluation.

"Lazarus, the survivor in Ryan, has gone from *in-control, to out-of-control*. This is apparent through the dramatic mood swings Ryan displays.

"Understand this: Lazarus is not gone. The survivor in Ryan is not dead. He is lost and confused. At this moment he

127

is wandering through a maze of corridors. In order for him to regain the keys to the doors, and once again gain control of his emotions, Lazarus must navigate his way through this maze. Together, we're going to listen to, and observe the occupants of Ryan's mind and let Lazarus help us guide him back home."

Once again Abdo looked at Regine, feeling her pain and confusion. He knew all of this was way beyond her understanding. He asked if she had any questions.

Regine could barely get the words out. "How many personalities are there, and will my son ever be the way he was?"

Abdo expected the second part of the question, but not the first. He knew Regine didn't care how, or at what cost—she just wanted her son back. The rest would be to be up to him, and Ryan.

Abdo pondered how much he should tell Regine. He thought about her question, and then said, "We want to stay positive. At this point we don't know how many personalities have developed, or their nature. Ryan is a strong young man. You know your son well enough to know he won't quit until he has won the battle. That is how he was raised. He has recovered when doctors told him he wouldn't. And while I myself must admit I don't truly understand, he has a remarkable, even uncanny, way of remedying himself."

Abdo walked Regine to the door telling her he would call later in the day with the dates and times of Ryan's upcoming sessions.

While Regine and Ryan paused at the elevator, Abdo closed his door. He stood with his eyes closed for a few seconds, and then withdrew into his office. He decided he'd done the right thing by not telling Regine about his additional concerns—she had enough on her mind.

Still, Abdo couldn't help but hope that one or more of Ryan's alter egos hadn't led him to do things, horrible things, which could never be remedied.

CHAPTER 43
July 24, 1968; evening

NERVES WERE FRAZZLED. The walls were closing in around the Quad members. The rickety table fan did nothing to squelch the summer heat and humidity. The smell of perspiration made the room physically nauseating.

"As if our lives don't suck enough," said the Watcher. "Until now, we've lived in our own little world. We did, thought, and said whatever we wanted. Nobody gave a shit. Now, all of a sudden, things are getting complicated."

"We have nothing to hide," said the Optimist. "You make it sound like there's something to find out about us. Other than ourselves, who cares what we do, or think?"

"Then why is some doctor asking questions about what I think, what I remember about my life, about my father?" the Watcher blurted in anger. "It's none of his fuckin' business."

"I think he's a pretty nice guy," the Loner stuttered.

The Watcher cut him off. "Dr Betaré, what kind of fuckin' doctor is he? One of those guys who takes anything you say and twists it around to make you look like you're nuts? I'm not telling him a fuckin' thing. He's nothing but trouble."

"Calm down," the Optimist said in a soothing voice. "Nobody here is nuts. None of us have done anything wrong. Let's not attack each other. We need to stick together."

Hoping to close the topic of discussion, the Watcher declared with disdain, "My past and my father are my business, nobody else's. You guys do what you want, but I'm telling him nothing."

Following a few moments of awkward silence, the Writer chimed in. "So, what do you guys think is going on with these murders? First Vespers is killed, then the Cockroach. It's all anyone is talking about, and it freaks me out that we just talked about them. The police are interviewing anyone who's ever had anything to do with them."

"Well, that leaves us out *question boy*," said the Watcher. "The only time we ever had anything to do with them was when they pushed us around and treated us like crap. I say someone did the neighborhood a favor."

"That kind of talk could get us into a lot of trouble, and don't call me *question boy*," the Writer warned. "I'm sure all of us, and anyone else who ever knew those S.O.B.s feels the same way, but you should keep those thoughts to yourself."

"We're the only ones here," the Watcher argued. "Are you going to tell someone else?"

"All I'm saying is, it wouldn't look good if anyone heard about the conversations we've been having. If I didn't know better, I'd think one, or all of us, had something to do with the murders," the Writer conjectured.

The Shadow Assassin agreed wholeheartedly.

CHAPTER 44

July 25, 1968

Morning:

HIS CELL IS DARK. Not peaceful dark. Disturbing, claustrophobic dark. The kind of dark that threatens to swallow you whole.

There are no windows, no pictures hanging. No distractions from the endless hours of loneliness. Visitors are forbidden. Nourishment is provided by an unseen entity during slumber.

Arising from the purgatory of his thoughts, Lazarus sobs and prays for the return to his days of innocence. He tries to erase the visions of torture and dismemberment plaguing his mind, consuming his dreams.

Soaked in perspiration, the screams in his head grow louder. He spreads his fingers, applying pressure to both sides of his skull, attempting to prevent detonation into a million pieces. *How do you erase nightmares? Silence the cries?*

"Do you really think you can keep me here forever? I will find a way out. Why won't you talk to me?" Lazarus shouts in futility.

The confining walls expand and contract. Possessing a life of their own, they give off a dim, pulsating, red-luminescence. Uneven floors make pacing a chore rather than a release of pent-up energy. A looped electrical cord, attached to an empty light socket coated with dried blood, dangles from the low ceiling like a hangman's noose.

The pounding in his head, the scent of his bodily waste, the aftertaste of his own vomit—distasteful as these sensations may be—all are welcome occurrences. They confirm he is still alive.

Morning's hope for a better day brings thousands of beads of condensation. The droplets quiver on the convoluted walls. Each converges toward its neighbor, eager to unite.

Lazarus places his face flush to the wall. He cheers the droplets tireless tenacity. During his years of solitary confinement, he has formed an imaginary friendship with the lifelike entities in an effort to maintain some semblance of sanity and contain his own loneliness. He envies the swells their final destination of solidarity, reminiscent of happier times spent with his own brothers.

Wetting his fingers upon the base of the wall, Lazarus contemplates the hopelessness of his situation. The depression that consumes him thrives in the chasm that has become his prison, his home, his life.

With two fingers inserted into the light socket, Lazarus considers the thought of ending his torment once and for all—an escape he has pondered a thousand times before. To his unseen captor he shouts, "One more inch and it'll all be over. Then, who will you have to torment, you son-of-a-bitch?"

Staring off into the nothingness that surrounds him, Lazarus wonders. *What's happened to my life? I was once a regular boy enjoying a child's simple pleasures. I had friends. Or was that someone else? I'm not sure anymore.*

In a pensive trance, one of his fingers makes contact with the power source. Jolted by the shock, Lazarus instinctively yanks his fingers from the socket. New emotions surge like an erupting volcano. He feels brought back to life. Jump started. His will to survive rekindled.

Hope renewed, he listens to the flow of fluids rushing through the plumbing concealed behind the damp cell walls.

"Talk to me, you son-of-a-bitch," he screams, knowing there will be no response. "Why have I been taken prisoner and isolated all these years? Why can't I get these terrible images out of my head? What is it you want? I know you can hear me. Show yourself. Confront me, you coward."

The gatekeeper stirs in silence, annoyed by the arrogance of its honored guest.

***

Afternoon:
On most days, Lazarus entertains himself by staring into an abyss of blinding fog created by the humidity of his habitat. He

utilizes the haze as a viewing screen and projects mental images of pleasant memories from days long past.

Today is different. If he squints and focuses, a faint road-map of veins and arteries appear, formed by cracks in the walls. *Have these always been here? Why haven't I noticed them before? Where did they come from? Has the electrical shock somehow enabled me to see these things? Are they actually here, or am I imagining them?*

Vague letters etched on the walls are coming into focus—a word—no, a name—Isok. Beneath the name is a string of scratches broken into increments of seven. It appears to be a calendar marking the passage of time. *Was someone else held prisoner here before me?*

The more he stares, the more he sees. Writings are strewn everywhere, although still somewhat of a blur.

It appears Lazarus' predecessor left a journal of sorts. His very thoughts have been transcribed onto the walls. Lazarus is hopeful that soon, these 'Writings of Isok' will become legible enough to read. Perhaps they will tell of Isok's travails and offer insight into his own fate.

Once again Lazarus confronts his elusive nemesis, "Do you see that, you bastard? I'm not alone. You can't hide forever. There are others, and together we'll find you, and then…"

"And then, what?"

Lazarus is at a loss.

***

Evening:
Something astonishing is happening. The day unfolds like no other before it.

Lazarus sits for hours, listening for the slightest hint of sound. He wonders if his captor, the gatekeeper, will be forced to make an appearance in light of the new circumstances.

Of late, Lazarus has detected a whisper of murmurs coming from somewhere beyond his detention walls. *Perhaps I'm hearing things that aren't there. Solitary confinement can cause moments of delusion.*

He ponders his situation. If he responds to the voices, his words may simply echo in space for perpetuity. Worse yet, maybe the voices he's been hearing are the echoes of tormented prisoners who preceded him.

Nonetheless, in the hope someone will hear him, he pleads for his invisible audience to pay close attention. His moments of clarity are growing fewer and farther between. Soon, he may not be able to elucidate his story.

"I am painfully aware that I no longer possess a constant stream of clear thought. My fantasies are my greatest ally in my struggle for survival. It is this understanding that makes these precious few moments of lucidity critical to me, and your ability to decipher my moments of possible delusion from reality, critical to you.

"My name is Lazarus. I am where I am, because I know too much. I know things the others have either forgotten or wish to forget. I represent memories too painful to address, and too important to dismiss.

"God help me, I remember the screams. People, both innocent and not-so-innocent, have been murdered and I was, and am, somehow involved.

"That is '*who*' I am. '*Where*' I am. is a more interesting question—a prison of some sort in an unchartered territory. I wish I could be more specific.

'*What*' I intend to do should be obvious—escape my captivity, return to my brothers, and make things right.

"As for the '*why*'—after much introspection I have identified my captor, *my gatekeeper*, if you will. It is '*fear*' that makes prisoners of us all, mercilessly taunting its holder, until confronted and overcome. It rules by intimidation, rendering its prey immobile before the battle ever begins. It ends today. I shall be its prisoner no longer.

"For most, there is no refuge from tormenting memories. It is my intent to search for, and expose, the truth and fears that have long inflicted hardship on the innocent members of my family, and set us free. And, if possible, make us one again.

"The '*when*'—very soon, I think. I can sense the moment approaching. The massive door that imprisons me has developed small cracks, which grow as I speak. Perhaps, the darkness of my life can be illuminated by the light now starting to seep in.

"The writings on the walls are becoming clearer, the sounds more audible. I'll be with you soon. I must go now and prepare myself."

The gatekeeper sits powerless against the proposed break-out; its prisoner has recognized the key that will unlock his door to freedom.

PART II
SECRETS

"Secrets are made to be found out with time."
—Charles Sanford—

CHAPTER 45
The 1930's

ABDO BETARÉ DESCENDED from Lebanese ancestry. A once-in-a-lifetime opportunity redirected Abdo's path to Austria, where he'd been offered the opportunity to further his education under the tutelage of his idol, and soon-to-be mentor, Sigmund Freud.

Freud was best known for his theories on the unconscious mind. His progressive studies in the areas of repressed memories and dream symbolism intrigued Abdo, who hoped to one day make his mark in the treatment of adolescent behavior.

In March 1933, Heinrich Himmler, the head of Hitler's Secret State Police, announced the opening of the first concentration camp in Dachau, a suburb of Munich, Germany. Designed to hold five thousand prisoners, Dachau soon overflowed with more than twice its intended capacity.

In 1936, after the disappearance of a friend and colleague at the hands of the Gestapo, Abdo joined the underground resistance movement. Those willing to risk their own lives for others numbered few and far between. The courageous non-Jews who did, became known as the "Righteous Persons."

By 1937, construction began on a new facility at Dachau, enabling the Nazis to increase their prisoner capacity and expand the number of experimentation facilities, gas chambers, and crematoriums.

In the early months of 1938, Anna Freud disappeared. Detained at Gestapo headquarters and interrogated for two days, she was returned home, her body unscathed but her mind overwrought with terror. Sigmund Freud and his family fled their homeland. Possessing influential connections, Freud obtained the documentation required to secure passage to France, and then England, where he would die a year later. Out of concern for his student and friend, Freud also procured transport documentation for Abdo, hoping he would one day join him.

August 1938 marked the completion of the expanded Dachau camp.

By November 1938, over ten thousand Jews arrived at Dachau following their arrests during Kristallnacht.

Jews throughout Europe ran for their lives. A mere handful of hospitals and courageous citizens provided shelter to the fleeing innocents. Small, underground rebel groups plotted in secrecy against the Third Reich, while they organized escape routes for Jews, by sea.

***

The leaders of the "Righteous Persons" had received confirmation of the existence of a parchment which Hitler sought. It seemed, with this document in his possession, Hitler believed he could not be defeated. He would rule the world.

Despite the illogic of Hitler's thought process, the fact that possession of such a document would strengthen Hitler's resolve gave the resistance reason enough to make certain he never obtained it. By thwarting his efforts to retrieve it, they hoped to cause Hitler to question himself, and falter.

Entrusted with the classified information detailing the status and location of an individual known only as prisoner No. 19, it was Abdo's mission to lead and secure the prisoner's rescue, if possible. If not, his mission entailed making certain Hitler never retrieved the information he was looking for.

The attempt to retrieve No. 19 from his Nazi captors proceeded as planned on the twenty-fifth of November. Intelligence stated security would be light. Time was of the essence—Abdo's instructions clear. Find No. 19 and rescue him. Or, eliminate him.

The "Righteous Persons" stood in disappointment as they arrived at No. 19's cell. The door wide open, No. 19 had been moved. They heard a commotion, men who sounded drunk, arguing. *How many are there?* Abdo made the decision to abort, their mission a failure.

Making their way through the compound they felt the heat of the roaring furnace. Their bodies cast eerie shadows over the corpses awaiting cremation. Five more seconds and they'd be gone. Abdo heard his name being called by one of his compatriots.

"Abdo, over here. This one's still alive."

Abdo hoisted the body over his shoulder. They needed to get the injured man to a hospital that would not only care for him, but also protect him.

"My friend, I'm so sorry, I called you by name. Someone might've heard. You can't take the chance. They'll hunt you down. You've got to get out of here. We'll make sure this man is taken care of. Go now."

While Abdo's intent had been to remain in Austria, unforeseen circumstances altered his destiny in the early hours of November 25, 1938. The paperwork provided by his mentor, months earlier, turned out to be a Godsend. After months in seclusion, hidden by the underground, Abdo Betaré's escape route from Germany had been finalized.

In May 1939, when Abdo first met Sandor Cain, boarding a ship destined to England, he had no idea he was talking to the man whose life he'd saved. The rescuer and the rescued stood side by side on their journey to freedom.

CHAPTER 46

May 1939

A CLOUD OF death loomed above an entire nation till it could endure no more. Then, the heavens cried. Its tears washed the blood of genocide from the cobblestone streets toward the harbor.

Two men stood silent, neither recognizing the other, rain dripping from the brims of their fedoras. From the corners of their eyes they measured each other with suspicion, neither man willing to be the first to flinch. In the distance, a hundred or more people, men, women and children, waited their turns on the gangplank of the black ocean-liner bound for freedom.

No luggage, no handbags, no jewelry, no belongings. "Leave with nothing but the shirt on your back," was the ultimatum afforded to a mere handful of the thousands of Jews seeking to emigrate. Mingled among the departing refugees were two fugitives, possessing forged papers.

"Do you know, sir, is that the RMS Georgic?" asked the pensive man standing unescorted. RMS, or Royal Mail Ship, was the designation given British ships contracted to deliver mail overseas. On this occasion it would also transport refugees from their homeland of Austria to the United States.

"Camouflage," responded the defensive man shielding his wife, no longer making eye contact.

"Pardon?"

"Camouflage. The ship is painted black, hoping to move undetected. The Brits are onto Hitler's game. They know that the same lunatics allowing us to leave may very well attempt to sink us once we've embarked. Our emigration offers the Nazis an opportunity to hone their fighting skills at sea. They are the hunters and we their helpless prey. I estimate we have a thirty-percent chance of reaching our destination."

"Now that doesn't pose a very optimistic future, does it? I'm Abdo. Abdo Betaré."

"Depends. Besides, it's thirty-percent better than if we remain here," the calculating man responded.

"Depends? Depends on what?"

"On whether Hitler has become a humanitarian, or, possesses an ulterior motive." The guarded cynic raised an eyebrow. "Perhaps his army is not yet accomplished at fighting off-land, and needs practice. I'd brace myself for a difficult voyage, my friend. I'm Sandor Cain, and this is my wife, Regine."

As evening settled in, ominous clouds hovered over the immobile vessel, foreboding the treacherous journey that lay ahead. At long last, the ship's engines roared, pistons jabbing like a tireless boxer. Diesel fumes never smelled so sweet.

Sandor remained stoically apprehensive.

***

To ease each other's anxieties, the two men spoke of their ancestral histories. Abdo shared an in-depth saga of his family's long line of physicians, indicating that he himself hoped to specialize in adolescent psychiatry. Sandor had found a friend, someone on his own intellectual level, whom he enjoyed conversing with, someone to whom he would open up. Within limits.

"My ancestors, in-fact, were named Cahn, not Cain. My great grandfather, Morris Cahn, immigrated to Austria in the mid-1800s, when Hungary was in a state of political change."

Abdo listened with genuine interest.

"Austria reverted from a dominant European power to a nation weakened by revolution. It struggled to combat internal uprisings, liberalism, and the forces of nationalism. Emigrant paperwork and its tedious follow-up were low on the totem-pole of priorities. Most information-takers were only semi-literate."

Abdo thought Sandor sounded more like a history professor reading from a book than a *real person* relating a personal anecdote. Nonetheless, intrigued by both Sandor and his story, he urged him to continue.

"Spelling errors were not uncommon. Family surnames were lost to the faulty pen stroke of unqualified administrators.

"In the blink of an eye, with the erroneous scribble of an 'i' in place of an 'h,' Cahn became Cain. Try as he may, once his naturalization papers were issued, my great grandfather found his efforts to correct the error futile.

"Thus began a new chapter in my family's history under a new surname."

***

For days on end, torrential rain pounded the Georgic. Twenty-foot swells hammered the ship from side to side, threatening to take the ship down. Nausea, anxiety, broken bones and concussions were everyday occurrences. Even one premature birth graced the RMS Georgic. Abdo's medical training kept him busy throughout the journey, assisting the ship's physician.

At storm's end, Regine gripped a guardrail. Chin raised and eyes closed, she rejoiced in the salty mist that sprayed her face. "Come Sandor, stand with me. The air is simply delicious. I feel so alive."

Sandor remained still. He entertained more relevant thoughts. *Where will we live? How will I go about finding a job?* Always the planner. He listened as other passengers questioned God. "Why have you spared us from the Nazis, only to test us at sea?"

Fools. Sandor sighed. *How have they managed to make it this far?*

Battered, but undeterred, the RMS Georgic docked at Ellis Island. The engines sputtered and shut down, their pistons throwing their final jabs. Once again they'd made it through fifteen grueling rounds.

Perched atop the ramp to freedom, the Captain and his First Mate offered up courteous smiles, wishing each of the departing passengers "good fortune" on his or her exciting new adventure. The travelers, in turn, disembarked, mumbling under their collective breaths about the harsh weather conditions and hellacious experience they'd endured.

Politely, the Captain nodded, wondering what they had expected.

"Thank God for bad weather, eh Captain," Sandor commented, hand extended.

The Captain stared for a moment, deciding whether or not this man was being sarcastic. Then he nodded and smiled.

"He's the only one who understands," the Captain shared with his First Mate.

"Understands? Understands what, sir?"

"The storm, the turbulence . . . they saved our lives. Those very conditions, First Mate, are the reasons we didn't come under attack."

Stepping onto Ellis Island, Regine spoke first. "Oh, my God. Take a deep breath, Sandor. This is what freedom smells like."

"Freedom doesn't have a smell, dear," Sandor corrected.

Abdo and Regine looked at each other, smiling. *Poor Sandor. Always so serious. He seems unable to take pleasure in life's natural beauty.*

***

In Vienna, Sandor had worked hard, earning respect as a gifted engineer. He'd proven himself both brilliant and self-motivated, demanding excellence of all around him, displaying zero-tolerance for incompetence.

In the new country they'd now call home, Sandor would once again prove his worth. Calculation dictated his every move. With the mind of a chess player, he remained several moves ahead of everyone around him. In record time, he climbed the ladder of an engineering think tank, and within two years ran the company's Research and Development division.

The Cains were well on their way to fulfilling their dreams.

Sandor's mindset had graduated to cautiously optimistic.

CHAPTER 47
September 1946
Washington Heights

"SANDOR, MY FRIEND. I'm afraid I haven't been very much help," Abdo confessed. "It's a good thing I've got my practice to fall back on. I'm certain I'd starve if I had to rely on my carpentry skills. I'm not even certain Regine will feed me after my pitiful display of incompetence."

Regine laughed at poor Abdo as she gazed out the window of their new two-bedroom apartment. Sandor remained in a world of his own, meticulously constructing baby furniture.

"Look Sandor, there are so many people walking about. And the children, look at all of them. I can't even count them, there are so many," she said rubbing her hand over her very pregnant belly.

In mid-December, upon Ryan's arrival into this glorious new world, Sandor looked into Regine's eyes. No words were necessary. *Life is now going to be what we dreamt it could be.*

Abdo, in the meanwhile, had found his perfect woman, Sonya. He proposed, and they married within six months of meeting. It was love at first sight for both of them. They shared a mutual respect that would never waiver

***

Three years later . . .

"IT'S A GIRL, Mr. Cain," the gregarious dark-skinned nurse boomed. "I been workin' here twenty years and ain't never seen nothin' like it. We told Miss Regine to push, and whoa, before the pu . . . met the . . . sh, that beautiful little girl of yours jus' flew outta there like a kid on a water slide. Lucky thing the doc's a good catcher."

Sandor's usually stoic face beamed. The words, "it's a girl," struck a chord of emotion that had been buried for years.

"A girl," he repeated, reconfirming what he'd heard. "And everything is in order? Fingers, toes . . . everything?"

"Don't you worry none, sir. You have yourself one precious little daughter there, Mr. Cain."

"And, my wife?"

"Doin' jus' fine, and waitin' to see you. You and the missus picked a name yet?"

"Willow," he said without hesitation.

"That be a mighty pretty name, sir. Why don't you come with me, and I'll introduce you to sweet baby Willow?"

CHAPTER 48
1952

FRIDAYS MEANT THE Cains and Betarés would be sharing dinner together. It had become a tradition. Sonya joined Regine in the kitchen while Abdo joined Ryan in the living room, awaiting Sandor's return from another late night at work.

"Hey there, Ryan. You're looking very busy. Mind if I ask what you're working on?"

"No sir. I'm drawing a dog named Snoopy. He's not a superhero. He's a lot like me. He thinks stuff, but doesn't talk. He makes me laugh. I already finished drawing Superman and Batman. Wanna see?"

"Don't I always?" Abdo smiled, trying to remember if he'd ever seen Ryan laugh. "Do you laugh a lot?"

"Not too much," Ryan answered in a hushed voice. "My dad gets angry. He says laughing is a waste of time. So, when I do laugh, I laugh on the inside, so he can't see. You won't tell him, will you?"

"That stays between us." Abdo relieved Ryan's sudden look of worry. "No puzzles to solve, or model ships to build today?"

"I dunno, maybe later." Ryan shrugged.

When Abdo excused himself to join the ladies in the kitchen, Ryan returned to drawing his talking dog, unflinching in every detail. Abdo snuck a quick peek in Ryan's direction. He couldn't tell if Ryan was laughing or not.

***

Two years later . . .

Ryan's uncanny ability to solve word puzzles evolved to a level that bewildered Abdo. "How do you do that?" he asked, watching Ryan, at age seven, reconstruct anagrams into words without effort.

"I dunno. The letters just kinda shuffle around in my head, and I see a word. It's easy. You wanna try? I'll help you."

Abdo smiled, declining the offer. *He has no idea how gifted he is.*

"Keep up the good work, Ryan. I'll just watch if you don't mind. You should…"

"Abdo. A word, please?" Sandor interrupted, clearly annoyed.

Stepping into the hallway, Sandor raised a hand. "I've asked you before. No praise. He'll become complacent. Please don't make me remind you again."

Sandor had changed. He'd become intolerant and abusive. He conducted himself as two distinctly different people—a kind, soft spoken, doting father with Willow, a strict, punishing tyrant with Ryan. Abdo's concerns for Ryan's emotional well-being grew. He wondered if Sandor recognized his own dual-persona. *This sharp little boy with a meticulous mind will never be sharp enough to satisfy his father.*

CHAPTER 49

May 1955

SANDOR TURNED OFF the lights. With the tip of his index finger he raised one of the closed venetian blind slats.

"I'm telling you Regine, we're being watched."

He became more compulsive and paranoid with each new day.

"Sandor, please talk to someone. There's no one there. No one is watching us. But, if someone is, we have to trust somebody. Talk to Abdo. We can trust him," Regine reasoned, trying to placate her husband's mounting fears. "Please Sandor, come to bed."

"Trust no one Regine. Do you hear me? No one. Where's Ryan? I have to talk to Ryan." Sandor's face reddened, taking on the look of a madman.

Frightened by the man she no longer recognized, Regine made one final plea. "Sandor, he's just a boy. He's only eight years old."

"Don't argue with me, woman."

Later that evening, tears rolling down her cheeks, Regine peeked through the crack of Ryan's partially closed door. He lay in the darkness talking to himself, or, perhaps to God. "Please, no more. Stop the voices in my head. Please, I'm scared. I'll be good. I promise. Please, make them go away."

Regine sat in horror, wondering what to do. The man she loved with all her heart now lay stripped of his humanity, his hopes, his dreams, left with nothing but a legacy of fear and discipline to pass on to his son.

Sandor appeared delusional.

When Sandor fell asleep, Regine dialed the phone. "Hello, Abdo. I need to speak with you."

***

Two weeks later . . .

"Childish games are a waste of time. I'm sick and tired of having this discussion," Sandor admonished Abdo. "He's my son, I'll decide what's best for him. I know what I'm doing."

Abdo backed off. Sandor had never used that tone with him before. Pursuing the topic any further would cause irreparable damage to whatever relationship still remained between them.

Deep down, in the saddest part of his soul, Abdo knew that one day, Ryan's fear and hostility toward his father would come to a head. On that day, all hell would break loose.

CHAPTER 50
January 1956

RYAN NEEDS FUN in his life. He doesn't need to share our demons. Regine thought those words often but never dared vocalize them to Sandor, who now exhibited a manic state of paranoia.

For years, without Sandor's knowledge, Regine had snuck Ryan his favorite comic books. They provided an escape from Ryan's disciplined reality into the fantasy world of Superman, Batman, and other superheroes.

"This is our little secret, right sweetie?"

Ryan pinched his thumb and forefinger, then zipped his lips. They both smiled.

***

Five months later . . .

The obituary read: *Sandor Cain. Beloved husband and father. Dead at forty-seven. Cancer.*

Ryan stood expressionless, watching his father's coffin lowered into the ground. He tried to remember the man in the box. Nothing came to mind, his memory a blank slate.

With Willow's small hand tightly in her grasp, Regine reflected back in time. She remembered the man whom she once loved so dearly. And, the man he'd become. Perhaps the cancer that ravaged his internal organs also consumed his mind.

As the casket lowered to become one with the earth, Regine's thoughts returned to the moment. She'd have to find a job, and cut back on expenses.

No tears. No sorrow. No feeling of loss. Ryan thought of nothing but his comic books.

CHAPTER 51

July 28, 1968; 5:00 am

SCUMACI LAY IN bed, thinking about the murders. He ran the facts through his mind over and over again, hoping something new would click in his head. Three weeks had passed since they'd visited the crime scenes and interviewed acquaintances of the two victims. Friends couldn't be found, and it seemed nobody missed the two less-than-upstanding citizens.

The investigation had progressed at a slow pace. More potential suspects popped up than they knew what to do with. They needed to find a common thread to tie the crimes together, if indeed one killer had committed both murders.

The Vespers investigation opened the door to lots of possibilities. A drug deal gone bad? Maybe a boyfriend of one of the mistreated girls decided to "off" the S.O.B? Or, perhaps, a pissed-off father might come forward claiming temporary insanity?

In the case of Billy Sane, a.k.a. the Cockroach, the list of suspects included anyone who'd ever met him. When interviewed a second time, the young lovers from the lawn reiterated the information they'd given on the night of the murder, offering no new recollections. "We heard the scream and ran for help." Having been passionately preoccupied, Scumaci could easily understand how they hadn't noticed anything prior to the scream. Remembering their genuine distress on the night of the crime, Scumaci believed every word of their story. He wanted to revisit the crime scene one more time on the off chance that they might have missed something on the first go-round.

Neither crime scene offered any visible clues, with the possible exception of the newspaper displaying the letters VIO circled on it. It didn't mean anything they'd been able to figure out yet. Maybe it didn't mean anything at all.

At five a.m., Scumaci's phone rang. Quinlan's voice sounded groggy and agitated.

"Get dressed. We've got another body. I'll meet you by the park's front entrance in twenty minutes."

CHAPTER 52

July 28, 1968; 6:00 am

"OVER HERE, CHIEF. You sounded a little annoyed on the phone, so I brought some cheese danish, in case you didn't have a chance to eat anything. Food always cheers me up."

"You're killin' me, Scumaci. I already need a shoehorn to get into my pants. Ya know, I was once skinny like you. You'll see. One day you'll go to bed skinny and wake up like me. It just happens."

"For real Chief, you were once my size? That's some scary shit."

"Fuck you, Scumaci. No, I was never your size. Go eat your fuckin' danish."

"You angry, Chief?"

"No, this early morning crap is just getting old, and Katie's pissed that I pulled an assignment like this right before my retirement. Two months to go and it can't come soon enough. Can you say, 'Hello, Tahiti'?"

"Tahiti's gonna have to wait, Chief. This is one sick puppy we're dealing with. The officer over there is waiting to take us to the scene."

"Okay, lead the way," Quinlan said, already exhausted.

It took a half-hour to make their way through the gardens, across the lawns, past the Cloisters and into the wooded area surrounding the uneven path.

Arriving at the spot, they stood frozen in silence, staring from thirty feet away. A beautiful sunrise, blossoming foliage, total silence except for nature's symphony, and a distorted, un-recognizable corpse duct-taped to a tree.

"This is one beautiful park. Too bad humans inhabit it," Quinlan grumbled.

The area had been cordoned off, so they walked the perim-eter to avoid contaminating any possible evidence. Once they'd maneuvered themselves to the point nearest the body they made their way over the yellow crime tape.

Scumaci gagged. "Man, I wish I hadn't eaten that danish. I think it's comin' up. Whoever did this is really sick. Let me see if there's any ID."

Using two fingers Scumaci picked a wallet from the vic-tim's back pocket.

"We've got one Phillip Vulchek. Twenty-four years old. Resides at 401 West 174th Street. Driver's license, social se-curity card, draft card—4F, and forty-seven dollars. Nothing seems to be missing. Robbery doesn't appear to be the motive. What can make a guy look like this, Chief? I can't tell where his face ends and his neck begins."

"We'll let the coroner determine cause-of-death. Let's take it slow and steady Vinnie, and see if we can figure out the sequence of events that occurred here."

CHAPTER 53

July 28, 1968; 8:30 am

AFTER TWO HOURS of scrutinizing the crime scene, Quinlan and Scumaci finalized their hypothesis. Scumaci summed up his thoughts for the report he'd have to write back at the station.

"The victim walked alone, along a remote path during the evening hours. Date to be determined. Evening seems most probable since the possibility of interruption would be at a minimum. Also, darkness would provide low visibility, allowing for the discreet placement of a hidden weapon.

"The site had probably been scoped out days earlier, maybe even weeks before the crime was committed. The preparation of the strike area, as well as the selection of tree to which the victim had been tied, indicates meticulous planning.

"Excess pieces of duct tape found stuck to a limb suggest earlier placement. Also, we theorize, a weapon had been positioned in a well-thought-out location, prior to the attack. The apparent lack of a struggle, by a well-built male in his late twenties, suggests the killer presented himself as no threat to the victim.

"The cause of death, if Chief Quinlan's assumptions are correct, displays a familiarity with the area and a morbid desire to watch his victim suffer. Blood—probably the victim's—was found on the pathway where the blow was struck. Rather than kill Vulchek on the spot, the assailant dragged his 'still-breathing' body to a specific tree to finish him off slowly in the woods. Rigor mortis has set in, which means Vulchek has been dead for at least twelve hours."

Scumaci paused for several seconds, wondering if he'd left anything out. Satisfied, he wiped his hands together, as though cleansing himself of the chore.

"How was that, Chief?" Scumaci asked, like a kid looking for approval from his dad.

Quinlan realized the death, in all likelihood, occurred days earlier, not hours. He based his assessment on the natural decomposition of the body, and the decay caused by the hearty appetite of the natural inhabitants of the wooded location. Scumaci seemed so proud of his summarization, Quinlan saw no need to correct him on the spot. They'd wait for the Medical Examiner to confirm the cause and time of death, and then he'd have Scumaci rework his report.

What the report wouldn't indicate was that the killer displayed sadistic creativity, enjoyed inflicting pain and humiliation, and as yet hadn't provided a consistent pattern of killing, or selected a weapon of preference. He did display a preferential time slot to commit his crimes, and all of his known victims were males in their twenties.

The press would eat up the tasteless potpourri of gore, and then spit it back out for the public to choke on. Making things worse, Quinlan knew his superiors would be all over his ass to get the case solved. If a scapegoat needed to be sacrificed, he would be it.

CHAPTER 54

July 28, 1968

ABDO SAT AT his desk, Ryan's file opened. He uncapped his fountain pen. Where to begin? The addendum would not address Ryan's medical problems. However, Abdo felt it necessary to document all information pertinent to Ryan's current state of mind.

"Supplemental Addendum to Ryan Cain File"
Days before his passing in June '56, Sandor Cain summoned me to his bedside. Skin yellowed, face drawn and body emaciated, he looked resigned to his own demise. It pained me to see my friend this way. The cancer, which had remained undiagnosed for a long period of time, ravaged his internal organs. It was only a matter of time before the inevitable occurred.

Regine held herself together as well as could be expected and, at the request of her husband, did not allow Willow to see him in his deteriorating condition. He wanted her to remember him as he was, not as he then appeared. Ryan was not so fortunate. He sat with his father, alone, every day, right till the very end.

I believe much of what Sandor said was outbursts of delirium. He endured extreme pain despite the high doses of morphine.

He spoke of murder and torture, which was understandable given his history. Images of the past are common under sedation. However, he also spoke of plots, and untold secrets, and people *still* out to get him.

He ranted that nobody was safe. "Ryan must know. He'll know what to do." There was more, but I can't remember. I'd never felt more helpless or tormented. It was so long ago, and I relive those emotions as though they occurred yesterday.

Sandor instructed me to remove an envelope from its hiding place atop his dresser. It had been opened and resealed, bearing a Berlin postmark dated March 24, 1933.

Sandor said it had been lost in the Austrian mail system, which was in total disarray, during and after Hitler's reign. The envelope had been delivered to him years later, in the United States, after the European Postal Service reorganized from the chaos created by the Third Reich.

He made me swear never to open it, but rather, "give this envelope to Ryan when the time is right. Not to Regine. Only Ryan." I had, and still to this day, have no idea what he meant by 'when the time is right.'

There's something I'm missing, I'm sure of it. It will come to me.

CHAPTER 55

July 29, 1968; 7:30 am

QUINLAN THREW COPIES of the *Daily News* and *New York Post* onto his desk, his worst fears realized. Front page, heavy bold fonts—"SHADOW ASSASSIN STRIKES AGAIN" and, "POLICE IN THE DARK, AGAINST SHADOW ASSASSIN." Residents would panic, and soon the tip-line would ring off the hook with well-meaning, but time-consuming bad leads.

Quinlan wished the newspapers would leave the police alone to do their jobs, knowing full well they never would. Everyone had a job to do, and they were doing theirs.

At five minutes to eight Scumaci strolled in without food in hand.

"What? Is there a bakers' strike?" Quinlan asked.

"Nah, I figured you already got enough on your plate this morning, Chief."

"You got that right. I take it you've read the papers. Somehow, I've never taken to being compared to the Keystone

Cops. Everyone's a critic. Don't they realize the bad guys start out with an advantage? They know who we are. We have no friggin' idea who they are."

"You know the routine, Boss. Someone commits a crime. The papers blame us for being too slow. Then, once we catch the guy, the papers take credit for pressuring us to do our jobs. And the world goes on."

"You're pretty much of a cynic for someone your age. No wonder I like you. The Medical Examiner is ready to talk to us. He's bitching 'cause I had him working all night. If I've got to be miserable, so does everyone else. How's that sit with you, Scumaci?"

"About the same as it sat with me when my date said it last night, Boss."

"Sorry I asked. Let's get down to the morgue."

Getting into Scumaci's vehicle, Quinlan noticed the empty cupcake wrappers and smiled.

Scumaci pulled out an eight-page publication printed on rag paper, the same kind of stock used by newspapers. "Here Chief, have you seen this one yet?" The signature box read, *The Heights Update.* "I checked it out, Chief. It's a neighbor-hood newsletter put out by a twenty-year-old journalism ma-jor. She started distributing these in supermarkets about six months ago with the intent of being discovered by a publisher. She's pretty good. Her name is Elaine Aubrey, but she uses a byline of *Scoop Aubrey.*"

Quinlan took the paper and began reading.

FEAR OF HEIGHTS
By Scoop Aubrey

It seems a lot more people than usual have a fear of heights these days—Washington Heights. Over the past four months there have been three gruesome murders committed in our Utopian neighborhood. Police have been conservative in giving investigative details. After all, they can't be telling the killer how close they might be to catching him. However, it would be nice to know they are making headway, and an arrest is close at hand. We can only hope we will be hearing some good news soon.

I'll spare you the nauseating details of the crimes. I'm certain you have read about them in your daily newspapers. All of the victims thus far have been males in their early to mid-twenties, and all attacks have occurred in the evening. If possible, avoid going out alone at night, and please do not assume that because you are not male, or in your twenties, you are safe. This is not meant to scare you, but rather to urge you to walk on the side of caution. As a resident of our community, I implore you to keep your eyes and ears open. Don't ignore anything you think might help the police catch this monster.

Who knows what evil lurks in the hearts of men? Only 'The Shadow' knows. The Shadow Assassin, that is, for that is the name given him by the over-imaginative press.

Do not despair, this lunatic will be caught and
Utopia will be restored.

Quinlan sat in silence, absorbing the article.

"You say she's only twenty? I like her style. She gets to the point. She's informative without the sensationalism. I think we'll have to meet her sometime. Somewhere down the road she may be useful in helping us nail this guy," Quinlan said with a glimmer of hope in his voice.

It was nine o'clock when Quinlan and Scumaci arrived at the morgue. An impatient Victor Golub awaited them. Golub, at age fifty-five, had held the M.E.'s position for almost twenty years, yet still possessed the enthusiasm of a rookie. A slight man with a big mind, he boasted a memory that put mere mortals to shame. His dark eyes hid under caterpillar-like eyebrows. A huge mole dangled from the left side of his chin like a giant raisinette. His wild frizzy hair and wire-brush mustache made people think of Albert Einstein. Victor thought that a compliment to Albert. Scumaci didn't think it a compliment to anyone.

Quinlan got right to the point. "Okay Victor, what can you tell us?"

"As suspected, the cause of death was suffocation," Golub said. "The victim endured a long, harrowing death. Your guy could have killed him within seconds, but instead chose to make him suffer."

"Was that poison-ivy shoved down his throat?" Quinlan asked.

"You're close. To be more precise, it's poison-oak. Both plants contain an irritating oily sap called urushiol. Urushiol triggers an allergic reaction when it comes in contact with skin, resulting in an itchy rash. Depending on the person, the allergic reaction can occur within hours, or take as long as several days to break out. The rash that results is a form of allergic contact dermatitis, or a swelling of the skin.

"Given the amount of poison oak leaves forced into the victim's mouth and throat, he didn't stand a chance. I can't tell for certain how long it took for his throat to fully constrict and block his air passage, but I can tell you this poor son-of-a-bitch suffered one terrible death."

"How long would you say he's been dead, Doc?"

"Based on the rate of decomposition, I'd say around ten days. Your perp thought this out well in advance. You don't handle poison oak unless you've come well-prepared. Otherwise, we could look for someone with their hands wrapped in bandages, and put this case to bed."

"No such luck, Doc. The entire scene indicated meticulous preparation. What else can you tell us?"

"He was struck on the back of the head, hard enough to knock him out, but not enough to kill him. I found traces of smelling salts inside the lining of his nostrils, which tells me the killer wanted him awake so he could watch him suffer. Also, I found adhesive residue on his mouth and limbs. The blood on his clothes is his own. Head wounds tend to bleed profusely. And, before I forget, there's one more thing. I found this small piece of paper lodged in the back of his throat along with the poison oak. I have no idea what it means, but that's your headache. It's in pretty bad shape, but it appears to have the letters 'VIO' written on it."

Quinlan and Scumaci looked at one another. VIO—the same letters circled on the newspaper found at the Vespers' murder scene. Finally, a clue, even if they didn't know what it meant.

By the time they left Golub's office it was almost eleven thirty.

"Vinnie, I know eleven thirty is an awkward time for you. Not quite lunchtime. Do you think you can hold out till after we make one more stop? I want to revisit the Cockroach kid's murder site again. Make sure we didn't miss anything. In particular, a VIO we may have overlooked."

"No sweat, Chief. I have a package of chocolate cupcakes in the glove compartment for just such an emergency."

Quinlan laughed. "I must be getting old. How could I have not seen that coming?"

CHAPTER 56

July 29, 1968; 11:45 am

BY THE TIME Quinlan and Scumaci arrived at the gazebo, the sun illuminated nature's beauty. An orchestra of assorted birds chirped in harmony.

"Over here, in the bushes, Chief. This is where Billy Sane's body was found. It won't be easy finding anything new after all this time. Remember, it drizzled that night, and this area has been reopened to the public for over a week."

"I'm not expecting to find anything," Quinlan admitted. "But we need to be thorough. It seems to me, if Sane's murder occurred between the murders of Vespers and Vulchek, and we found VIO at both of those scenes, we should find it here too. But we didn't. So let's start looking."

"Maybe we should have Golub check out the kid's body again," Scumaci suggested. "Give it a thorough once-over. Make sure *he* didn't miss anything,"

"You don't know Victor Golub very well, do you? If you did, you'd know better than to suggest he'd missed something. The guy is the definition of thorough. Anyway, before we left his office, I asked him to take a look at the body one more time, for which, I got a dirty look and a head nod saying he was offended, but he'd do it. He won't find anything new. He doesn't miss stuff."

"Sorry, Chief. I'd say a fifty foot perimeter around the spot where the body was found should cover it. Does that work for you?"

"Sounds about right. This could take a while, so let's get started. These leaves on the ground might be hiding what we're looking for."

Two hours of kicking up dirt and crawling on their hands and knees rummaging through fallen foliage produced nothing. Frustrated, Vinnie pounded the heel of his shoe on a nearby boulder. When the boulder became dislodged, Vinnie bent down and pushed with both hands.

"Hold on a second, Scumaci. There's something under there. Let me grab it."

Quinlan stood, examining a moisture-soaked scrap of what appeared to be a page from a comic book. Written on it, the letters VIO.

CHAPTER 57
July 30, 1968

ABDO PICKED UP the previous day's *New York Times*. The sudden, hectic pace of his life had prevented him from keeping current on both world and local fronts. He skimmed through several sections while sipping his morning coffee. A small filler-article caught his eye. *Another Murder in Washington Heights*... details to be released at a later date.

The article acknowledged the discovery of a male body during the early morning hours of July twenty-eighth by an undisclosed hiker. More information would be made available once family members had been notified.

Between visits to Regine, sessions with Ryan, and reading up on the murders in Fort Tryon Park, Abdo's life seemed all-encompassed by Washington Heights, its residents, and its tragedies. Readying to leave home for his office, Abdo's phone rang. Regine's voice displayed an unsettling nervousness which had become the norm.

"Have you read today's paper?" she inquired.

"No, I've just finished going through yesterday's. What's wrong?"

"There's been another murder in Fort Tryon Park, and the name of the young man who was killed is the name Ryan talked about in his sleep. I'm sure of it. Can you look? What's going on, Abdo? What does it mean?"

"Calm down, Regine. I read about the murder in yesterday's paper. No name was given. What paper are you looking at?"

"*The Post*," she said, trying to catch her breath.

"I have the *Times* right here. Let me take a look. I'll see if they have an update in today's edition." Abdo rustled through the pages. "I'll call you back in a few minutes, Regine. Stay calm. I'm sure everything will be all right."

Abdo found the article. More specifics had been released by the police. '*The body found in a wooded area two mornings ago has been identified as Phillip Vulchek.*' Abdo came to a shrieking halt. The name seemed familiar to him, too. He'd check his recording of Ryan's alter egos conversing ten days earlier, on the evening of July 20th.

This isn't good. The estimated date of Vulchek's death fell within a day or two of the incriminating recording. Abdo needed to think. *What implications does this have? What responsibility do I have to report this to the authorities? Does patient-confidentiality dictate that I not report it?*

Slow down, he warned himself. *I'm getting ahead of myself. Ryan's mention of Phil Vulchek's name might mean nothing.* He wished he believed that.

181

I've comforted myself. Now I have to do the same for Regine. That will be more difficult. Dreading the call, he reached for the phone.

CHAPTER 58
July 30, 1968

THE SHADOW ASSASSIN sat, enjoying his morning newspaper, on the coping of the masonry wall in front of his Washington Heights residence. He loved reading his own press. Recognition by the media filled him with an air of importance. So far, it seemed the police had little or nothing to go on, only what he'd intended for them to find.

The Shadow Assassin, what a great name they've given me. I shouldn't have to share it with anyone.

When neighbors walked past, he offered a polite smile, thinking about what method he would choose to kill each and every one of them. He was the wolf and they were unsuspecting sheep.

In his mind he formulated a greeting for all who passed, but spoke only to a mere handful.

"Hey there, Mr. Simon. How about those Giants? Think they can stay hot?" He pictured himself gutting the cheap cock-sucker who never tipped when he received deliveries.

In the distance, the Assassin spotted the cute redhead who published her own so-called local newspaper entitled *The Heights Update.* He had a genuine respect for the cub-report-er's spunk. He felt Scoop Aubrey displayed a style of her own, but lacked the content he looked for in a writer. *Where's the sensationalism, the adulation?* Not once, did she make him ap-pear larger-than-life, the way respectable newspapers did. He thought she needed a lesson in writing that only he could pro-vide. She lived just a couple of blocks away. Perhaps one day he'd give her the interview of her life.

He put those thoughts aside. The Shadow Assassin needed to finalize the plans for his next murder. Before retreating for lunch, he acknowledged one last neighbor.

"Morning, Miss Cornblatt, how are you today?" *Enjoy your day, you mean-spirited bitch. In a few days you're going to die.*

Back at his apartment, the Shadow Assassin walked in on an unwelcome scene. The instant the door shut behind him, he found himself assaulted by a barrage of aggression from his other-self.

"Where the hell have you been?" Get a grip on yourself. You think this is just about you? We've got planning to do. Your anger is out of control. You're going to get us caught."

"Chill, brother. I know what I'm doing. Remember, without me you're nothing."

CHAPTER 59

July 30, 1968; evening

THE WATCHER, Loner, Optimist, and Writer sat in their meeting room, overloaded with brain-pounding thoughts. If only the voices in their heads would shut-up. Dr. Betaré's sessions with Ryan had started the wheels turning, and now they wouldn't stop. When Ryan was asked questions, the Quad members gave up unintended answers. Weeks of daily introspection produced a draining effect on all of them, some more than others.

"Someone say something," the Watcher blurted out.

"I'm all talked out," the Loner confessed. "Dr. Betaré has me thinking about things I don't want to think about. I've never felt so lonely. I hate who I am. The doctor tells me I have to confront my issues in order to overcome them. He says with time I'll feel better."

"I'd say you've benefited already," the Optimist said.

"Whatta ya mean?"

"This is the most you've ever said at one of our meetings, and it's the first time you've ever confided something personal to us. I like you, and respect you more today than ever before. You're trying something to make yourself a better person. I'd say that's great progress."

The Loner felt a little better, until the Watcher had to open his big mouth. "I like you better when you don't talk. I don't have friends, other than you guys—if you can call us friends, and I'm not lonely at all. By the way, which of you guys told the doc about me going through the alleyways and watching people? I'll bet it was you, Writer."

"It might have been me. I'm not sure," said the Writer. "I didn't know it was a secret. You think you're invisible? While you're watching people, people are watching you. Everybody knows you prowl the night. Besides, the doc and I have more important things to talk about than you. He says I should let people read my writings. He thinks my stories could make a difference in peoples' lives. So cut us some slack, you're no better or worse than the rest of us."

"Have you let Dr. Betaré read your work?" queried the Optimist.

"Not yet, I'm not ready. Maybe in the future."

"And what enlightenment do you bring to us today?" the Watcher asked the Optimist, unable to hide his sarcasm.

"Dr. Betaré and I agree on a lot of things. We both believe things will work out in the near future; and the four of us are going to be great friends. And, you'll be glad to know, we agree that someday Lazarus will come back to us."

Shockwaves rippled through the Quad. It was the break-through moment Abdo had been waiting for. One of the Quad members referenced his name—LAZARUS. The dike had sprung a leak. Out of fear and desperation, the Watcher would try to plug the hole, but piece-by-piece, the wall was now primed to fall. Soon the floodgate of emotions harnessed within Ryan Cain's mind would come rushing out.

The Optimist knew Lazarus would be listening for the first drop of hope. Somewhere far away, the prison of Lazarus' exile was being breached.

CHAPTER 60
July 31, 1968

IRONY OF IRONIES, the jolt of electricity transmitted from the light socket had saved his life. Lazarus sat in his cell, his mind growing clearer. He estimated a week had passed since he'd first heard the voices speaking his name. Tracking time in darkness and silence proved an imperfect chore.

He no longer doubted his sanity. *I'm not hallucinating. The voices beckoning me are becoming louder and clearer.* An aura of peace embraced him as the walls around him began to crumble. The light pouring through the growing cracks of his cell door provided clarity, like a ray of sunlight breaking through a solar eclipse.

Events progressed faster than anticipated. The voices grew more comfortable calling his name. His resurrection appeared imminent. Soon, he would embark on his journey.

Chapter 61
July 31, 1968; midnight

THE REVELATION STRUCK like a call from the IRS—unexpected and impactful. Abdo's nerves felt on fire. He sprung out of bed and ran to his desk to retrieve the envelope. A chill ran down his spine. He realized now, some thirty years later, that his mission on that terrible day had been fulfilled.

Ghosts of the past returned to haunt him. *That's what I failed to recognize when Sandor called me to his bedside so many years ago.*

"Still alive, still alive." Sandor Cain was No. 19, *the prisoner I'd been sent to save.* It all seemed surreal. Abdo laid awake the rest of the night, trying to grasp at the deeper meaning.

In the morning Abdo reviewed his entries of the past few days, and began writing.

In his final hours, Sandor Cain refused medication. He asked Regine to bring their son to him, and to leave them alone. Sandor needed to be lucid for his final conversation.

Knowing the impact that my meeting with Sandor, days earlier, had on me, I believe it possible that the content of Sandor's conversation with Ryan may have caused heightened emotional distress resulting in Ryan's memory loss and gradual disintegration of identity. I do not know if the horrors harnessed upon the shoulders of this sensitive boy have thrown his psyche into a state resulting in his committing the current murder spree.

"Personal Insights in Reference to June 10, 1956, Sandor Cain's Death"
There are an infinite number of paths which can lead to an individual's ultimate destination. Each man must determine the method and path best suited to his journey. To go from point A to point B one man will fly, another may drive, yet another may choose to take a long-term odyssey by walking.

One man will take his trek a day at a time, while the other will plan, and attempt to foresee every possible obstacle that may stand in his way.

One will rely on luck to deal with whatever blocks his path. To the other, there is no such thing as luck. Every contingency is planned for.

The time involved, the lessons learned, and the preparation for what awaits will differ for each individual.

Life and death journeys should not be navigated by children, yet that was the path thrust upon young Ryan Cain on the day of his father's death.

More to the point, I should say, *upon Lazarus*, the preordained survivor within Ryan Cain's persona.

From the moment of his conception Ryan had been groomed to be a thinker and a planner. The only games allowed in Ryan's young life were those which enhanced thought, planning, and strategy. Mistakes, even as insignificant as a wrong checker move, were met with harsh punishment.

Sandor Cain could not help but be who he was … a product of his environment and the life he had been subjected to. He'd grown up in a world of discipline, horror and cruelty. He believed that in this world you must be on the top of your game every second of every day, or you would be crushed by others. Sandor's feelings would not be swayed—*anything other than perfection leaves you, and your loved ones, vulnerable to disaster.* Nothing could, or would, ever alter Sandor's perception of the world.

While Sandor's intent was well-meaning, his methods and the expectations he placed upon his son would be judged unreasonable (by others). Some may even consider his parenting child abuse.

A child needs affection and joy in his life. In retrospect, I see that Ryan's sole escape from his rigid upbringing had been the comic books which his mother snuck into his room—most specifically: *The Fantastic Four*, his favorites.

After meeting with Ryan for the past week, I believe Ryan's persona possesses five distinct identities. I have spoken with four of the five. They have taken on monikers which I believe are symbolic of Ryan's comic book heroes. I have concerns over the anger and rebellion issues that one of the personalities displays.

I will expound on their personalities as our sessions progress. I will ask Regine for *The Fantastic Four* comic books Ryan still harbors in his closet. It is my belief that his subconscious has created its own fantastic four, referred to as the Quad, to save himself. The fifth persona, Lazarus, is buried somewhere in the depths of Ryan's mind.

If I am correct, these five personalities have always been present within him, with Lazarus playing the dominant role. The others serve as normal recessive emotions.

It is my hope to subdue the dominance of the Quad and to draw Lazarus back into control of Ryan's consciousness. I feel certain he is in there, awaiting the opportunity, and mapping with meticulous care the journey for his return. When he is ready, I will be waiting to help him.

I hope, at that time, he will confide in me what transpired between him and his father on that fateful day. Then, together, we will cope with the devastating truth.

CHAPTER 62

August 1, 1968

UNABLE TO SLEEP, Abdo rose at the crack of dawn, his mind replaying his list of things to do. He crawled out of bed and readied himself, all the while attempting not to wake Sonya. It would be a busy day. The thought of Ryan, somehow involved with the Washington Heights murders, hammered his brain.

First order of business: go to the library and review articles covering the murders. Abdo didn't care to read those types of stories, however, the prevailing situation changed everything. He now needed to read them all. Before leaving, he kissed his wife's forehead. *Sleep well my love.*

Abdo arrived at New York's main library, located in midtown Manhattan, minutes before it opened. *Protectors of knowledge,* he thought to himself, pausing in front of the two large concrete lions standing guard at the base of the stairway. *Please share your strength and wisdom with me.*

Once inside, Abdo retrieved the materials he sought. He took a deep breath. The articles turned his stomach. Visualizing the graphic scenes, he focused on how surreal this nightmare had become. *Is one of Ryan's alter egos a monstrous serial killer?*

The names of *all* the victims corresponded to the names on the recordings of Ryan's sleep-talking conversations. *Coincidence can no longer be factored into the equation.* The recordings, made with the intent of helping Ryan, would now make him the prime suspect in a murder investigation.

Abdo needed answers. *Patient confidentiality dictates my silence, but my conscience demands disclosure. I can't stand by while innocents are slaughtered.* He called Regine, confirming he would stop by to pick up Ryan's collection of comic books.

Leaving the library, a wave of nausea overtook him. Abdo braced himself against one of the stone lions. Regaining his composure, he gazed up. "Stand strong noble beasts; the guarding of knowledge, and the protection of information are honorable endeavors, and not chores for the timid."

CHAPTER 63

The Writings of Isok
"Now You See Me..."

You think people are who they say they are? You think loved ones always tell you the truth? How can you know someone else if you don't even know yourself?

Everyone has secrets. Some are small and trivial, significant only to those who harbor them; while others are so painful, their possible exposure could devastate lives. I'll tell you one of mine, if you'll tell me one of yours. No? I didn't think so. But I'll tell you one of mine anyway.

It was a hot summer's day in 1960, and I remember opening my eyes and saying, "What the fuck? Where am I?" I was no longer in my cell. I was in a schoolyard with other kids. That was the first time I had physically been out of my domicile and in the presence of other 'real' people.

There was a bully picking on some kid named Ryan Cain. It didn't seem to me like it would be much of a fight. The bully appeared to be a few years older than Cain. His name was Flint. Whether that was his first name, last name or even his real name, nobody knew, and everyone seemed too afraid to ask. I didn't give a shit. To me, he was simply an angry son-of-a-bitch who liked to beat up other kids.

I'd heard a couple of guys saying that Flint's father beat him pretty good on a regular basis. So, maybe there was a reason he was such a dick.

As always, Flint gathered a crowd, declaring he was going to kick somebody's ass. It's amazing how excited people get to see somebody else get their ass kicked. Like my father taught me, violence is inherent in the nature of man. Today was Ryan's turn to get beat up. He looked pathetic.

Ryan scurried to leave the schoolyard as Flint kept pushing him, but the crowd was circling and there was no escape. An ass-kicking seemed inevitable.

Ryan watched wrestling on television and practiced the moves all by himself. It's odd, I don't know how I knew that, but I did. His plan, which had merit, was to avoid a fist fight so he might not get hurt too badly.

While the cheering vultures lusted for the oncoming slaughter, Ryan moved closer to his attacker to avoid punches. As he'd hoped, it became a wrestling match. Then, Flint had Ryan in a headlock. There was total silence.

All of a sudden I was in Ryan's place.

Again I said, "What the fuck."

I swung my arm over and around the arm holding my head, pushed my forearm against the side of Flint's head, pinned him to the ground and applied pressure.

After so many years of solitary confinement I was out, and in a fight. It was like having your first orgasm.

No one else seemed to notice it was no longer Ryan fighting, but rather me . . . Isok.

For an instant, Ryan took my place, and whispered in Flint's ear, "I give, you win." He let Flint up. I thought, this kid must be an idiot.

Standing back and watching Flint attack Ryan again, I became lightheaded. Once more, it seemed to be my turn. I had Flint back on the ground and immobile within three seconds. That was the moment I snapped. My brain caught fire, and my blood coursed through my body as I whispered into Flint's ear. "You did this to yourself, asshole, take a good look at your life," and then, I wrenched his arm out of its socket. His scream was deafening.

In that instant, I felt the emotions of a lifetime. I was invigorated and horrified at the same time.

I retreated back to my cell leaving Ryan feeling sick to his stomach, while I, on the other hand, felt great.

To the best of my knowledge Flint never appeared in that schoolyard again. I've often wondered what became of him.

My point is . . . everyone has the capacity for violence. It's how we deal with the emotion that defines who we are as men. We are the sum of the choices we make.

CHAPTER 64

August 5, 1968

THE ASSASSIN EYED his prey. Ethel Cornblatt had aged like cheap wine. Once palatable she was now bitter and soured beyond redemption.

At five-foot-seven, the matronly spinster carried thirty pounds of fat around her midriff, and another twenty in her butt. Her amusing body formed a bold-faced, capital-letter "S"... on legs. Her stern face, with caked-on make-up, appeared frightening, highlighted by the bright red lipstick she always wore. Her hair sprung from her scalp emulating the needles of a startled porcupine, while her cold, yellow eyes squinted in condescension. Waddling in small steps of self-perceived superiority, Ethel appeared to have a broomstick shoved up her ass.

In her late fifties, Ethel lived alone. *Big surprise,* the Assassin mused to himself.

Maintaining few acquaintances, and fewer friends, Ethel appeared to regard herself as the brightest woman alive. When she walked down the street people turned the other way.

Common opinion was that Ethel hated children, and, of course, they hated her back. Funny, when you consider Ethel spent twenty years teaching fifth and sixth grade at the local public school.

The Shadow Assassin studied Ethel's routine for almost three weeks. He knew how and where she spent her days, what time she picked up her mail, and that she attended a cooking class every Wednesday evening, stopping to pick up groceries on her way home.

It took no great effort to gain access to neighborhood buildings. Entry was as easy as pushing buzzers and waiting for someone to buzz back, or, waiting for a tenant to enter and then slithering in behind him.

On the evening of Wednesday, August 5th, the Assassin positioned himself on the stairwell to the left of the northernmost elevator. He knew Ethel would return around eight thirty.

The plan seemed simple. Once she entered the building, he would walk down the stairs pretending to be on his way out. If she didn't carry a lot of packages he would walk out the front door and wait for another night. Ditto, in the event someone else entered the lobby with her.

If, as on previous Wednesdays, she struggled with cumbersome packages, he would offer to help her carry them. She, of course, would afford him the great honor of helping her. And once inside her apartment the games would begin.

The only other possible deterrent would be if he offered to help and someone else got out of the elevator, getting a good look at his face. In that case, he'd help her with the bags and call it a night.

Fate smiled upon the Assassin. At eight forty-five p.m., Ethel plodded through the building's front entry huffing and puffing. Her arms bear-hugged two grocery bags and she gripped a small watermelon with her gnarly fingers.

Descending the stairs toward the lobby the Assassin set his plan in motion.

It almost didn't work. At first, when he offered to help her, she chided him. "You! What are you doing in this building? You don't live here." Then, glaring at him, as though he weren't good enough to help her, she declined his offer with a curt, "No, I'm quite capable of handling it myself."

The Shadow Assassin couldn't believe it. All his planning had worked to perfection, and the bitch said "no". He wanted to kill her right on the spot but restrained his anger and walked toward the exit door.

Then, to his delight, arrogant as ever, she called out, "You there, all right, you can help me. This one time."

The shrill sound of her voice was music to his ears. The Shadow Assassin's heart raced. He couldn't wait to get the high and mighty Ethel Cornblatt alone.

CHAPTER 65
August 6, 1968; early morning

THE *9-1-1* CALL came in at four forty a.m., which meant another early wake-up call at the Quinlan household. Quinlan called Scumaci and arranged to meet at the crime scene around five twenty. Right on time, Scumaci arrived, wiping powdered sugar from his lips with a Dunkin Donuts' napkin. "I made a quick stop on the way. I'm no good on an empty stomach. Didn't figure the 'vic' was going anywhere. What's up?"

"It appears we have a change in pattern. The victim is female, in her fifties. One Ethel Cornblatt, a retired grade school teacher. One of her neighbors was headed out to walk his dog when he noticed Miss Cornblatt's door ajar. He called in to her. When there was no answer, he gave the door a nudge and found her lying there. Said he'd read about the new *nine-one-one* initiative, and called it in. For once I think the politicians may have come up with something useful.

"Anyway, she's in the kitchen, her head is rotated a full one-eighty. Her grocery bags and their contents are splayed in the foyer, and a watermelon rolled to the far side of the living room."

"We sure it's our guy, Chief? It doesn't fit our killer's M.O."

"It's him all right. Go take a look."

Cornblatt's panic-stricken face stared at the ceiling, her body prone.

The letters VIO were scribbled in red lipstick onto the victim's exposed back. Police had withheld the VIO signature from the press, hoping to avoid copycats and false confessions. Now, a new signature had been added to the mix… a compass needle accompanied by the letters *N, S, E,* and *W,* on the victim's right shoulder blade.

Quinlan loomed over Scumaci, who knelt over the body.

"So, what do you think? Is it our guy, Vinnie?"

"It's our guy all right, but I don't get it. I'm more confused now than when this psycho started his killing spree. What's with the north, south, east, west thing?" Scumaci shook his head.

Quinlan opened the window and scanned the streets. "I don't know what it means, but based on the placement of the body those symbols are accurately displayed. It means something to our killer, but I'll be damned if I know what."

"I'm not so sure," Scumaci said. "What if he's messing with our heads, leaving a false clue to send us in the wrong direction? No pun intended."

"Yeah, well, there's that possibility too."

CHAPTER 66

August 6, 1968; afternoon

QUINLAN ASSIGNED THREE officers to go door-to-door, asking if anyone had seen or heard anything the previous night. What the officers learned was that the death of Ethel Cornblatt didn't generate much sorrow or compassion from her neighbors. While everyone expressed concern over what had occurred and wanted the killer caught, no one implied Ethel Cornblatt would be missed.

At four thirty that afternoon, Officer Ian Tomlinson prepared to call it a day. He'd planned on returning early the next morning to continue canvassing the neighborhood. As he exited the building's front door into the courtyard, a young woman and her son, who appeared maybe five or six years old, walked toward him.

Couldn't hurt to ask one more. "Pardon me ma'am, I'm Officer Tomlinson with the NYPD. We're investigating the murder that occurred here sometime last night. My fellow officers, and I, are checking to see if anyone saw or heard anything unusual. Do you have any information that might help us?"

The woman seemed like a nice lady. She was the only person who showed any genuine sorrow over the death of her neighbor.

"I'm sorry. I didn't know Miss Cornblatt very well. Just to say hello. I wish I could help, but I didn't hear or see anything. My name is Cindy Kaden, and this is my son Mitchie."

As he thanked Mrs. Kaden for her time and began walking away, Tomlinson heard the boy whisper to his mother.

"Hey Mom, I saw Miss Cornblatt last night."

CHAPTER 67

August 7, 1968; morning

IT WAS EVENING when Quinlan received the message from Officer Tomlinson indicating he'd found a witness in the Cornblatt case. Given that it was a six-year-old boy, Quinlan decided to wait until the following morning to interview the child. He called Cindy Kaden at eight p.m., thanked her for her cooperation, and confirmed a mid-morning interview with her son. He requested Mrs. Kaden be present for the questioning, even though he knew she'd be there whether he'd requested her presence, or not.

As Quinlan and Scumaci pulled up in front of the Kaden residence, the radio announcer shared the day's weather forecast with his perspiring audience, "It's gonna be a scorcher today." Shirts and trousers sticking to the car's vinyl upholstery, both cops flipped the radio the finger at the same time.

Quinlan hated putting a kid through the interview process, especially in a capital crimes case. He instructed Scumaci to remain silent while he did the talking. "It'll be less intimidating if only one of us asks the questions." Quinlan didn't want this to come across as an interrogation, and frighten the boy.

They rang the bell in the entryway, announced themselves, and were buzzed in. Standing in front of apartment 2-D, Scumaci struck his best kid-friendly pose. Quinlan looked at him in disbelief and burst out laughing. "Thanks Scumaci, I needed that. But seriously, I said be non-threatening, not pathetic. Pretend you're about to be offered free-dibs at your favorite pastry shop. That should get the expression I'm looking for."

Cindy Kaden greeted the officers with trepidation. She invited them into her home, and introduced her son, Mitchie. The boy was slim with curly hair, and an impish smile. He wore shorts, sneakers and a Superman tee-shirt. He looked like a kid you wanted to hug.

"Hi there, Mitchie. I'm Chief Quinlan and this is my partner, Officer Scumaci. You can't tell by looking at him, but there are two things Officer Scumaci loves more than anything else in the world—donuts and baseball. I'll bet you like those things too, don't you?"

"Yes sir, I like donuts a lot, especially jelly donuts. Raspberry jelly is my favorite, but my mom only lets me eat one a day. I could eat a hundred if she'd let me."

Quinlan took to the kid right away. There'd be no problem talking to him.

"Now Mitchie, I'm going to ask you some questions, but first I want you to tell me about seeing Miss Cornblatt last night. Is that okay with you?"

Mitchie spoke in an animated style. "Sure. It was late last night and we forgot to get our mail 'cause Mom got real busy and stuff, doing other things like talking on the phone and helping me with my homework."

Cindy Kaden interjected, "It was around eight forty-five when we realized we hadn't gotten our mail."

"Mom, I'm telling the story. Oh yeah, and Mr. Officer Stumani, I really love baseball too. When you were a little kid you were probably just like me. Are jelly donuts your favorite?"

Scumaci smiled, rolled his eyes, and gave Mitchie a thumbs-up.

Quinlan needed to redirect the conversation. "Okay Mitchie, you're doing great. Can you tell me how you happened to see Miss Cornblatt, and what she was doing at the time?"

"Well, we didn't have our mail and I asked Mom to let me go down and get it. She didn't want to let me go 'cause I'm too little, but I kept asking and then the phone rang again and so I took the keys and went down while she was on the phone. That's when I saw Miss Cornblatt with that man."

"Where, exactly, were you, and what were Miss Cornblatt and the man doing when you saw them?" Quinlan prodded.

"I was under the stairs where the mailboxes are, and I can reach ours 'cause it's on the bottom row and I'm jus' tall enough to open it. I heard people talking and I peeked my head out to see who it was. It was Miss Cornblatt and a man I couldn't see too good. She looked angry and she scares me, so I pulled my head back really fast so they wouldn't see me." Mitchie took a deep breath.

"Did you hear what they were talking about?"

"I don't know zactly, but when I looked the first time she was falling down with her bags, and the next time I looked the man was carrying a bag in one hand and playing catch with the watermelon."

"What do you mean when you say he was playing catch with the watermelon?" Quinlan said.

Mitchie ran down the hall and into a room. When he returned he was holding a pink rubber ball. He held the ball in the palm of one of his hands, tossed it up a few inches, and caught it again in the same palm. Then, he smiled with pride. "That's how he did it, only with the watermelon."

Quinlan asked, "Do you remember which hand he used, Mitchie?"

"The one without the bag," Mitchie beamed.

"Was it this hand or this hand?" Quinlan asked holding his hands out one at a time.

Mitchie thought about it for a minute and said, "This one," pointing to Quinlan's left hand.

"Are you sure?"

"Yeah, I'm sure, cause they were on the other side of the building from me and the hand with the watermelon was on the side where the elevator is."

"Now Mitchie, can you tell me if the man was tall or short, fat or skinny?"

"He was pretty much regular. I remember he was taller than Miss Cornblatt. And he was wearing one of those cool shirts with a hood."

After several more minutes, it became evident Mitchie had told Quinlan everything he could remember. He hadn't gotten a close enough look to recognize the man, but enough to confirm he was white. He also confirmed the man wasn't old, but not a kid like himself, meaning the perp fell somewhere between the ages of six and sixty.

Quinlan ruffled Mitchie's hair, complimenting the great job he had done remembering so much. He likened Mitchie's assistance to that of a superhero, like Superman.

"You hear that, Mom? I'm like Superman." Mitchie flexed his little biceps.

Cindy Kaden assured Quinlan that the things her son had told them were true—at least, as true as he remembered them. "He's not prone to making up stories, or fibbing."

Before leaving, Quinlan promised Mitchie that if he needed to come back to ask more questions, he'd bring donuts.

As the officers left the apartment Mitchie called out. "So long policeman Spumoni, I bet if you're good Chief Quinlan will get you a donut too. Try a raspberry one."

Scumaci winked at his new friend.

CHAPTER 68
August 7, 1968; afternoon

SCOOP AUBREY WAS a go-getter. She harnessed unlimited energy for things she enjoyed, which at the moment included writing, clothes, and shopping for good deals.

People who didn't know Scoop well thought her a cute, kind of ditsy girl. Those who did know her thought the same, but also viewed her as one sharp cookie. She'd graduated college before turning eighteen, and would be entering her final year of studies at Columbia University Graduate School of Journalism at the start of the new semester.

Scoop sat before her make-up mirror looking into the reflective soul of the face staring back. Gazing deep into her green eyes, framed by a sprinkling of freckles, her mind churned the possibilities for her follow-up story on the Shadow Assassin. *It needs to be great. "Scooping" the big newspapers will help me make a name for myself.* She smiled at the thought.

As she stroked her long, straight auburn hair, parted in the middle, her path became clear. *I'll investigate on my own. Check out the crime scenes; meet with neighbors, family members, and the building superintendent. Maybe I can get an interview with the police officers handling the case.* The deadline for the next issue of *The Height's Update* was just days away. She threw on her size-five jeans and spent the next fifteen minutes deciding which top to wear.

Scoop suspected the upcoming days and weeks would be tough, given the nature of the crimes and the devastation of the families she planned to interview.

If Scoop Aubrey, Cub Reporter, had known how dangerous things would become, she might have chosen to stay home. Then again, probably not.

CHAPTER 69
August 7, 1968; evening

ABDO SORTED THROUGH, and read, over a hundred comic books—*Superman, Batman, Spiderman, Green Lantern, Flash,* and *The Fantastic Four.*

He reflected on Ryan's youth, picturing him in his mask and cape, playing superhero. Whenever Sandor wasn't home, Ryan ran free, playfully ridding the world of bad guys. *It seems a lifetime ago.*

The past three weeks of therapy proved revealing. Abdo gained a heart-wrenching insight into the sad life of Ryan Cain. Through Ryan's rare moments of control, and the intervention of his other personalities, Abdo discovered loneliness and fear in a boy so desperate for companionship he'd created his own best friends. Sandor's harsh criticism had broken Ryan down to a state of low self-esteem and self-loathing.

Abdo knew well, through his years of treating depressed patients, if you beat someone down long enough you instill a sense of worthlessness, especially in a child. Sandor's compulsive drive to make his son perfect created the polar opposite result of what he had intended.

Referring back and forth between Ryan's recorded conversations, and interaction between *The Fantastic Four* comic book characters, Abdo found distinct parallels.

The Fantastic Four superheroes embodied a close-knit family with idyllic intentions and bad judgment. They reinforced the concept that family ties and loyalty could be equally strong in a group of misfits, as in a society of normal humans. They would never betray one another.

The Fantastic Four consisted of Mr. Fantastic, The Invisible Girl, The Human Torch, and The Thing.

The character of Mr. Fantastic overanalyzed everything and talked way too much, thus driving his compatriots crazy, much like the Optimist. The Invisible Girl, by definition, possessed the ability to become invisible, the way the Loner described himself.

The Human Torch was a showoff and troublemaker with the physical ability to literally heat things up. Abdo thought it might be a bit of a stretch comparing the Writer with The Human Torch, but it still remained to be seen if his detailed documentation of the Quad's meetings and activities might heat things up as therapy progressed.

That left The Thing, and the Watcher. The Thing, who griped and bickered a lot, began as deformed, underprivileged, and argumentative, not much of a reach for Abdo to compare to the Watcher.

The unfolding of tragedies that led to the deterioration of Ryan's behavior, combined with the ongoing murders, left Abdo no choice but to request the use of hypnotherapy in Ryan's future sessions. Progress was being made, but not fast enough, given the circumstances. Peoples' lives hinged on the progress of Ryan's treatment. Hypnosis would bring quicker and more substantive results.

Tomorrow will be the first of many intense and emotional days to come. With both a touch of hope and dread, Abdo readied himself.

CHAPTER 70
August 8, 1968

ABDO DRESSED IN a hurry and ran out to purchase more newspapers. The morning edition of the *Times* had announced another murder. The headlines succeeded in attracting attention: "Teacher Taught A Lesson" and "Night School A Killer."

Back in his apartment, Abdo read with great concern. The name Ethel Cornblatt didn't ring a bell. He couldn't remember Ryan making reference to that name on any of his recordings. He savored a momentary feeling of relief.

Abdo called Regine to see if he could stop by for a chat. He told her not to buy or prepare any food. He simply wanted to talk for a while.

Abdo arrived minutes before noon. They greeted each other with a hug and made their way to the living room. On the table sat a plate of cut-up fruits and cheeses. Abdo said nothing; he smiled and took an apple slice.

"Just tell me, Abdo," Regine said. "What's happened? Don't make me suffer while you wait for the right moment to get to the bad news. I know this is hard for you too. Please, tell me now."

"I need to know if the name Ethel Cornblatt means anything to you." Abdo got right to the point.

"You mean the woman I read about in today's paper? No, I don't know her."

"How about Ryan, does he know her?"

"I don't think so. How would he know her?"

"She was a retired fifth grade teacher who taught at Ryan's elementary school. Is it possible he knew her when he was in grade school?"

Regine's face flushed. She began to tremble.

This isn't going to be good. Abdo sighed. "Tell me Regine, I need to know."

"I didn't remember until you mentioned grade school. That was so long ago. Ethel Cornblatt was Ryan's fifth grade teacher. Ryan was ten years old. After Sandor died, Ryan struggled. His grades went down. He wasn't himself."

"Tell me what happened," Abdo prodded.

"I was called into school one day. The teacher asked Ryan to point out some place on a map and he couldn't do it. Then, she asked him to point to north, south, east and west, and he couldn't do that either.

"Miss Cornblatt humiliated him. She took him from classroom to classroom asking him to point out what she already knew he couldn't do. Ryan lashed out, and I was called to pick him up. He wasn't physical; he just yelled at her.

"I don't use bad words Abdo, but that woman was a bitch. She scarred my boy for a very long time. It was only after the school made Ryan take an I.Q. test that Ethel Cornblatt shut her nasty mouth and left him alone. I wish you hadn't made me remember." Regine's eyes were moist.

"Why did she leave him alone after the test?"

"They told me I.Q. tests show a person's potential, and Ryan's score rated him a genius." Regine spoke with pride. "Those were their words. I'm sure Miss Cornblatt expected him to be stupid, but instead, Ryan's I.Q. was probably higher than hers."

Abdo then proceeded to explain his theory about Ryan's escape from reality through identification with *The Fantastic Four* comic book characters. Regine became upset. She immediately came to Ryan's defense. "You don't really think Ryan did those awful things, do you? You've known him all his life. He's been through so much. None of this is his fault. Blame Sandor. Blame me. I should have protected him. Please, don't let anything bad happen to my Ryan. We have to help him."

Abdo put his arm around Regine, offering her a shoulder to cry on.

"None of this is your fault," Abdo reassured her. "Given Ryan's connection to *all* of the murder victims, I think it best to attempt hypnosis at future sessions. However, the decision will be Ryan's, and Ryan's alone." *For everyone's sake I hope he consents.*

CHAPTER 71

August 9, 1968

THE SHADOW ASSASSIN closed his eyes and thought about the time he'd spent with his victims. Drool oozed from the corners of his mouth, settling on his chin. He'd reached a painful decision. The investigation into the murders had intensified. A person couldn't walk a city block without bumping into a cop. While he craved his on-going blood lust for vengeance, and the adrenalin rush each new kill initiated, to continue would be his undoing. It was time to lay low.

Police patrolled everywhere. They hid in alleyways and behind bushes watching for anything or anyone appearing suspicious. Everyone in Washington Heights became a slide under a microscope. Cops and reporters scurried about looking for leads. Even the snoopy little redheaded girl calling herself 'The Scoop' was asking annoying questions. *The nosy little bitch.*

Who would have thought it, a 'nobody' like me, the talk of the town? I'm all anyone talks or thinks about. I'm a celebrity. He felt more alive than ever before.

The decision was made. *If the temptation becomes too great, I'll take a day off and go to the beach.*

CHAPTER 72
August 9, 1968

QUINLAN SCHEDULED a squad meeting. He'd been able to get in touch with everyone involved in the case except Victor Golub. He left several messages and hoped Golub would show.

Thus far, the investigation suggests no apparent rhyme or reason for the killings. Quinlan was anxious to get the meeting started. *This lunatic can strike anyone, at any time, and we're no closer to catching him now than day one. Heads are going to roll, and mine will be the first.*

Quinlan instructed Scumaci to pick up 'a little something' for the boys to eat while they kicked ideas around.

"Hey Chief, I sure hope I'm getting reimbursed for this, it ran me forty-seven fifty," Vinnie said, arranging the pastries in a decorative design.

"Forty-seven fifty? I said get something for the four or five of us to munch on. I didn't ask you to cater a wedding," Quinlan responded, eyeing the culinary display.

Officers Cohen and Tomlinson entered the room together at seven forty. Victor Golub followed at seven forty-five.

"So this is where our tax dollars are going," Golub snorted, helping himself to a cup of coffee and a cheese danish. "I might request a transfer here myself. Do you guys always eat like this?"

"Only on the days Scumaci's in charge," Quinlan said.

"I haven't heard any complaints," Vinnie added with a big donut-powdered smile on his face.

Quinlan let the boys enjoy themselves for a few minutes, then got down to business.

"Okay, from the top. To save time, I've outlined each victim's info." He pointed to a blackboard. Scribbled across the top were four major headings—Vespers, Sane (a.k.a.Cockroach), Vulchek and Cornblatt; under each heading: two categories—Public Knowledge, and Undisclosed.

VESPERS
"Public Knowledge"
Age 22
Killed on April 17, 1968.
Bully, drug dealer, ladies' man.
Lived alone in basement apartment.
Previous run-ins with the law.
Head split open with hedge trimmer.
Body found by superintendent.
No witnesses.

"Undisclosed"
Sneaker print found in blood pool at scene—size eight.
Newspaper with circled letters "VIO" found at scene.

SANE (a.k.a. Cockroach)
"Public Knowledge"
Age 20
Killed on June 27, 1968.
Bully, no friends.
All around scumbag.
Sealed juvenile record.
Dismembered.

"Undisclosed"
Adopted.
Killed father.
Molested sister.
Peeping Tom.
Comic book page, with letters VIO, found at crime scene.

VULCHEK
"Public Knowledge"
Age 25
Killed between July 18-22, 1968.
Bully, tough guy.
No record.
Tied to tree and suffocated in park—early morning.

"Undisclosed"
Lived with girlfriend.
Suffocated with poison oak.
Struck with blunt object, then moved.
Smelling salts used to revive and make victim suffer
after being tied up.
Small piece of paper with letters VIO found in throat.

CORNBLATT
"Public Knowledge"
Age 57
Killed on August 5, 1968.
Single; never married.
Retired public school teacher.
Murdered at night in her apartment.
Broken neck.

"Undisclosed"
Disliked by neighbors.
Reputation as always angry and nasty.
Neck rotated—one-hundred-eighty degrees.
Witness—young boy.
White male seen helping victim prior to murder.
Witness description suggests left-handed assailant.
Witness describes man as taller than victim.
Letters VIO printed on victim's back in red lipstick.
Compass indicating north, south, east and west
drawn on victim's shoulder blade.

The flip side of the blackboard held an assortment of observations and questions, with space for anything new that the group might come up with.

1. Anger issues.
2. Displays no fear of youthful, virile males.
3. First three victims: white males in their twenties.
   Why switch to a fifty-seven-year-old woman?
4. Significance of the NSEW symbol?
5. 'Perp' leaves '*VIO*' clue. Why? What does VIO represent?
6. Do crime specifics indicate left or right-handed?
7. How does he pick his victims?
8. What sets him off?
9. How did Vespers' killer get away unnoticed with what must have been blood-soaked clothes and shoes?

After reviewing the items on the boards, Quinlan asked for new input.

"You can add the button I found clutched in Ethel Cornblatt's right hand to your list," Golub chimed in. "It's quite possible she ripped it from her assailant's shirt before he killed her."

"Hey Chief, how about we check out old, unsolved murder cases in Washington Heights similar to our boy's M.O.?" Cohen suggested.

"Good idea. You and Tomlinson get on it, and keep me posted," Quinlan said, adding both new items to the list.

"Victor, do your thing with the bodies and let me know if anything new turns up. At this point, I'm willing to take an educated guess on height, weight, and body type. Vinnie and I will check with the newspapers to see if we can get any info on who's been providing them with their tips."

Meeting adjourned, Scumaci rounded up the left over pastries. *Who says you can't have your cake and eat it too?*

CHAPTER 73
August 9, 1968

SCOOP HAD READ and reread every article related to the Shadow Assassin murders ten times over. She was ready to do her own due diligence. Her first stop would be the Vespers' crime scene, and a visit with the superintendent who discovered the body.

Scoop felt unsettled, but excited, as she arrived at the basement location. She pushed beyond her fear and anxiety, inching her way through the dreary underground maze. Arriving early, she hoped to take a look around before meeting with Mr. Sussman.

She located the precise spot of the crime with ease. Faded blood stained the concrete floor. Torn yellow tape hung from the door jamb of the deceased's dwelling. To her right, columns of stacked newspapers stood tall. In the farthest corner of the basement a locked storage gate secured an assortment of garden and maintenance equipment. Among the array of old rusting tools hung a new hedge trimmer. Its unsoiled blades were a dead giveaway. *A replacement for the murder weapon.*

Scoop was startled by an angry shout, "Hey you, what are you doing there?" She jumped at the sound of the voice, then relaxed seeing the building's superintendent approaching. Scoop recognized the fifty-ish Otto Sussman. Over the years she'd passed this building many times while he tended the landscaping.

"You scared me. I'm Scoop Aubrey. I called yesterday inquiring if you might be able to spare me a few minutes of your time."

"You should have come to see me first," he scolded. "It's not safe for you to be down here alone."

"You're right. I should have come to you first. Sorry. Is there some place we can sit and talk?"

They took the conversation outside to a small courtyard. Walking behind Sussman, Scoop contemplated the best way to go about her interview.

Seated on a bench, Scoop displayed an interest in Otto Sussman, the person, rather than Otto Sussman, the source of information. They began to talk, and while telling Scoop his life story Sussman lost some of the attitude. He'd grown up in Germany, and was taken away from his parents by the Nazis at age seventeen. For a year he worked at hard labor in one of the concentration camps. Then, due to overcrowding, the Nazis released a limited number of prisoners, of which he'd been one. "My release was too good to be true. I knew I could be picked up again at any time. So I searched for a way to flee the country.

I was fortunate. I met the right people and got out of Germany just in time. First I ended up in Sweden, and then in November 1938, I came to the United States. I never heard from my parents again."

"The tattoo on your left forearm," Scoop asked, "did you receive that while in the prison camp?" Scoop hoped she wasn't being too forward.

"Yes, the Nazis used numbered tattoos for identification. As soon as a prisoner entered the camp he was tattooed and logged in. It was the same for men, women and children. The only differences were the letters used to identify gender, race and religion."

"You've led a very difficult life Mr. Sussman. I'm so sorry."

"I was a lucky one. I got out," Sussman offered. He appeared to become drained by the conversation. "Then, I met my wife."

"Here in America?" Scoop asked.

"Yes. But, not till fifteen years later. She was widowed with two daughters. We hit it off from the moment we met. I went from bachelor to family man, overnight."

"Just one more thing, if you don't mind my asking. Is there anything new you can tell me that I might be able to quote in my story? Perhaps something you thought unimportant that might give me a leg-up on everybody else? How about the gated cage where you keep your tools and gardening equipment? I noticed it's locked. Is it always locked? Might it have been left unlocked that night?"

"I'm very careful with my tools. I could lose my job. What are you implying?" The anger in his voice had returned. "We're done here, Miss Aubrey. I've told everything I know to the police. You can leave me your number, if you like. If I think of anything else, I'll call you."

PART III
REVELATIONS

"Life is a hell of a thing to happen to a person."
—David Rossi—
Criminal Minds

CHAPTER 74

August 10, 1968

THE DOOR CRUMBLED, evaporating in a puff of smoke. Freedom beckoned from across the open threshold. Before venturing his first step Lazarus paused to reflect upon the events which led to his current residence.

He remembered the day, twelve years earlier, when Ryan's father with his dying breath called his son to his bedside. Real or imagined, Sandor shared the imminent danger he foresaw threatening the lives of his family. Ryan's mind spun out of control. Knowledge and memories present one moment disappeared in the next. His life seemed unsalvageable. Fear and anxiety consumed him.

In the blink of an eye Ryan's devastation sent Lazarus reeling on an inward spiral transforming him into a time traveler of sorts. A chill ran through Lazarus as he passed a voyager moving in the opposite direction. Lightheaded, Lazarus careened through a myriad of tunnels deep inside Ryan's brain, reaching his final destination in a lower level of consciousness. What he didn't realize at the time, what he couldn't possibly have known, was that he himself possessed an alter ego, named Isok.

Wham. The cell door slammed shut. Darkness and silence encompassed him.

Within moments of his arrival, Lazarus identified his location. His transference had propelled him through cranial space and time, depositing him at the Beach Street Station of Ryan's subconscious.

In a time which seemed a million years ago, Beach Street represented Ryan's quiet place, the place he would go in his mind seeking comfort. At night, while Ryan slept, he and his alter egos frolicked on Beach Street, their retreat to paradise, an escape from their tortured existence. Though not real, those memories reflected bright and joyous moments, moments critical to Ryan's survival at the time.

Beach Street now afforded the perfect setting for Lazarus's needs. The darkness shed an illuminating light on reality. It enhanced thought without distraction, an opportunity to view himself, from the inside out, with the tranquility needed to reflect on his predicament. It provided a fortress for strategic planning.

Following twelve years of solitude, Lazarus suspected Beach Street would *one day* become his final resting place. *But not today.*

Through the blackness, the light of freedom shone in. The time was at hand for Lazarus to again traverse the tunnels of Ryan's mind and announce his return. Lazarus stepped through the doorway of enlightenment.

CHAPTER 75

August 10, 1968

SCOOP KNEW BILLY SANE by sight and reputation only. She'd found him repulsive. While she had no desire to delve into the slime pit the "Cockroach" dwelled in, it came with the job. Scoop resigned herself to get it over as soon as possible. She decided against viewing the crime scene and called to arrange a visit with the Sanes at their home, around noon. Scoop liked midday interviews. Most people had already taken the opportunity to sip their coffee, read their paper, and take care of the previous day's leftover chores.

Scoop scanned her surroundings as Rosa Sane opened the door and invited her in. What she saw was not at all what she had expected. The apartment was small, but tidy. Mrs. Sane and her daughter, Lucinda, both appeared well-kempt and colorfully attired.

Scoop opened her interview with an appropriate, "I'm so sorry for your loss."

Mrs. Sane's response caught Scoop off guard. "Thank you, but don't be sorry. He was the devil. From the very beginning he brought nothing but pain and heartache. Maybe now that he's gone my Lucinda and I can have some peace."

"I'm sure there must be some good things about him you can hold on to," Scoop offered.

"Then, I'm sure you didn't know my son." Mrs. Sane hesitated. "I'm sorry; I'm being a very bad host. Please, sit down. Can I get you something to drink? Water? Perhaps a soda?"

"No, thank you. I'm sorry for upsetting you. I hope you'll forgive me."

"There's nothing to forgive, you were trying to say the right thing. But sometimes there is no right thing to say. Sometimes the ugly truth stands on its own. Now, what can I do for you?"

Scoop took an unexpected liking to the Sanes. The fact that she despised Billy had biased her expectations of his family. She felt ashamed for her rush to judgment. "As I mentioned on the phone, I'm a journalism student at Columbia Graduate School, and I publish my own neighborhood newspaper. The big papers are so busy sensationalizing everything, that a lot of the time they miss important details. Putting out my own paper has been a great experience, so if you could fill me in about what happened, in your own words, that would be great." Scoop noticed Lucinda hadn't shifted her gaze off of the floor, or said a word, the entire time.

"I don't know that there is anything I can tell you that I haven't already told the police and other reporters a hundred times," Rosa said. "I know it is terrible for me to say, but Billy was a bad person. God knows that my Arturo and I wanted so much to love him when we adopted him, but evil must have been in his blood.

"Every night, for the past two years, I've gone to bed thinking my sweet Arturo would still be alive, beside me, if we had never seen that boy. Billy killed my husband and did terrible things to my daughter which I've only recently found out. I cannot bring myself to talk about it. Billy's murder was a gift from God. God, forgive me." Rosa crossed herself.

Scoop felt regret as she stared into the pain-filled eyes of the two women. "I'm so sorry for your misfortune, and for asking you to relive it. It was thoughtless of me. I should leave you alone now."

Approaching the door, Scoop couldn't help but comment on Lucinda's outfit. "I hope you don't mind my asking, but where did you ever find that top and skirt? They're so beautiful. I don't think I've ever seen anything like them in the stores."

Lucinda blushed while her mother boasted of Lucinda's God-given gift for designing clothes. "My sweet angel, she makes her clothes with her own two hands. One day, I promised her, we will be able to afford an electric sewing machine. Things have been so difficult since Arturo's death. But my angel, she never complains."

Scoop walked to Lucinda, took her hands, and told her how gifted she was, and that she should never give up on her dreams.

On her way back home Scoop couldn't get Lucinda's sad tortured face, and the inference of what her brother had done to her, out of her mind.

Perhaps Rosa Sane was right. Sometimes the ugly truth has to stand on its own. Billy's murder was a gift from God. God forgive me.

CHAPTER 76

August 11, 1968

ABDO FELT TORN between legality and responsibility. He needed to check the laws pertaining to doctor-patient confidentiality before hypnotizing Ryan. He felt an obligation to protect Ryan, but couldn't in good conscience risk another individual being attacked, or killed, as a result of his silence.

As he approached Manhattan's main library for the second time in less than two weeks, Abdo again paused by the grandiose lions guarding its entrance. "You're still standing, my friends. I envy you your stature. I'm sad to say you are holding up much better than I am. I wish you could embody me with some of your strength, for I'm going to need it."

Once inside, Abdo located the article he wanted to review. It told the story of a New York murder case which had gone to trial a few years earlier, in 1965. It involved a young man who had been fighting with his wife. The man sought guidance from a psychiatrist known for treating patients with violent rage, self-esteem issues, and personality disorders. The man told the psychiatrist of homicidal urges he was struggling to control toward his wife. He feared what he might do and sought help.

The doctor, uncomfortable with the position he found himself in, agreed to treat the patient only under specific conditions. The man's wife would be informed of his violent tendencies, all sessions would be recorded, and the doctor would be granted unlimited discretionary permission to provide all insights and recordings to the proper authorities if he deemed it necessary.

Once the patient agreed to the doctor's terms of treatment, the doctor sent a letter explaining the situation to the man's wife. Two years later she was reported missing under strange circumstances, and the man was arrested for her murder.

The doctor became the central figure in a legal debate that had been going on for years. Does a psychiatrist's duty to warn the potential victim of a violent patient negate a patient's right to confidentiality in a court of law?

It seemed medical ethics and legal rules of law differed greatly. From the medical community's point of view, the psychiatrist's obligation is to safeguard his patient's confidentiality, no matter how self-incriminating his treatment confessions may be. The legal system however, fights for the physician's personal obligation to provide the truth and protect the innocent. The debate still continues.

The article hadn't cleared up Abdo's legal obligations as he hoped it would. There no longer seemed any way to avoid the issue. Abdo knew what he'd have to do.

CHAPTER 77

August 11, 1968

OPERATORS RESPONDING TO *9-1-1* calls had their hands full. Thousands of anxiety-ridden citizens deluged the under-manned system. Dispatchers had been instructed to forward all queries related to the Shadow Assassin case to a dedicated line located in the Washington Heights Precinct. History had shown that the smallest, most insignificant detail often ended up breaking a case. Within two weeks, one hundred and eleven calls came in. Each and every lead would be evaluated to determine its credibility for follow-up. Quinlan assigned Cohen and Tomlinson to tip-assessment.

At seven p.m. the line rang for the one hundred and twelfth time.

"Thirty-fourth precinct, Officer Tomlinson speaking, how can I help you?"

"Hello, is this the number for people with information about the killings in Washington Heights?"

"Yes sir, you have the right number. Can I have your name please?" Tomlinson was growing weary of well-meaning, none-theless, useless leads.

The caller proceeded. "I've been out of town for the past several weeks, so I didn't know about what's been going on here. My daughter-in-law was ill, so I went to help my son take care of her. Anyway, she's better now and I'm back. I've been hearing about these murders. It's all very disturbing. Then, I remembered. I'd called for a taxi to take me to the airport. Just as the cab pulled up, a young man rushed by me. I didn't give it a second thought at the time, but now that I think of it, there was blood on the front of his shirt. I thought he'd hurt himself and was rushing to get home, or get medical attention. I had other things on my mind and continued on to the airport. I don't know if it means anything. It may have nothing to do with the killings, but I thought I should call you."

Tomlinson tried to calm the man down; he could hear the quiver in the man's voice. "You did the right thing sir. What night and time did this occur?"

"It was June 27th, at about quarter-to-ten in the evening. I remember because I was running late, and was nervous I might miss my flight."

Tomlinson straightened up in his chair. The date and time coincided with the "Cockroach" murder. *Maybe this lead will pan out?* "Did you recognize the young man with the bloody shirt?"

"Like I said, it was dark and he appeared to be in a hurry, but it did kind of look like a young fella I've seen playing ball in the park. I enjoy watching the boys play on the weekends. Anyway, I think his name is Ryan. I don't know his last name, but I'm sure the other boys at the park could tell you. I did the right thing by calling, didn't I?" The man seemed to be attempting to catch his breath.

"You did exactly the right thing. You've been a great help, sir. I'm sorry I didn't get your name." The line clicked to silence.

CHAPTER 78

The Writings of Isok
"The Unknown Soldier"

Let me start at 'my' beginning. I was born at a very early age.

Now that may seem a strange, even stupid, thing to say. But when I say 'born,' I don't mean came out of my mother's womb born. That was Ryan Cain's birth. I'm talking about my identity, who I am. That doesn't occur upon the first inhalation of oxygen. Identity is nurtured.

No, I was conceived, my life-seed planted, on Ryan's fifth birthday, along with my five siblings. It was at that precise moment our father extricated and incubated us into our own separate cubicles of horror within Ryan's mind.

To be honest, I lay dormant for another four-plus years, within the soul of my brother Lazarus.

I am Isok, the representative savage beast, searching for justice to assure survival, deep within Ryan Cain.

I am the sole entity of Ryan Cain's existence that carries the complete recollection of our father's mental, emotional, verbal and psychological abuse upon us. I am the last wall of protection separating the human Ryan Cain from the inhuman.

I am Isok, the protector, the one borne out of necessity to do the deeds that must be done. I am thankful for each and every day I am locked away in the recesses of Ryan Cain's mind.

I am the capacity for devastation and retribution, created and magnified beyond reasonable limits by our late father.

I am the unspoken brother of Ryan's other alter egos. More to the point, I am the sixth stepbrother once removed. The one no one knows.

And while they do not know me, there is a psychic bond between us, as within twin siblings, which makes us aware of each other's existence.

I am not acknowledged, but I am feared, and often fear is necessary.

I am the 'unknown soldier' given the honorable, yet unenviable chore of protecting 'the One.'

CHAPTER 79
August 12, 1968

ABDO LISTENED OVER and over again to the Quad's conversations. With Regine's permission he'd kept a tape recorder running during the eleven-to-one time slot, when the foursome conjured together.

For almost two weeks Abdo had gained insight into each of Ryan's persona. Indirectly, each of the Quad members provided useful input, their personalities unable to resist the temptation to interject their emotions. Therapy produced positive changes. Ryan displayed less hostility and more moments of clear thought. Now, Abdo needed to speak directly to each of the Quad members.

Conventional methods would take time, and current circumstances dictated the necessity for a faster progression. Ryan had agreed to try hypnosis. In a trance state, Abdo would be able to draw out Ryan's alter egos. Under hypnosis, Ryan would unleash the part of his subconscious harboring his counterparts.

Abdo escorted Ryan into his office, directing him to a leather chair across from his desk. Beyond the uncomfortable silence, the truth awaited discovery,

"I'm going to play a recording for you. Are you ready?" Abdo asked. "We're going to try to unravel a complex mystery novel whose characters will be read, scrutinized, picked-apart, and in time—understood."

Ryan nodded.

Ryan focused his attention on the four males in conversation. At first he showed no visible reaction. He didn't outright say it, but in his mind he thought, *these guys are more screwed-up than I am.*

Once the boys-without-faces spoke about revenge and murder, declaring "vengeance is ours," Ryan became more aware of the sound of their voices. *They all sound a lot like me, with slight variations.* Ryan became tense and nervous. He felt faint.

Abdo turned off the recorder and spoke in a soothing voice.

"Those voices are you, Ryan. They speak while you are asleep. They display emotions existing within you. What we need to determine, is whether your alternate personas merely vent through you verbally, or if they are capable of transforming you to physically do things you would otherwise never consider."

"You mean I could be the lunatic everyone is looking for? That can't be. I would know. I couldn't do those things and not know. Could I? What's happening to me? I should have died in that hospital."

249

"Slow down, Ryan. I know this is difficult. But, I don't want you jumping to conclusions. The human mind is very complex. There is still much we don't understand about how the brain compensates in times of stress and trauma. Let's take this one step at a time. Please trust me to do what is best for you. We need to get to the truth, and I believe hypnosis is the approach we should utilize. Do you feel ready to proceed down that path, or do you need time to think about what I've said?"

Ryan's speech became rapid. He leaned forward to rest his elbows on Abdo's desk. "I know you're advising me as my doctor, but also, you're my friend. If this is what I need to do, let's do it. I trust you. I'm so unhappy. I wish I could escape my miserable life. I've had thoughts of ending it all. But, I'll never act upon them. I remember the effect my sister's death had, and continues to have, on both me and my mom. I'd never put her through that again."

After a brief pause Ryan uttered, "Let's get started."

CHAPTER 80
August 12, 1968

IT WAS ALMOST noon by the time Scoop reached the site of the Vulchek murder. She possessed many talents, but finding her bearings wasn't one of them. She'd lost her way several times before reaching the location.

Scoop wore jeans, a long-sleeve shirt, and high-top sneakers. She also brought a pair of rubber gloves. A multitude of vegetation grew in the wooded areas of the park and Scoop bore no desire to get a rash on her pale, sensitive skin.

The trampled area where the police had congregated, desecrated the otherwise beautiful landscape. Barricade tape still marked the scene. On any other day, the location where Scoop now stood heralded the beauty of Mother Nature. Today it displayed mankind's ugliness and disregard for human life.

Scoop formulated a mental picture of the poor soul taped to the tree. A chill ran down her spine. She moved closer to the exact spot. Adhesive residue from the duct tape used to restrain Vulchek still stuck to the tree's limbs.

Scoop observed everything around her. She decided she was wasting her time, but believed—*if you want to be good at something you can't be lazy.*

As she turned to leave the 'death-tree,' she spotted two squirrels nibbling on something. She knew not to get too close even though she loved animals. Scoop squatted down. The squirrels were chomping away at a comb. Half of the comb's teeth were missing, and there appeared clusters of, what looked to be, matted hair and dandruff.

The squirrels might have found the comb elsewhere and carried it to the tree, but the fact that it now rested a few feet from the where the victim was found, made Scoop think she should save it for the police. Under other circumstances she would have left and gone to call the police; however, she feared the industrious squirrels might abscond with their new found treasure.

Reaching into her bag, Scoop removed a sucking candy and tossed it near the squirrels. As she'd hoped, they abandoned the mangy comb for the sweetness of the candy. Scoop whisked up the comb with a tissue and made her way home.

CHAPTER 81

August 12, 1968

ABDO THOUGHT IT wise to take a short break before starting hypnosis. He sensed Ryan's anxiety. Hypnosis would unearth issues, making things worse before making them better.

Abdo could see the pain in Ryan's eyes, but not the images causing it.

"Ryan, I want you to understand my intent. The human eye and mind work together to form the world's most perfect camera. Everything we see or imagine, real or suggested, creates a picture that is stored in our memory banks. Those memories can bring us immense pleasure, or insufferable pain.

"In your instance, the images stored in your mind became so unmanageable, that out of necessity for survival, you created alter egos to take on the burden. Each of your personas carries visual images the others do not possess. You survive by delegating the responsibility of sustaining your memories. I intend to speak with *all* of your personas, and see if I can piece together *all* of the images, to create a unified, complete picture of what is going on."

Abdo paused, allowing Ryan a few moments to take in the concept, then continued in a calm and soothing voice. "I want you to close your eyes and visualize a quiet place. Somewhere you feel at ease. Can you do that?"

"Yes."

"Where are you?"

"I'm at the beach."

"Can you describe it to me?"

"It's warm and there's a breeze coming in from the ocean. I like the wind in my face. I'm sitting under a willow tree and birds are flying overhead. I'm alone, and that's okay. I like sitting by myself, looking out at the breaking waves. I've come here many times. It's the one place I feel safe and at peace."

"You're doing great, Ryan. Now, I'd like you to take slow, long, deep breaths. I want you to concentrate. Inhale. Feel your lungs and stomach expanding. Hold. And release. You can feel your lungs and stomach retracting. In . . . and out." Abdo was thankful for small blessings. While some patients experienced difficulty with deep breathing exercises, Ryan appeared at ease.

"Now, I want you to count backward from one hundred. You're going to begin to feel drowsy, lightheaded. Let yourself go. You're doing great. I'm going to speak with the personalities who share your thoughts and memories. I want you to immerse yourself deep within your mind and send them out one at a time. When we're done, I'll snap my fingers and you'll awake feeling refreshed." There was a pause, then a response.

"What's going on?" questioned a timid voice.

"Who are you? Abdo asked in great anticipation.

"My friends call me the Loner. You can call me that if you want."

"It's nice to meet you, Loner. You mentioned friends. Do you have many?"

"Three. Well, four. But one I haven't seen in a long time."

"Would those be the Watcher, the Writer, and the Optimist?"

"Yes, how do you know that?" The Loner looked surprised.

"And who would be the friend you haven't seen for a long time?" Abdo continued.

"Lazarus," the Loner said with sadness. "He disappeared one day, a long time ago. Sometimes I think I hear his voice. And then it disappears again."

"We'll talk about your friends another time. Today, let's talk about you. Would that be all right?"

"I'm certain they'd be more interesting."

"I'll bet you have a lot more to say than you think. Can we try, Loner?"

"Okay. What do you want to talk about?"

"Why don't we start with how old you are? When were you born?"

"December 14, 1951. It's funny. I remember the day, but I wasn't a baby. I was turning five. How can that be? I never thought about it before. I was unhappy. It was my birthday and I was alone, locked in my room. I remember my mom and dad fighting about how I had to grow up and be a man. Then my dad came into my room and I was crying, so he laid into me real good. My dad always scared me because he yelled so much. Nothing I did was good enough. Things always went better for me if I was quiet and did what I was told, so I did. I remember being lonely, and him telling me how disappointed he was in me."

Note to Chart: The boy's been told so many times that he isn't good at anything that he's come to believe it. He is an empty shell, bordering on self-destruction.

"Did your dad ever hit you?" Abdo asked.

"No, but I was always afraid he might. He had a look in his eyes that I can't describe, but I'd sure like to forget."

"How do you feel about your dad?"

No response.

When the Loner finally spoke he said with an air of guilt, "You know, I didn't cry when my dad died. People were in our house, and I could hear them saying, 'Look, he's not even crying.' I couldn't. I don't know why. I always felt bad about that." The Loner sat with his head down.

"Why don't you tell me about the day your dad died?"

"I don't feel much like talking anymore."

"Can you try to tell me what you remember about that day, and then we'll call it quits for today. You're doing so well."

"I don't remember much. My dad was yelling when he told my mom to send me in. But I couldn't go in. I was scared. So I stayed outside the door while Lazarus went in. The Watcher listened from outside with his ear to the door. You need to talk to the Watcher if you want to know about that day. But I have to warn you, he doesn't wanna talk to you."

CHAPTER 82
August 12, 1968

SCOOP DISCARDED HER sweaty clothes and jumped in the shower. The cool water working its way down her body was just what she needed. She remained in the sobering flow for a full twenty minutes, trying to wash away the feeling of filth she'd gotten at the crime scene.

Towel dry, hair brushing, body lotion, deodorant, make-up, clothing selection, full-length mirror perusal, and final approval, took about an hour. Scoop felt ready to reenter the world and have a chat with the police.

She dialed the local precinct and was put on hold. A few minutes later Officer Vincent Scumaci came on the line and introduced himself.

Scoop told the story of how she'd come into possession of a comb.

"So, you're *Scoop* Aubrey, the newspaper gal?" Scumaci caught her off guard.

He's heard of me? "That's me, guilty as charged. How do you know who I am?"

"Don't sound so surprised. I've read your *Height's Update.* You've got talent. As a matter of fact, I'm looking forward to reading your follow-up on the murder investigation. Any hints for an avid reader?"

"I could tell you, but then I'd have to kill you. Sorry. Not a good thing to say to a police officer. I don't know what my article will say, but I'll come up with something."

Scumaci smiled. He'd liked her writing, and now he liked her wit too.

"I'll tell you what. The Chief and I will be in your area tomorrow. Why don't we swing by around noon and you can give us the comb."

Scoop hung up and spent the next ten minutes selecting an outfit for her meeting with Scumaci and the Chief.

CHAPTER 83

August 13, 1968

THE NEWSPAPERS IDENTIFIED Chief of Detectives, Thomas Quinlan as lead in the Shadow Assassin murder investigation. Abdo called early hoping to catch the Chief in his office. After identifying himself, he explained that he had information, which he felt obligated to share but preferred to relay in person.

At ten a.m., Abdo entered the 34th Precinct, located at Amsterdam Avenue and 184th Street. The men-in-blue hustled about while phones rang off the hook. The officer at the front desk raised his hand, signaling Abdo he'd be with him shortly. After a few minutes, the Desk Sergeant motioned Abdo forward. "How can I help you, sir?"

"I have an appointment with Chief Quinlan. My name is Dr. Abdo Betaré."

"The Chief is expecting you. Top of the stairs, turn left, third door on your right."

Arriving at the open doorway, Abdo gave a gentle tap.

Quinlan rose with his hand extended. "Doctor Betaré, I'm Chief Quinlan and this is Officer Scumaci. Please, have a seat. Can I get you a cup of coffee? I should warn you, what they say about stationhouse coffee is true."

Abdo declined with a smile.

"So what can we do for you, Doctor? Or should I say, what can you do for us? You said you have information regarding an ongoing murder investigation."

Abdo remained silent for a moment deciding where to begin. "This could take a while."

"Take as much time as you need. Begin whenever you're ready."

"Chief Quinlan, are you familiar with a condition called multiple personality disorder?"

Quinlan acknowledged he'd heard of it, but only in a general sense.

Abdo continued. "Multiple personality disorder is a condition in which two or more distinct identities or personality states alternate in controlling the patient's consciousness and behavior."

Quinlan and Scumaci straightened up in their chairs as though that would help them understand what the doctor was talking about.

"Everyone has different sides to their personalities," Abdo explained. "Sometimes we're serious, sometimes playful. Sometimes we're angry, sometimes happy. These changes are brought on by daily experiences, or alcohol or drugs. Multiple personality disorder is different. In these patients, more than one identity exists within an individual's mind. These identities control behavior.

"Multiple personality is almost always triggered by abuse and/or by overwhelming stress. Inner conflict becomes so intolerable that the mind is forced to separate incompatible or unacceptable information from conscious thought.

"The person with multiple personality disorder maintains his or her primary identity. He or she is usually depressed, guilty, passive, and dependent. Other identities within the same person have their own names, likes, and dislikes. There may be as few as two identities, or significantly more.

"Multiple personality disorder is very complicated. The goal of treatment is to integrate the personalities into a single entity. However, integration is not always possible. In those situations, the goal is to achieve a harmonious interaction among the personalities which allows for more normal functioning."

Quinlan scratched his head. "Where exactly is this going, Dr. Betaré?"

"I have a patient, a young man whom I've known since his birth. His father died in his presence when he was nine, his sister committed suicide when he was eighteen, and shortly thereafter he spent nearly two years in a coma after falling victim to a vicious assault. I have his files with me. His life has been one trauma after another. His name is Ryan Cain."

"How does Ryan Cain fit in with the homicides?" Quinlan asked.

Abdo explained about the call he'd received from Regine and the events that followed. "I've made a copy of Ryan's medical history and duplicates of tape recordings in which Ryan's alters engage in conversation. Once you've reviewed them, I'm certain you will understand both Ryan's and my concerns."

"You're aware that what you've told us might incriminate your patient?" Quinlan asked.

"Indeed. I have Ryan's written permission to share this information with you. We're in full agreement that it is in everyone's best interest to determine what is going on, even if it implicates him."

"We'll need to meet with Ryan and, dependent upon how things go, we may have to detain him," Quinlan advised.

"We understand that you'll do what is necessary. However, I'm in the process of utilizing hypnotherapy to restore Ryan's memories. He is a very receptive subject. It is my hope you'll be able to conduct your investigation without interrupting Ryan's treatment."

"Let's take it one step at a time, Doc. You were right to contact us. We'll review everything you've brought us, and then arrange to meet with Ryan. In the meantime, it would be a good idea if your patient remains in someone else's company at all times. I'm sure you understand."

"Already taken care of, Chief Quinlan. I've got it covered. Please get back to me as soon as possible."

Once Abdo exited, Quinlan instructed Scumaci, "Check out the good doctor."

CHAPTER 84

August 13, 1968; evening

THE ADRENALIN RUSH from the kills was addictive, the withdrawal pains intense. The murders, which started out as revenge, had evolved into a 'fix' the Shadow Assassin now craved to feed his own existence.

He sat in his dingy eight-by-ten room eyeing the flaked, dirt-grey paint. Sweat permeated his drenched undershirt. He sniffed his arm pits. The stench gave him a rush. It reminded him of the thrill of the kill. He loved it.

A mouse scampered along the baseboard, attracted by the molded piece of cheese set in a trap. The Assassin ogled the rodent. *Eat or be eaten.* Without hesitation, the Assassin leapt forward whisking the mouse from the floor. With the look of a madman, prisoner firm in his grasp, he sensed that the mouse understood what was coming next. He lurched forward and bit the head of the mouse off its body, spitting it to the floor.

The door burst open, his partner in crime furious. "What the hell is going on? I told you, this crap has to stop. Get control of yourself. We need to lay low. At least till things cool down. It shouldn't be that hard. We've managed to remain invisible for so many years. Now go clean yourself up, you're a fuckin' mess."

CHAPTER 85

August 14, 1968

BY THE TIME everyone arrived, Quinlan had laid out an assortment of donuts and a pot of coffee. When Scumaci passed, Quinlan mumbled, "Three dollars and seventy-five cents, including tax." The officers quickly inhaled the pastries. Golub showed ten minutes later.

"Okay men, we've got one solid suspect and one new lead in the form of a comb. It was turned in by a civilian, the lovely Ms. Scoop Aubrey. Isn't that right, Vinnie?" Quinlan enjoyed an occasional jab at his young protégé. He could tell Scumaci was smitten with the redhead. "First, let's go over what you guys have come up with. Victor, start us off."

Victor Golub cleared his throat while the others prayed he wouldn't rant into one of his technical lectures. "I've got one addition which seems interesting. Let me give you some history on . . ."

Cohen and Tomlinson laid their heads on the table dreading the lesson about to come. The Chief intervened. "Victor, we've got a lot to cover. Please give us the short version. That goes for everybody."

"All right, if you geniuses don't want to be educated, here it is. Your killer is both left and right-handed. The Cockroach kid had his weiner whacked by a righty, and the Cornblatt woman had her neck broken by a lefty. I came to these conclusions based on the direction in which her head was twisted, and the angle of the cut on the kid's genitals. I apologize if that was too lengthy."

"So Victor, you're saying our perp is ambidextrous..."

"Or, we have more than one killer," Golub finished Quinlan's sentence.

"Let's move on. Who's next?" Quinlan urged.

Tomlinson dove right in. "We've taken over a hundred calls, most of which have been a waste of time. However, we had a call from a guy who says he saw a young man, whose name he thinks is Ryan. He says the kid seemed to be in a hurry and had blood on his shirt. He remembers the time and day because he was rushing to get in a cab and catch a flight to visit his son and ailing daughter-in-law. Day and time are a perfect fit for the Sane kid's murder."

"Who's our witness?" Quinlan inquired.

"That's where we have a problem, Chief. He hung up without giving his name. I asked a couple of times, but he ignored the question."

"Great. An anonymous tip." Quinlan seemed frustrated. "Any last name on this Ryan person?"

"No, but the caller mentioned he'd seen the kid playing ball in the park. Cohen and I asked around. The name we came up with is Ryan Cain."

Quinlan and Scumaci eyed each other for a long moment.

"Vinnie, did you check out the doc? Is he legit?"

"Squeaky clean, boss. Great rep. Nobody has anything bad to say about him. He appears to be on the level."

Without delay, Quinlan informed the team of his previous day's meeting with Dr. Betaré, and their discussion about his patient—Ryan Cain. He followed up by playing the tapes Dr. Betaré provided.

Everyone listened with great interest as the members of *The Quad* vented their anger and hatred for three of the four murdered victims. The Quad members hadn't stated they'd killed anyone, but the tapes would make for damaging circumstantial evidence.

Cohen jumped out of his chair. "Did you guys hear that?"

"What?" the others chimed in.

"Go to the end of the tape. Vengeance is ours. VIO."

Quinlan smacked his hand down hard on the table. "Holy crap. I've listened to these tapes a dozen times and didn't make the connection. Good work, Harvey."

"And, by the way," Cohen added. "I've completed compiling the list of unsolved violent crimes committed in Washington Heights over the past twenty-plus years."

The Chief put his hand up. "Hold onto it until we meet again. Right now we need to get a search warrant for Ryan Cain's home. Finally, we're getting somewhere. Good work, guys."

CHAPTER 86

August 14, 1968

"CAN YOU HEAR me?"

"I hear you, don't rush me."

"With whom am I speaking?" Abdo asked.

"You wanted to talk, so here I am."

"You're the Watcher?"

"Score one for the *know-it-all* doc," the Watcher said.

"Are you afraid of me?" Abdo questioned.

"I'm not afraid of anything, or anyone."

"In that case, can we chat?" Abdo hoped to maneuver the Watcher into sharing his feelings.

"Chat? Yeah, we can chat. What would you like to chat about?"

"Tell me about yourself?" Abdo suggested. "What you like, what you dislike. What makes you happy, what makes you sad? Or, we can talk about anything else that you'd like to get off your chest."

"I'll tell you this, Doc. I don't like being told what to do, or not do. I like people who mind their own business. I like being with my friends, even though they drive me crazy, and I like getting even with my enemies."

"What is it about being with your friends that you enjoy?"

"What kind of question is that? They're my friends. You have friends, don't you, Doc? What do *you* like about your friends? They're a part of me. And, even though they're a pain in my ass most of the time, they're family."

"So family is important to you?"

"Don't you get embarrassed asking stupid questions? They couldn't survive without me. Between them they can't make the simplest decision. Anything that needs doing is left up to me. The others are talkers."

"Do you enjoy that responsibility?"

"I do what needs to be done. These guys get pushed around and beaten up, and take that crap with a smile on their faces. But I know how they really feel behind those fake smiles. They feel like shit. So, I do what I have to. I protect my own."

Abdo avoided asking the Watcher if he'd ever committed any physical acts of aggression. "Is that what you did on the day your father died? Take charge and protect your own?"

The Watcher was quick to respond. "I did what I had to do to stay out of his way."

"But on the day he died, you were present? You couldn't bring yourself to go in and see him, but you did listen at the door after Lazarus went in. Why did you do that?"

"I could tell something bad was going to happen. Don't ask me how I knew, but at the instant Lazarus closed the door to my parents' bedroom a chill ran through me."

"Did you feel like you wanted to be in the room with Lazarus and your father?"

"Hell no, I hated my father. Nothing was going to get me in there. I couldn't hear much of what was said. My father's voice was weak and Lazarus didn't speak."

"Can you tell me what you did hear?"

"I've never spoken about that day. And yet, bits and pieces of what I heard play over and over again inside my head."

"Isn't it time you unburden yourself, and share those moments with someone?"

The Watcher sat close to tears, looking down at the floor. When he raised his head he recounted what he'd heard.

"Like I said, I could only make out a few words here and there, but that was more than enough. My dad talked about torture in great detail. Then he said, 'they're here and coming to get us.' He said he'd been hard on us because he had to be. He kept repeating, 'You have to watch and listen to every word, and observe every gesture, of everyone around you.' He said he loved us. He sure had a funny way of showing it.

"I can't talk about the things he said they did to him and others. It was too awful. My brothers and I fall asleep to the cries of innocents being tortured. He kept repeating, 'they're here.' Then, there was something about 'You can do it. Is okay.' I didn't know what the hell he was talking about.

"All of a sudden, in mid-sentence, there was silence. My mom went in a few minutes later. She screamed and started crying; and when the door opened, there was my dad. He wasn't moving or anything. Lazarus was nowhere to be found. He'd disappeared. That was the day I became who I am. I hate who I am, who I have to be. I wish Lazarus was here."

CHAPTER 87

August 15, 1968; early afternoon

WARRANT IN HAND, Quinlan and Scumaci ascended the final flight of stairs to the sixth floor residence. Quinlan bent over and took a deep breath. "Damn elevator, figures it would be out of order today."

"It's good exercise, Chief. You've been complaining about your waistline." Scumaci could poke fun as good as he could take—within respectable boundaries.

A muffled voice off to their right called out, "Don't matter what day or time you come, you'll still be walking up and down the stairs." Wearing a tool belt, the grease-stained man climbed out from the elevator shaft. "Damn elevator is a piece of crap."

"NYPD. Who might you be?" Quinlan inquired.

"Gunther Heber. I'm the superintendent, and also, unfortunate enough to live on the top floor of this repairman's dream. NYPD, what are you doing here? Has something happened?"

"Nothing to concern yourself about, Mr. Heber. Can you direct us to the Cain residence?"

"End of the hall, on your left. Apartment sixty-eight."

Regine's heart sank when Quinlan and Scumaci flashed their badges. "We've got a warrant to search the premises, ma'am. Is your son home?"

"What is this about? He's at a doctor's appointment. Should I call and let him know you're here?" Regine's fingertips quivered at the edge of her lower lip.

"No need, we'll send a patrol car if necessary. Would you be kind enough to show us to your son's room?" Quinlan could see the woman was lost to fear and confusion.

"Scumaci, you take the bathroom and closet. I'll check the bedroom."

Although located in Washington Heights, there was a distinct difference between this apartment and the ones closer to the park. It was like comparing a child to his grandparent . . . one vibrant, one run down. Ryan's walls hungered for personality. The paint throughout the apartment was chipped and flaking. Ryan's bed remained unmade, and a mousetrap sat on the linoleum floor in the far corner of the depressing room.

"Chief, check this out," Scumaci called out. "The kid's a packrat. He has six pairs of sneakers, all different sizes. And one appears to have dried blood on it."

"Put gloves on," Quinlan instructed. "Then, bag it for Golub."

"That's not all, Chief. I've got a flannel shirt with a missing button. I'll bag that, too. We'll see if it matches the one in Ethel Cornblatt's hand."

Quinlan poked his head in the closet. "Take the comic books too." He grabbed a *Fantastic Four* from the top of the pile. Skimming through, he came to spot where a page had been torn out.

"There must be ten combs in here. I'll bag 'em all," Scumaci called from the bathroom.

Quinlan approached Regine. "Mrs. Cain, can you tell me why your son keeps so many pairs of sneakers, and combs?"

"He doesn't throw things out," Regine explained, teary-eyed. "He's always been a junk collector. But as long as he keeps it all in his space, I don't have a problem with it. If he gets comfort from his old things, I want him to have them. Please tell me, what's going on?"

"We'll be removing multiple items for the police lab to check out," Quinlan explained.

"What is this about? What has Ryan done? There must be some mistake." Regine's knees started to buckle. Quinlan took hold of her shoulders.

"Here ma'am, let me help you to the sofa. You best have a seat. I'll get you a glass of water." Quinlan hated giving bad news to loving family members.

"I'm sorry I can't share any other information with you. We'll know more once we've examined these items more closely."

As Quinlan and Scumaci exited the apartment, Ryan and Dr. Betaré reached the sixth floor landing. Ryan ran to his mother's side while Abdo remained in the hallway with Quinlan.

"Sorry Doc, it doesn't look good. We're taking some things with us, but we'll be back if the lab confirms our suspicions. We have to keep tight reins on Ryan till we get this sorted out. I'll be posting an officer in the hallway."

Half way down the first flight of stairs Quinlan stopped. He turned back to Abdo. "One more question, Doc. Is it possible for one personality to be right-handed, and another left?

Abdo thought for a moment. "I've seen no research on it."

"Thanks for your help. We'll be in touch."

CHAPTER 88

August 15, 1968; morning

ABDO WAS PLEASED with the willingness of Ryan's personas to speak with him. In many multiple personality cases it took months, even years, to draw out an alternate identity.

Abdo stared into unfamiliar eyes. Hopeful eyes. *The Optimist. Finally, an opportunity to speak with a positive side of Ryan's personality.*

"Hello, Doctor," the Optimist greeted. "I believe you know who I am. I've been looking forward to talking with you."

"And I with you. What shall we talk about?"

"I suspect Ryan's well-being would be a good place to start," the Optimist said with apparent concern.

The response left Abdo at a momentary loss. *Alternate personalities don't acknowledge the existence of the primary identity. To do so is to recognize that they themselves have been created in someone else's mind. How can this be?*

"You know Ryan Cain?" Abdo asked.

"Yes, and I know the Loner, the Watcher and the Writer too."

"Then, you know you are a creation of Ryan's mind."

"I do. A very important creation, I would say. Wouldn't you agree?"

In total befuddlement Abdo asked, "How long have you known? How did you find out? Do the others know?"

"You left out, 'Why do I still exist if I know I'm a creation of Ryan's mind?' the Optimist said. "And, in answer to your question: no, the others are not aware. Let me tell you about myself. I think you'll find my story interesting.

"I believe I was conceived at the moment of Ryan Cain's birth," the Optimist began, "as all humans are born with an inherent grain of optimism in their souls. However, my explosion of consciousness came during an unexpected adventure—a journey on which Ryan and I visited with God.

"I see the skepticism on your face. It is a difficult concept to accept, but as surely as I am sitting here talking to you right now, Ryan sat and conversed with God. Thus my 'coming-out,' so to speak, evolved. Would you care to hear the whole story?"

"Please," Abdo urged.

"It was July 19, 1962. I remember it like it was yesterday. Ryan had returned home from school and his mom called him to her bedroom. From the tone of her voice, it didn't sound good. A trip to Mom's room meant only one thing. Head down, wearing a sad face of apology, Ryan readied himself to take the blame for something he didn't even know he'd done.

"'What is this, young man?' Regine demanded, opening her closet door. There, standing upright in the corner was a 26" Schwinn bicycle. Regine had put the word out. If anyone knew of a used bike for sale, she'd be interested. The call came that morning.

"The black three-speed, with hand brakes and the coolest tires ever, idled in its hiding place, staring at its new owner. 'Don't just stand there kid; let's go for a ride,' the bike seemed to cry out.

"'This is great, I can't believe it. I gotta take it out for a ride. Right now. Okay, Mom? Please.' Ryan was speed-talking. When he finally stopped, his mouth formed a smile that ran ear to ear. He couldn't remember feeling so happy, ever. It was the best day of his whole life.

"His mom smiled. 'Dinner will be ready in forty-five minutes. Don't make me come looking for you.'

"Plenty of time for a short ride to Bennett Park, Ryan calculated in his head. He maneuvered the bike toward the front door and turned around. 'You're the best, Mom. Love you.'

"Ryan coasted into Bennett Park. Benches lined the playground, and a four-foot-high, steel-spiked fence encompassed the two-square-block perimeter. Families enjoyed the close of a beautiful day; toddlers laughed on the swings and see-saws, while older kids played ringolevio. July nineteenth was turning out to be a perfect day, in a perfect park, on a perfect bike . . . until tragedy struck.

"Cruising, without a care in the world, the wind blew through Ryan's speckled hair. The baseball cards attached to the spokes of his wheels made the coolest 'tick, tick, tick' as he sped along the pavement. Exhilaration overtook him. Ryan lost focus of where he was going. He was moving too fast, getting ready to execute a turn at one of the park's four corners. From out of nowhere, two women with baby carriages blocked his path. *No time to stop.*

"The razor-sharp spikes inched closer to his speeding head.

"Under his breath, Ryan uttered, 'Sorry, Mom.'

"And that's when it happened. A millisecond from death, God reached out and swept Ryan into his arms. He, or more accurately, *we* were literally in the presence of God.

"For the ten seconds in earthly-time that it would have taken Ryan to get from spot A to spot B on his bike, we were God's guests. I know how this sounds, but please allow me to go on."

Abdo nodded.

"Ten seconds in human time equates to ten years in heavenly time. Ryan, and I through Ryan, conversed with God for ten years. Can you imagine? God explained the mysteries of life. We'd been taught the answers to questions that mankind has been asking since the beginning of time. It was glorious. Everything made sense. Then, it was time to return.

"God told us the knowledge we'd gained would remain within us when we returned to earth, but we would not have conscious access. He told us of challenging times ahead and of the ultimate joy we would one day attain.

"As God returned Ryan to his bicycle, he was no longer in danger. Instead, he was situated on the other side of the park, safe and sound. Ryan's future had been written."

Abdo sat dumbfounded. He'd heard Ryan's version of the bike ride, and closing his eyes, and being on the other side of the park when he reopened them. He'd listed it as "Ryan's Miracle" in his chart. But this was incredible. This was an alternate personality being nurtured and experiencing the event with Ryan.

"Speechless, huh Doc? Ryan and I have conversed with God. He told us everything will be all right. Is it any wonder I'm an unwaivering optimist?"

Abdo remained paralyzed in his chair.

"If I may," the Optimist proceeded, "let me add my own personal insight on your dilemma. The Loner and Writer will be willing subjects in your efforts to integrate all of us back into Ryan's subconscious. However, the Watcher is another story. He will present a challenge. You see, he would find it very difficult to believe he doesn't really exist in physical form."

Abdo couldn't get his words out. The Optimist spoke in a sane, rational manner. He did not try to convince Abdo to believe him. To the contrary, he seemed to understand that anyone who had not lived the experience would have trouble accepting it.

"Can I ask you one more question," Abdo begged.

"Of course. Whatever I can do to help."

"What are your feelings toward your father?"

It was the Optimist's turn to sit in silence. Once content with what his response would be, he spoke in a well-thought-out and constructed tone. "My father, our father, was a difficult man to know. His life's experiences left him a damaged shell of the man he'd once been. His endless relating of the horrific experiences he endured and witnessed has now left us… damaged goods. At night, when I and my brothers go to sleep, we are prisoners of unearthly screams placed there by our father. We endure so Ryan can forget."

Abdo interrupted. "The Watcher has referred to the screams as *the cries of innocents*."

"That seems an accurate description," the Optimist concurred. "I couldn't have phrased it better.

"However, in answer to your question, I know harsh feelings exist among my siblings regarding our father. I can well appreciate their animosity. I also understand that the mistakes our father made were out of concern. He was a tormented soul and a hard man to love, but I harbor no ill feelings toward him. He journeyed to a place no man should ever have to go. He'd been to hell's doorstep, and found his way back. And, while his methods were extreme, he did what he thought best for his family. How can I hate him for that? Does that answer suffice, Doctor?"

"There are no wrong answers," Abdo responded, "only insightful ones. I appreciate your candor. It has been a pleasure speaking with you."

"And with you, Doctor."

CHAPTER 89
August 16, 1968

SCOOP DECIDED HER follow-up story on the "Assassin" crimes would have more of a personal, rather than investigative, angle. To publish a story based on guesswork would be unfair to both her readers and herself.

YOU CAN'T TELL A CROOK BY ITS COVER: LOOKING BEYOND THE OBVIOUS
By Scoop Aubrey

Things aren't always as they appear. People are not always who you think they are. My experiences of the past few weeks have taught me this valuable lesson. So now, I keep an open mind. I look beyond the obvious and seek out the heart of a person rather than the facade they project, or worse, the one I imagined.

I now search for understanding beyond what people show me, because sometimes good people hide their kindness behind feelings of insecurity, while bad people disguise themselves to appear as angels.

Similar to a book, a crook's cover can be deceiving. A pretty picture or intriguing title preconditions us to believe we are looking at a great book. Judging people is like judging a book. We have to read beyond what the author puts in front of us. Sometimes the truth is buried beneath layers of deceit.

I have met many people of late, and through my own flaws, have approached some of them with preconceived notions which later made me ashamed of myself.

It has occurred to me ... perhaps the reason the Shadow Assassin has remained elusive is because the picture on his book jacket is misleading. Perhaps when we look at him, he is the person we would least suspect.

CHAPTER 90

August 16, 1968

"WITH WHOM AM I speaking?" Abdo inquired.

"I'm the Writer."

"It's a pleasure to make your acquaintance. I'm Dr. Betaré. Might I inquire how your writing is going?"

"There are good days and bad. There's so much material to sort through. Sometimes it seems overwhelming, but I think my book will be interesting when it's finished."

"May I ask what it's about?"

"It's about the Quad, of course. I document our lives. No one listens to us now, but one day they will."

"And how do you get material for your book? Do the members of the Quad divulge their experiences and share their emotions with you?"

"I believe our objectives are not dissimilar from one another, Doctor. It's a matter of asking the right questions and directing people to share what's on their minds. Deep down, everyone wants to talk. You simply need to be a good listener."

"That's a very astute observation. Would you mind if I turn the tables and ask you questions?"

"You already are. It's your book we're working on here, Doc. Ask away."

"In your years of researching the Quad do you recall the mention of a suicide in 1964?"

"I do, but wish I didn't. It was a terrible period in all of our lives, especially the Loner's. As if he wasn't depressed enough, the poor soul found Willow hanging from a basement pipe with a suicide letter on the floor beneath her. Ever since, he's been devastated with guilt for not anticipating her actions. He feels he should have done something to save her. He could never reconcile the event in his head. To this day, he swears she wouldn't have killed herself.

"Willow was pregnant. She'd confided to the Loner who the father was, and that she was afraid to tell him about the baby."

"And when she told the Loner who the father was, how did he react?" Abdo asked. "Did he tell his mom?"

"He told no one. His sister made him swear, and now he carries the burden of her suicide deep in his soul."

"So he has never spoken of this to anyone, but you? Why do you think that is?"

"Like I said, everyone wants to talk, and I'm the only one who showed an interest. After his sister told him who the baby's father was, the Loner confronted him. It was out of character for him, but he wanted to make certain the father took responsibility.

"That meeting didn't go well. The father couldn't have cared less about Willow or the baby. He laughed, which made the Loner furious. That's when the Loner threatened to expose him to the police as the neighborhood drug dealer. After that, things got worse. They got into a fight, and from what I understand, while this guy was beating on him, the Loner grabbed for whatever was in reach and swung. He put a nasty gash down the left side of the daddy-to-be's face. It left one hell of a scar."

"Was that the end of it?" Abdo asked with concern. "Did they ever confront each other again?"

"I don't know. I do know the Loner has always suspected Willow's suicide was in fact a homicide, and that son-of-a-bitch with the scar was at the top of the Loner's list of suspects."

"Did the father-to-be have a name?"

"Yeah, Vespers. Derek Vespers."

CHAPTER 91

August 16, 1968

THE FOUR MEN sat in hushed contemplation. There were no donuts. No jokes, no high fives, no frivolous banter. Each of the officers had read through Ryan Cain's lengthy medical history, listened to the tapes of his multiple personalities in conversation, and reviewed Dr. Betaré's notes of how Ryan Cain had deteriorated to his present state.

"I didn't foresee it going down this way," Scumaci said. "I expected the killer to be a monster." The others concurred. They sat in silence feeling empathy rather than contempt for Ryan Cain's tortured soul.

Quinlan entered the room with the same mixed emotions as the others. Putting his personal feelings aside, he opened the meeting. "Okay, gentlemen, let's review what we've got. One: The blood on the sneaker found in Ryan Cain's closet has been confirmed as Derek Vespers'. Two: The button found in Ethel Cornblatt's hand is a match for the missing button on the flannel shirt found in Ryan Cain's closet. Three: The torn page with the letters VIO written on it, found at the 'Cockroach' scene, came from *The Fantastic Four* comic we retrieved from Ryan Cain's closet. Victor, although it seems moot, what did you get from the comb found at the Vukchek crime scene?"

Golub toyed with the mole on his chin as he spoke. "It's a match to the comb retrieved from the suspect's home. The dry, crusted residue caked at the base of the comb's teeth is psoriatic flaking from the boy's scalp."

"It appears we've found our killer, gentlemen," Quinlan said. "So, why don't I feel happier? Is there anything else to go over?"

Golub spoke up. "There is one more thing I'd like to point out. The hair and skin flakes on the comb Ms. Aubrey brought in are at least ten years old.

"We know the kid's a packrat," Scumaci offered. "Maybe he grabbed an old comb that day."

"With everything we've got, I don't think the age of the hair on the comb is going to make a difference," Quinlan surmised. "I've made arrangements for Ryan Cain to be contained in the psychiatric ward at Bellevue rather than city lockup. Once we make the arrest, I'll call Dr. Betaré and set up a time to interview Mr. Cain with the doctor present. I'm going to need his help in understanding who I'm talking to." Quinlan began to exit the room when he turned to his men. "Cohen, take Tomlinson with you and pick up Ryan Cain on suspicion of murder. Mirandize him and make certain he understands his rights."

Above the chatter, Tomlinson called out. "Hey Chief, I've still got that stuff you had me dig up."

"File it away. We've got our guy"

CHAPTER 92

August 16, 1968

HYPNOTHERAPY HAD GONE well. Abdo tried accessing the Watcher, who had opted not to respond on his previous attempt. "Watcher, are you there?"

His voice sounded different, timid. "Hey Doc, you have a few minutes?"

"Of course, I was concerned when you missed our last meeting. What's on your mind?"

"I didn't feel much like talking then."

"And you feel like talking now?"

"I'm not sure. I've been thinking."

"And?"

"I'm confused."

"About?"

"The way I feel."

Abdo continued. "When last we spoke you said you hate the way things are now. You wished Lazarus would return."

The Watcher appeared drained. "I don't know what I want."

"I'd like to show you something. May I?" Abdo presented the Watcher with a current photograph of Ryan Cain. "Do you know this young man?"

"No. Should I?"

The Watcher's response came as no surprise. *Each of the Quad members perceives his physical appearance differently.* "His name is Ryan Cain. He's had a tough life, much like your own. What he needs now is for his friends to help him find his way home."

The Watcher squirmed in his chair.

Abdo continued. "Ryan experienced emotional trauma as a child. To compensate, his mind created alternate identities to help him cope. Without those identities he wouldn't have had the strength to endure the horrors thrust upon him. Those personalities were, and are still, his saviors. The condition I've described is known as multiple personality disorder."

"Why are you telling me this? You think I have multiple personalities?"

Abdo paused, concerned about the Watcher's mental state. "Because you are one of Ryan Cain's personalities."

The Watcher lost it, his coiled anger unraveled into hysteria. "What the fuck are you talking about?"

Abdo needed to be careful as the Watcher was the primary bearer of Ryan's anger. He implored him to remain calm.

"Whattaya mean remain calm? Let me outta here. Where are the Loner, Writer and Optimist? I wanna see them, now."

"You can't. You each occupy a separate state of consciousness, but share the same body—Ryan's. Inside his head, you can interact. However, out here with me, you can only communicate one at a time. You were created by Ryan's mind when he was a child. The occurrences on the day of his father's death propelled you, and your *brothers*, into the roles you currently fulfill."

The Watcher's face turned red with anger. "If that's true, why didn't Lazarus fulfill a role?"

"That's a good question." Abdo tried to appease his patient. "At the time of the incident, it was Lazarus who entered the room with Ryan. It was during the meeting, of which you heard bits and pieces, that Lazarus was propelled deep into the recesses of Ryan's mind."

"This is bullshit." The Watcher stood, ready to leave.

Abdo felt empathy for the lost soul before him. *There's no turning back now.* "Please sit down. I know this is overwhelming, but multiple identities confronting each other can lead to violent actions. At the moment, Ryan exists in a state which he cannot survive. That puts you all at risk. The number of identities in Ryan's mind must be reduced to one—Lazarus. Be assured that neither you, nor the others, will ever disappear. You'll simply move to a more stable location in Ryan's mind. You'll take on a less stressful role in Ryan's life. You'll be happier, and Ryan will be healthier. Please think about it."

"What makes Lazarus so special? "Why does he get to stay instead of me?"

"You each have a role to play. This is Lazarus' time. Be assured that once Ryan is again one with himself, Lazarus will join you and the others. You've stated that you wished Lazarus would return. Help me bring him back. I need your cooperation to finish this."

They were about to call it a day when something the Watcher said caused Abdo to think back to Ryan's childhood. Something Ryan had said a long time ago gnawed at Abdo's mind. *Were they the playful words of a child playing superhero, or an indicator that I'd missed?*

Abdo decided to ask the question he had been holding back on.

"Watcher, have you ever killed anyone?"

***

Seven years earlier . . .

In 1961, Ryan's favorite comic book, *The Fantastic Four*, was first published. Every Monday, Ryan sat on his bed rationing out the tip-money he'd earned making deliveries for the local florist and dry cleaners. He sorted his pocketful of change into three piles. *Two dollars for Mom, thirty-five cents for two slices of pizza and a soda, and thirty cents for two new comic books.*

Always the first to arrive, an impatient Ryan stood by the newsstand, his sweaty hand clutching his coins.

"Must be Tuesday," the vendor bellowed with a smile.

The delivery driver threw the bundled publications to the curb. "Here ya go, son. Let me grab you a copy from the middle. Here's one in mint condition."

"Thank you, sir," Ryan replied, already engrossed in the cover art. In *The Fantastic Four*, Ryan found a family of characters who, like himself, differed from other people. When he returned home, Ryan retreated into his room, absorbed in the fictitious adventures. At evening's end, he'd wander the apartment imagining what it would be like to be a superhero, declaring, "One day, I'll deal with the bad guys."

CHAPTER 93
August 16, 1968

QUINLAN TOOK A deep breath as he entered Manhattan's Bellevue Psychiatric Hospital. He'd visited the facility before and dreaded every moment. The waiting room resembled a microcosm of purgatory. Beyond the swinging doors hell awaited all who dared enter. He peered through the entry's 6" x 6" shatterproof glass window. Patients sat on the floor. Some banged their heads against the walls.

Quinlan flashed his badge to the receptionist and was buzzed access to the hallways of the lost. Before him stood, sat, and sprawled an assortment of criminals whose consciences were either non-existent, or out-to-lunch. Their shouts of lunacy bellowed in an equal opportunity barrage of English, Spanish, Italian, and a few languages Quinlan didn't recognize.

Proceeding down the corridor, Quinlan sidestepped the residents medicated with the drug of the day, chlorpromazine. They were easy to spot. Their faces were blotted, their skin colors an unnatural pink, and their life forces drained from their bodies.

Quinlan reached the high security ward, which housed inmates awaiting arraignment or trial. He didn't want to think about Ryan Cain who, if found guilty, would be moved in with the general population. *The corrections system doesn't have an accommodation suited to Ryan's particular circumstances. If proven guilty, he doesn't belong on the streets where he'll be a danger to others. But, incarcerated with violent psychopaths, he'll never survive.*

The alternative to Bellevue was even worse. Under ordinary circumstances, a person arrested in Manhattan landed in the Tombs. There, prisoners were sorted by the nature of their crimes. Burglars and robbers occupied one floor, while prisoners arrested for more severe crimes such as murder and arson were kept on another. Quinlan knew Ryan Cain would be lost to the system if placed there, so he'd arranged for incarceration at Bellevue.

When Quinlan entered the room, Abdo sat at Ryan's bedside, appearing calm. Quinlan knew better. He'd been reading faces all his life. *I know fear when I see it. The doc is putting up a good front for the sake of the kid, but he knows the score.* Abdo started to get up. Quinlan waved him back down. "You can stay, Doctor. It will be helpful for all concerned. First of all, I need to ask Ryan if he has a clear understanding of the multiple personality disorder with which he's been diagnosed."

Ryan nodded.

"Please, I need to hear you say it."

"Yes, I understand my condition."

"In that case, this next question is for both of you. I'm having trouble understanding how and when your personalities take over or, if in fact, I'm speaking to one of them right now. How do I know with any certainty who I'm speaking with at any given moment? And, how will I know if the situation changes from question to question?"

"Allow me to put your mind at ease," Abdo responded.

Quinlan picked up on the quiver in the doctor's voice. "Go ahead, Doc."

"Prior to hypnotherapy, Ryan's personalities did in fact impose themselves into conversation. Out of frustration they craved to be heard. Now free to speak their piece during sessions, they are more than happy to remain in the background. I assure you; you are and will be speaking directly with Ryan."

"Okay then." Quinlan scratched his head. *This case is giving me a headache.*

"Let me ask the most obvious question right up front. Did you kill any of the people you've been accused of murdering?"

"I'd like to say no, but all I can say is, not that I know of. I wish I could be more helpful for both our sakes."

"Do you think any of your alter egos are capable of committing such violent crimes?"

Ryan thought and responded with the truth. "I wish I could tell you, but I'm just learning about them myself. If you're asking me do I think it's within me to do the things I'm accused of, I would say no. However, I'm as confused as you are."

Quinlan pressed on. "You do concede that you knew, and disliked all of the victims?"

"Yes," Ryan admitted.

"Well Ryan, what do you think should be done, if in fact one of your alter egos, through whatever means Dr. Betaré has explained, caused you to perpetrate these crimes?"

"That's not for me to decide. I try not to think about it."

"I've got to be honest with you, son. I hope you're innocent. However, there is an overwhelming amount of evidence that says you killed four people. Items retrieved from your home implicate you for each and every one of the murders. That being said, there are things that trouble me. That's not meant to give you false hope. The evidence against you is staggering. The way things stand there isn't a jury that could help but find you guilty."

Quinlan stood to leave. "I appreciate your honest answers, son. I don't get much of that in my line of work. You hang in there a while longer. I've got some things to check out. I'll be back in touch soon."

Abdo escorted Quinlan into the hallway. "Thanks for arranging for Ryan to be kept at Bellevue. I researched the alternative. Do you really believe there's a chance Ryan didn't commit these crimes?"

"Like I said Doc, there are some things I want to look into. When I said 'hang in there,' that included you too. The kid's lucky to have you on his side."

Quinlan exited the warehouse of lost souls. He'd never felt so happy to reenter the insanity of the streets. At least it was the kind he understood.

CHAPTER 94

August 17, 1968; morning

LAZARUS SAT IN wonderment, observing the fireworks. They were both glorious and frightening. *It's happening.*

As the Quad members confided their deepest and darkest secrets to Dr. Betaré, synapses fired in Ryan's mind, mimicking an electrical storm. The rains poured, as distorted images flowed in streams of emotions. Vessels buried beneath the convolutions of Ryan's brain washed aside debris, clearing a path for Lazarus' journey. He could see the light in the distance. It would take time, but escape from damnation seemed imminent. The walls of hell would soon dissolve to smoldering rubble.

With each session's disclosure, Lazarus swam further upstream toward a heightened reinstatement in Ryan's life.

Memories infiltrated Lazarus' thought banks. Good memories, bad memories, but mostly painful memories overwhelmed his consciousness. Emotional flashbacks played like an 8mm video reel projecting vivid images of the tormented life of the child named Ryan.

With the help of Dr. Betaré, and the link to Ryan's consciousness growing stronger, Lazarus hoped to soon be conversing with Dr. Betaré himself.

Get ready, Doc. Here I come.

CHAPTER 95

December 1938

HANS AND GERHARDT Schtroeber had served as guards at the Dachau camp for almost two years when their transfer orders arrived—*Report to the Reichstag in Berlin.* To work under Hitler's direct command was a supreme honor. They marched to a new found enthusiasm.

Two months later, all was lost. The Schtroebers were on the run. They had killed No. 19. Injected him with medication earmarked for the Führer. The Führer would most certainly be unforgiving and kill them in a manner most foul.

The brothers wasted no time. A call to a friend, a fellow soldier at Dachau, set their escape plan in motion. It would be a long and dangerous trek over the German terrain. Dachau was located more than three hundred miles south of Berlin.

They dyed their hair, donned civilian clothes, and began making their way along the less traveled roads heading south. In their wake remained the corpses of men, women and children who had possessed what they needed—food, money, and safe-harbor. The Schtroebers could ill afford to leave witnesses as to their whereabouts. A month later they reached the town of Dachau.

Their contact had procured the requested items. From the Nazi storage lockers, overflowing with confiscated identification papers and personal effects of camp prisoners, the brothers would assume new identities.

With forged travel permits, the Schtroebers boarded an ocean-liner bound for the United States.

CHAPTER 96

August 17, 1968; evening

ABDO CALLED FOR a meeting of the minds. Circumstances dictated a need to expedite both Lazarus' return and the rekindling of Ryan's memories.

In turn, each of the Quad members was summoned to consciousness. Abdo explained the dire reality of their futures. "What happens to Ryan happens to you. If Ryan goes to prison, you go as well. There'll be no walks in the park, no writing stories while sitting on the lawn, no beautiful girl named Robin. If you think your lives have been hell up to this point, you're in for a rude awakening. You're well on your way to a life sentence of wall-to-wall psychos, murderers, rapists, pedophiles, and junkies. The bullies you talk about are saints compared to the miscreants awaiting you in prison. Now, tell me everything you know about Ryan's life."

Abdo paused to let his words sink in.

"Are any of you involved in the crimes Ryan is charged with? I need to know. No more messing around, no more secrets. Once incarcerated, there's nothing I will be able to do to help you. This is your last chance."

The plethora of information provided by the Quad portrayed a clear picture of Ryan's painful existence. Disturbing memories revealed on-going emotional and psychological abuse caused by his father. Ryan was haunted by Willow's death. Loneliness and guilt consumed his psyche.

Notable also, were two omissions from the Quad's recollections of Ryan's life: the day Sandor called Ryan to his bedside before dying, and the participation in any murders.

Abdo processed the new information. *The absence of knowledge regarding the events at Sandor's deathbed is understandable, as only Lazarus was present at the time. The absence of knowledge regarding the killings is a good sign, but proves nothing. My description of what would happen to them if Ryan were found guilty could easily have caused the intentional omission of those memories.*

The Watcher squirmed as though he wanted to say something, but couldn't bring himself to do it. Abdo gave it one last shot. To each Quad member he made one final plea. "Now is the time to clear your conscience. Everything said here is forgiven. We've reached the moment of truth. As one goes, you all go."

The Loner, Writer and Optimist each assured Abdo he'd told everything he knew. The Watcher put up resistance. "Why should we trust you? For all we know you'll get us into more trouble than we're already in. You don't know a damn thing about us, or what we've been through."

"I know more about you than you know about yourselves."

"Like what?" the Watcher challenged.

Abdo fired with both barrels. "I know the Loner is sad, insecure and dejected. He lives in his head because he doesn't feel a part of the team. He compensates because he doesn't think he is worthy of a real life.

"The Writer is curious and afraid of failure. He is overwhelmed by his knowledge of others, which is why he shares so little of his own thoughts and feelings.

"The Optimist keeps you all sane. He fills your lives with hopes and dreams despite the horrors you've experienced.

"Lazarus is the level-headed one . . . a born leader, a visionary. While I've not yet met him, I imagine he goes to sleep every night hoping he made the right choices in protecting all of you.

"And you. You're angry, cynical and impatient. You hide your emotions behind childlike outbursts, but that's not working anymore. You want to escape the prison you've created for yourself.

"If you want to know how I know these things, it's because I'm good at my job. You're in serious trouble. Now please let me help you. Let me help all of you."

The Watcher broke down. A look of submission overtook his face. In a whisper, he said, "I think Willow was raped. I think they were all raped."

Tears of guilt poured down the Watcher's cheeks. He held his shaking hands before his face trying to hide his shame.

While shocked, Abdo remained calm. "How do know that, did she tell you?"

The Watcher regained his composure. "I've already told you I spend a lot of time cutting through alleyways. What I haven't told you is that over the years I've often been to the alley overlooking Derek Vespers' apartment."

Abdo encouraged the Watcher to continue. "What happened there? What did you see?"

"I didn't see anything. But I'd been hearing girls yelling for him to stop for years, and I did nothing about it. I'd always see the girls in the park a day or two later, and they seemed okay. So I minded my own business. I swear I didn't know Willow was one of them. Not until the Loner told us Derek Vespers was the father of Willow's baby. Then it hit me, but I couldn't tell the others. They'd hate me. I hate myself. It's my fault. If I'd told somebody about the girls screaming Willow might still be alive. What have I done?"

As painful as it had been, a fragment of guilt's causation was now exposed and with time might be lifted. All emotions carried by his alter egos were also borne in Ryan's subconscious.

"As far as you knew, the young girls you heard screaming were not abducted," Abdo said, trying to alleviate some of the Watcher's guilt. "No one ever filed charges. I'm certain that over the years, you've heard many things that seemed out of order. How could you have been expected to know which instances required action, and which did not? There was nothing you could have done for those girls." Abdo didn't really believe what he was saying; however, there was nothing to be gained by pursuing other possibilities. Not now. Vespers was dead, and relieving the Watcher's guilt seemed more beneficial toward Ryan's recovery.

The Watcher's demeanor improved as he absorbed the logic of Dr. Betaré's comments. The burden of his secret now shared appeared to lift an enormous weight from his shoulders.

Abdo achieved what he'd intended. He now understood the tremendous guilt Ryan carried over his sister's death. He would confide his findings to Ryan and determine where they'd go from there.

CHAPTER 97

August 18, 1968

SCOOP FELT UNSETTLED. She reviewed the notes of her interview with Otto Sussman. Something one of her elderly Jewish neighbors once told her registered in her memory. She was talking with sweet Mrs. Lehman a few months earlier. She didn't remember how the topic came up, but Mrs. Lehman shared stories of her childhood, and revealed her experience in the Auschwitz concentration camp. She was one of the few survivors liberated at the end of the war.

If Scoop's memory served her right, Mrs. Lehman had said, "First the Nazis used mandatory camp badges made of colored inverted triangles to identify prisoners. The triangles varied in color based on the reason the prisoner had been placed there." She recalled triangles were made of fabric and were sewn onto the jackets and shirts of the prisoners.

Later, she recalled, "The camp changed from the triangles to sewing numbers onto the prisoners' clothing. However, with the death rate increasing daily, it became difficult for the Nazis to keep track of the corpses' identities because clothes were removed and given to new prisoners. The Nazis then began writing the numbers on the corpses' chests with indelible ink to help keep their records in order. When that method no longer seemed practical the Nazis began tattooing numbers on the prisoners' left breast using metal stamps. Ultimately, they settled on tattooing identification numbers on the left forearm."

Scoop sat in the library, scouring history books for information to confirm or deny Mrs. Lehman's recollections. If Mrs. Lehman was correct, and who should know better than a camp survivor, Scoop wanted to see if she could find the dates when each process of inmate identification was implemented.

Hours of research provided the answer. *Mrs. Lehman knew what she was talking about.* The practice of tattooing inmates with identification numbers originated in Auschwitz, where Lehman was imprisoned.

In March 1942, the tattooing process became the standard in every camp. In short order, when metal stamps became financially impractical, the tattooing of identification numbers was performed with a single needle on each prisoner's left forearm.

What Scoop was having trouble understanding was, *if Otto Sussman was a prisoner in 1938, and fled Germany later the same year, why does he have an identification number tattooed on his left forearm, if the Nazis didn't initiate that particular process until 1942?*

CHAPTER 98

August 18, 1968

ABDO TOSSED THE folded section of the *New York Times* onto the bed, exposing the half-completed crossword puzzle. He took a seat across from Ryan.

"Ryan, I'm not sure how much more we can hope to accomplish before your arraignment. I believe your alter egos have told me everything they know. We've made tremendous progress. For the next few days, it's just you and me."

"Zygote," Ryan said.

"What?"

"Twenty-four down, a six letter word for a fertilized egg before cleavage. Zygote. And seventy-eight across—a person who hates or distrusts all people—misanthrope."

"Lazarus?"

"Yes, Doctor. Back from the dead."

"Where have you been?"

Lazarus kept his answer simple. "Solitary confinement."

"Are you aware of what's transpired since you disappeared?" Abdo asked.

"I'm quite certain I don't know everything, but my return has been guided by your sessions. I've followed the voices for days. Without the outpourings from the Loner, Watcher, Writer, and Optimist, I'd have been lost forever. I have you to thank for my return. Also, thank you for your sincere efforts in trying to help *all* of us. However, now I believe I can be of help to you. You wanted to know about the day our father died? Allow me to fill you in."

"It was 3:47 pm on June 10, 1956. I remember looking at the clock. Regine came to Ryan holding back her tears. She caressed his cheek and ran her fingers through his hair. 'It's time,' she said.

"Ryan stood outside his parents' bedroom door, numb with anticipation. His legs shook. He felt certain they would collapse beneath him as he worked up the courage to enter the room. His stomach churned. He wanted to see his father, but didn't want to see his father. He opened the door.

"Ryan had never seen his father unclothed. He never wondered why. Now he understood. He became lightheaded at the sight of his father's undraped body. Sandor was a horror to behold. His skin had turned a yellow-gray hue as he approached death. His eyes were ochre crusted. Drool oozed from the corners of his mouth as he coughed up phlegm. Thick scars and burns covered Sandor's torso and legs. The number 19 had been branded onto his sunken chest.

"Earlier that morning Sandor had discontinued his morphine drip. He needed to be lucid when he spoke to his son. His arms bore no muscle tone, yet he managed, with his bony fingers, to grab Ryan by his tee-shirt and pull his scrawny body toward him. The stench of Sandor's breath made Ryan nauseous.

"Sandor positioned his mouth to Ryan's ear and whispered. 'I'd hoped never to relay these stories, but it is now necessary.' I don't know if Sandor was aware at the time that he had been relaying horrific stories to Ryan every day since Ryan turned five. This recounting, however, surpassed the gory detail of previous telling.

"He told Ryan about Kristallnacht and his weeks of incarceration by the Nazis. He described his rescue by people he'd never been able to thank, and of his and Regine's journey across the globe to their eventual sanctuary in the United States.

"Sandor then went on to explain how Hitler was consumed by a piece of parchment which he believed was in Sandor's possession. He explained that he'd had no idea what Hitler was talking about. Only years later did it become clear when, while living in Washington Heights, an envelope arrived from an Erik Jan Hanussen bearing a Vienna postmark dated 1933.

"Sandor didn't believe in the prophecies of a charlatan, but then things started happening.

"Hanussen had enclosed a letter accompanying the long sought parchment, stating his vision had been a recurring one, upon which he had taken no liberties. He acknowledged the chicanery of other prophecies during his reign, but swore these were genuine. He begged Sandor Cain not to dismiss them.

313

Hanussen's letter predicted his own death upon the presentation of the prophecies to Adolf Hitler on March 25, 1933.

"Sandor said he had entrusted the parchment to Abdo for safekeeping, and that Abdo would present him with the parchment when time was right, not a moment sooner.

"Sandor's pain became excruciating as he doubled-up. He continued in broken sentences. 'Have to know. They're here. Nazis—they're here. Saw them. Sure they saw me.'

"At this point I become hazy. I remember free-falling until I reached the cell which I inhabited for countless years. The rest of Ryan's conversation with his father is vague. I tried to listen, but there was an overwhelming reverberation of echoes through my passage.

"Again, I recall hearing something like 'mother, sister, you kill, Is OK! Is OK!'

"That's all I remember."

Abdo understood that Ryan's conscious-self had no indication that his personality had broken down into multiple personas. In truth, none of the personas knew of the existence of the others in the beginning, yet it was their coexistence keeping Ryan alive. It was only as conflicting emotions overlapped that Ryan's *alters* became acquainted.

Abdo now possessed a more complete picture of the trauma that had erased Ryan's memories and sentenced Lazarus to solitary confinement. Perhaps, with the information gained from Lazarus and the others, Ryan's healing could begin.

Just when Abdo thought he saw the complete picture, Lazarus looked up and added, "There's one more thing you should know."

CHAPTER 99
The Writings of Isok
"Buried Truths"

Prior to our father's death my brothers' personalities held a more prominent role than my own. They were more suited to Ryan's particular needs at the time. They became real in that they functioned on a daily basis and over time became conscious of one another's existence. I, on the other hand, remained nestled in the prison of Lazarus' soul. On some level you may look upon Lazarus, and me, as alter egos of each other. When one thrives the other is suppressed. It is a constant battle of extremes present in all mankind.

My 'out-coming' came on the day of our father's death, when he instructed Regine to bring Ryan to his bedside. My memories of that day seem to be just that... mine and mine alone. Sandor clutched

Ryan's scrawny body as he spoke. He described being forced to watch as others were tortured; people were skinned alive. He spoke of women and children being dismembered. A further detailing of the long list of horrors seems unnecessary.

Ryan was nine years old. He couldn't cope with what his father had thrust upon him. That became my responsibility. Then it happened. My cell door unlocked. I was free. I could feel a rush of blood as Lazarus was ushered in and I was summoned out. I was to be the protector. I was the one who would succumb to violence, if necessary, to protect 'the One.'

"They're here, in Washington Heights," my father said. "I saw them. The same faces I saw in my cell. They're coming for you. Monsters. I can't stop them. Up to you. Can't happen again. Protect mother. Sister. You kill, before they kill. You kill. Is ok! Must do it. Is ok! Is ok!"

Then he was dead.

My father's dying words sealed my identity. "You kill. Is ok! Is ok!"

I am ISOK. Is ok!

CHAPTER 100

August 18, 1968

QUINLAN TRUDGED INTO the squad room feeling uneasy about the case. Passing Scumaci's desk he paused to look down at the new edition of *The Height's Update*. "Mind if I borrow your paper? I wonder what insights Scoop Aubrey has to offer. God knows I need some inspiration."

"Be my guest, Chief. That girl's got a good head on her shoulders."

Quinlan made his way back to his office with a cup of steaming hot coffee and Scoop Aubrey's insights in hand. "YOU CAN'T TELL A CROOK BY ITS COVER: LOOKING BEYOND THE OBVIOUS! The Chief liked it already.

As he finished reading the short but to-the-point article, Quinlan thought, maybe this young reporter can teach my old butt a thing or two.

"Scumaci. Get in here."

"What's up, Chief?"

"This story by Ms. Aubrey has me thinking. There are un-answered questions that have been bothering me for a couple of days now. Maybe in our haste to get this case solved we've ignored some inconsistencies."

"Like what, Chief?"

"Here's what I don't get. We've got this kid, who for the first twenty-one years of his life has displayed no tendencies toward physical violence. All of a sudden he's an accomplished assassin. It doesn't feel right.

"Now, I guess it's possible he snapped and started kill-ing people he'd hated for years. I'm no expert on this multiple personality thing. What I don't get is the methodology. These crimes don't look like the creations of a beginner. They reek of a history of sadistic violence. Let's not forget, three of these vic-tims were bullies, and one a drug dealer to boot. They weren't easy targets. If a novice planned these killings, wouldn't he pick the fastest and safest method?

"Also, the button we found from one of Ryan Cain's flannel shirts. Who wears flannel in the summer?

"Then, there's the sneaker print. The blood was on a size eight sneaker. Ryan Cain wears a size ten. Why would he have worn a pair of sneakers, if in fact he could even fit into them, so tight as to hinder fleeing if it became necessary?

"Lastly, Ryan Cain loves those comic books. According to the doc, they represent his escape from the reality of a miserable childhood. I don't think he'd deface them to leave us a message.

He could have used any piece of paper and achieved the same effect. The doc says this kid has a genius I.Q., yet he's made several mistakes. Would he be that careless?"

"If one of his identities *wants* to get caught, he might," Vinnie suggested. "Or, maybe he just hasn't perfected his skill set."

Quinlan shrugged. "There's something wrong here. I can feel it. We're missing something and this kid could spend the rest of his life in jail because we're not seeing it. Let the guys know we're on for another meeting—tomorrow at two. I think Scoop Aubrey hit the nail on the head, 'Sometimes the truth is buried beneath layers of deceit.' We're digging deeper."

CHAPTER 101
August 18, 1968

FOLLOWING RYAN CAIN'S arrest, Harvey Cohen had a little free time on his hands. He decided to immerse himself into
the long list of unsolved violent crimes committed over the past
twenty years. While most cops found this kind of work tedious,
Cohen loved it. He realized Ryan Cain would have been only
two years old at the time of the earliest crime he'd pulled.

Cohen reduced the pile of case files from a little over three
hundred to an even dozen. All but one of the remaining cases
had been murders. The other was a beating which left the victim
in a vegetative state.

Cohen made notes on each file. He set parameters based
on instinct, and created a chart consisting of columns indicating victim's age, gender, nationality, religion, profession, date
of crime, victim's residence, method of crime, officer in charge,
and investigation results.

Cohen knew that if Ryan Cain was the killer, the exercises he was going through were for his own enjoyment. Happy as a kid with a new toy, Cohen became absorbed in the laborious task of sorting information and making notes of things to follow up on.

By day's end, Cohen had his fill of bludgeoning, stabbings, impaling, shootings, and hit-and-runs. He was eager to go home and unwind to reruns of his favorite TV series, *Dragnet*.

CHAPTER 102

August 19, 1968; morning

QUINLAN ARRIVED AT his office bright and early. It was going to be a busy day. The desk sergeant poked his head in the doorway. "There's a Scoop Aubrey on the line for you, Chief."

"Put her through."

"Good morning, Ms. Aubrey. What can I do for you?"

"I was hoping to come down and go over something with you. And maybe get an interview at the same time. If you recall, we met briefly the other day. I gave you the comb I found. I'm a reporter."

"Of course, Ms. Aubrey, I remember you quite clearly. I'm familiar with your *Heights Update*. Officer Scumaci, whom you've also met, has shown me your current article. Your work is very enlightening. However, I'm afraid this isn't a good time for me."

"Please hear me out, Chief Quinlan. I've been doing re-search on my own, and I don't know if it means anything, but

I'd like to share what I've found with you. I promise, I won't take more than ten minutes of your time."

Quinlan thought for a moment. "I have a meeting scheduled at the station for two o'clock this afternoon. If you can be here at one forty-five, I'll give you your ten minutes."

"One forty-five, I'll be there. Thank you, Chief Quinlan."

"I'm looking forward to meeting you, Ms. Aubrey," the Chief said, and actually meant it.

CHAPTER 103

August 19, 1968; 9:00 am

DESPITE HIS DIRE situation, Ryan awoke with a fresher and clearer mind than he had in years. The sessions with Abdo had been a blessing. Perhaps the restored memories of his father's words brought hope, as well as danger. Even in the bleakest hours of Sandor Cain's life, he had assured his son that there was a reason for everything that happens.

That being said, preparation when doing battle is still the key to success. His father would always say, "You need to be ten moves ahead of your opponent. Life is a chess game."

Subconsciously, during the two years of his coma, Ryan reconstructed and embellished upon a list of *survival lessons* his father had taught him. In his mind, he referred to it as his "Rules of Engagement."

As he prepared for the long day ahead, Ryan knew the words of his father would affect the outcome of his future.

CHAPTER 104
August 19, 1968; noon

BEFORE EMBARKING ON the drive to Bellevue, Quinlan instructed Scumaci to pull over at a local candy store. Quinlan returned sporting a huge lump in both his left and right trouser pockets. He also carried a crème-filled Devil Dog which he tossed to Scumaci, the way he'd toss a dog a bone. Scumaci scarfed down the chocolate cake in record time.

"Thanks Boss, what's with the enlarged testicles?"

Quinlan smiled. "You'll see."

The trek from Bellevue's entryway, through the hospital's hallways, to Ryan Cain's domicile again proved to be an adventure. *This place would be hell for a sane person to be stuck in.* Upon reaching Ryan's room Quinlan and Scumaci found their suspect and Dr. Betaré engaged in casual conversation.

"You're both looking as well as can be expected. How are you holding up?" Quinlan asked.

"We're both doing better, thank you." Abdo stared at the bulges in Quinlan's pants, resisting a comment. "We've been making great progress."

Quinlan asked, "Can I speak with Ryan?"

"Would you prefer I leave?"

"No Doctor, that's not what I meant. You should stay, by all means. What I meant was, is Ryan available for me to speak with?"

Ryan spoke for himself. "I'm right here."

Quinlan put his hand to his chin, much the way Sherlock Holmes did when sharing a logical deduction. "I've given the evidence a lot of thought, and truth is… it's too damn perfect, and inconsistent with what we know about you. There's the flannel shirt, the missing button, the wrong size shoe, I mean c'mon."

"Here's my dilemma. Doctor Betaré has informed me you've been tested and scored at a genius level. In my experiences, I've found there's a fine line between genius and insanity. How can I be certain you didn't plant all of these clues, knowing I'd find them to be too perfect? You could even have called in the anonymous tip. How can I be sure you're not playing me?"

Abdo responded. "Your killer is a sadist, and while Ryan's personalities display anger and rage, none of them exhibit that type of cruelty."

"Still, I have only your word on that," Quinlan said.

Abdo and Ryan stood as Quinlan walked toward the door placing his hands in his pockets. In an instant, Quinlan turned and lobbed a ball to Ryan's right side.

Ryan waited for the ball to descend and made the basket catch in his right hand, the way Willie Mays would have done—palm facing upward.

Without pause, Quinlan's other hand came out and tossed another ball, this time to Ryan's left side. In a catlike motion, Ryan's left hand snagged the ball mid-air, shoulder height—palm-side down.

"How do you feel about taking a field trip?" Quinlan asked Ryan. "I've already made the necessary arrangements. You think you can tear yourself away from this place? There's something I need to check out, and you need to be there."

"Sure, but what's the ball thing about?" Ryan asked.

"Maybe, I just saved your life?"

Quinlan smiled.

CHAPTER 105

August 19, 1968; 1:45 pm

AT ONE FORTY-FOUR, Scoop Aubrey entered the 34th Precinct—out of breath and looking lost.

"Excuse me. I have an appointment with Chief Quinlan at one forty-five."

"You're cuttin' it pretty close there, Ms. Aubrey. The Chief instructed me to send you right up, but only if you arrived on time. Up the stairs to your left, second door."

Quinlan could see why Scumaci was smitten by the young reporter. She had a look of pure innocence. Quinlan extended his hand and offered her a chair. "What can I do for you today, Ms. Aubrey?"

"Please call me Scoop. Everyone else does."

She explained how she'd decided to interview the Sanes and Otto Sussman on her own. She described Sussman's eagerness to talk about his experience in a concentration camp, the tattoo he'd been given as an identification number, and his unusual release due to overcrowded conditions. She then relayed how Sussman met his wife fifteen years after he arrived in this country.

"And, your point?" Quinlan asked.

"Here's the thing. Sussman says he immigrated to the United States in 1938."

"And?"

Scoop felt like a real crime reporter. "And, the Nazis didn't initiate the process of tattooing numbers on their prisoners until 1942. So, why does Otto Sussman have an identification tattoo on his arm, and where did he get it?"

"I'm impressed, but I'm not sure how it relates to the murders."

Scoop was on a roll. "It's a strange thing to lie about. And, another thing. You know how he talks about his wife, like they have this great love. Well, I did some digging."

"And?"

"Sussman's wife died less than a year after they married in 1953. I'd sure like to know if there was a life insurance policy, and who the money went to."

"Again, that's very interesting, but there's no law against his talking about his wife as though she were still alive. I admit it is strange, but not illegal. Is there anything else, Scoop?"

"There is. When I met with Mr. Sussman, I spotted the bin at the rear of the basement where he stores his maintenance and gardening tools. It was secured. Later, I asked him if it was always kept locked. He became agitated. He insisted that whenever he removes tools he locks up afterwards. If that's true, how could anyone else have obtained the hedge trimmer? The lock wasn't broken, was it?"

Quinlan rubbed his chin. "You've been very busy, and you bring up some interesting questions. My two o'clock meeting regarding this case is about to start. Would you care to sit in?"

Scoop couldn't believe it. *Sit in on a police brainstorming session?* She almost jumped out of her chair. "And how."

"One thing, Ms. Aubrey," the Chief added. "Everything that goes on in this station house is police business. You are not to repeat, or print, a word of what you hear. Am I making myself understood?"

CHAPTER 106

August 19, 1968; 2:00 pm

THE MEETINGS GREW larger. Scheduled to attend were Quinlan, Scumaci, Cohen, Tomlinson, Dr. Betaré, Ryan Cain, Scoop Aubrey, and Victor Golub.

At quarter past two, Golub entered the room huffing and puffing. "Sorry I'm late. A gal outside the precinct caused a traffic jam. It took half an hour to get everyone calmed down and back on their way. I didn't get a clear look at the *young lady*, but I'd like to give her a piece of my mind."

Scoop's left shoulder crunched up against her left cheek while her eyes shifted to a coy stare directed toward the ceiling, away from the irritated Golub. Her shoulder-cheek move reminded Ryan of someone, and her pixyish stare of innocence made him smile. It seemed ironic that in a room filled with cops, no one else spotted the unintentional confession of Golub's notorious "young lady."

At the same time Ryan watched Scoop, Abdo took a mental picture of Ryan confined to his chair, yet smiling. He had a good smile, one Abdo hadn't seen in a very long while.

Quinlan introduced everyone and presented the issues he was encountering with the evidence against Ryan Cain. He explained it was the article written by Ms. Aubrey that had prompted him to reevaluate the case. "I want you to think about this. We have recordings of Mr. Cain's alter egos stating they hated three of the four victims, but never once do they admit to killing them, or discussing the method of the murders. Why? They didn't know they were being recorded. We need to come at this from a different angle. Sherlock Holmes stated it best when he said, 'There is nothing as deceptive as an obvious fact.'

"We've been handed the killer. Somebody's yankin' our chain. As Scoop alludes to in her article, we need to, 'look beyond the obvious.' I want everyone to assume Ryan Cain *is not* the perpetrator, and go from there."

Quinlan paused in case anyone wanted to interject. With no takers, he continued. "There are other things that bother me about this case. How did a bloodied attacker go undetected after killing Derek Vespers? How did the killer get his hands on the hedge trimmer if, as Mr. Sussman so adamantly claims, he always locks up his gardening tools when they're not in use?

"If that's not enough to make you think twice, try this. This morning, Victor confirmed his previous findings. He assures me the rotation of Ethel Cornblatt's head indicates a left-handed assailant, while the cutting angle of the blade to the Cockroach's genitals indicates a right-handed attacker.

"Mitchie Kaden says he saw a man tossing a watermelon with his left hand. Later this evening I'll be meeting with Mitchie and his mom for a little experiment. If things turn out as I expect, Ryan Cain will be cleared.

"You see, gentlemen, I've gone through Ryan Cain's medical history with Dr. Betaré, and Ryan Cain has a congenital defect of his left forearm rendering him incapable of doing what the evidence, and an eye witness account, have told us occurred."

Tomlinson spoke up. "So we're looking for a sociopath who is trying to frame Ryan for the crimes? How would this individual have access to the people's names that Ryan talks about in his sleep? What would his motive be, and are we dealing with one or two killers?"

"Those are the questions, all right," Quinlan agreed. "Mr. Cain, can you think of anyone who would have reason to try to do this to you? Other than in your sleep, can you recall telling anyone about your feelings toward the victims?"

Ryan spoke tentatively. He wasn't comfortable in conversation, let alone speaking to groups of people. "To the best of my knowledge, I've never consciously spoken of my feelings about anyone, to anyone."

"Is there anyone you can think of who would want to hurt you?" Quinlan asked.

For fear of appearing crazy, Ryan hesitated before telling the group of the conversation he had with his father on the day of his father's death. With concerned reservation he described his father's torture under Hitler's regime, and his father's supposed sighting of one or more of his torturers while living in Washington Heights. "'They're here. They're coming to get you.' Those were my father's last words."

"But that conversation took place twelve years ago," Scumaci pointed out. "If someone intended to harm you, why would they have waited so long?"

Ryan thought and replied, "I can't answer your question, unless maybe it was simply a matter of waiting for the right opportunity to come along. Maybe harming my father was the primary goal, and the rest of us were an afterthought. Then again, maybe my father only *thought* he saw the men who'd tortured him. He wasn't in the best state of mind at the time."

Quinlan asked, "Dr. Betaré, do you have anything you'd like to throw into the mix?"

Abdo thought for a moment and decided not to complicate matters by bringing up what Lazarus had shared with him—the introduction of the new personality, Isok. *The addition of an alter ego belonging to an alter ego goes far beyond my own comprehension. God only knows how much it will confuse everyone else. Technically, Isok is not a creation of Ryan's mind, but rather of Lazarus'.* "No Chief, I'd say you've covered it all."

Scoop took the opportunity to ask if she could present her findings on the tattoo discrepancy.

Wanting to leave no stone unturned, Quinlan gave Scoop the floor. Afterward, he closed the meeting. "Okay people, tomorrow, same time, same place. I want results. Let's put this case to bed."

CHAPTER 107
December 1938 – April 31, 1945

April 31, 1945
THE VOICE ON the phone spoke in a whisper. "Everything's been taken care of. Go quickly, Mein Führer. I count the moments till we are together again." She paused. *Is this a good time to tell him?* "One more thing, my love . . ."

***

1938 - April 30, 1945
Throughout the war years, Hitler was said to have created no less than six doppelgängers.

Doppelgängers were loyalists who eagerly offered up their own lives to ensure the safety of the Führer's. Plastic surgeons altered the sacrificial lambs' appearances down to the smallest of scars and birthmarks. Dental reconstruction replicated the Führer's in every detail. The imposters were then trained to mimic the Führer's speech pattern and physical mannerisms.

The most proficient doppelgänger, a man named Gustav Weler, was selected by the Führer himself for the supreme honor of dying in Hitler's place. Hitler's medical files, x-rays, and dental records burnt red-hot. In their place were substituted the files of the chosen martyr. When the time came no one would be the wiser. Hitler would be free to vanish from the spotlight.

Following the Schtroebers' blunder in November 1938, Hitler's hope of retrieving the prophetic parchment was lost in the wind. Paranoia consumed him. Doom lurked at every turn. With great care, Hitler implemented the measures he'd initiated years earlier to secure his own survival.

Beginning in January 1939, Hitler pilfered hundreds of millions of dollars from the Nazi coffers, transferring the monies into a Swiss bank account. Opened under an assumed identity which he'd created, the funds awaited his beckoning.

By late October 1944, Hitler saw the end of his dream approaching. He made arrangements for the immediate transfer of his Swiss numbered accounts into various U.S. assets. He'd instructed his intermediary to pay the necessary bribes to backdate fund transfers as well as the acquisition of his new residence. Altered documents confirmed transactions as occurring in 1932.

In January 1945, Hitler underwent total facial reconstruction. He was unrecognizable to anyone. The bodies of the plastic surgeon and his assistant held the dubious distinction of becoming the final entries into the *ledger-of-death* attributed to the *might-have-been* ruler of the world.

In April 1945, Hitler instructed his contact in the United States to finalize all arrangements. A new life awaited the Führer. He'd selected his new city of residence. Abraham Lerner was about to make his grand debut on the New York City stage.

In the courtyard of Hitler's Berlin bunker the burnt body of an unknown doppelgänger was found lying next to the scorched bones of Eva Braun ... the remains of an apparent double suicide.

As far as the world was concerned Adolf Hitler died on April 30, 1945.

***

April 31, 1945
"One more thing . . ."

She reconsidered. "Never mind, my love, I'll tell you when I see you."

"I'll contact you when it's safe," Hitler instructed. "Be well, Eva."

The line clicked off.

CHAPTER 108

August 19, 1968; 8:30 pm

QUINLAN ARRANGED FOR Mitchie to view a reenactment of what he'd seen on the night of Ethel Cornblatt's murder. After assuring Cindy Kaden her son would be in no danger, she agreed, with reluctance. They planned on eight-thirty that evening.

In the time it took Scumaci to pick up Ryan, Quinlan stopped off to purchase two bags of groceries, a small watermelon and a couple of jelly donuts. At eight-thirty, Quinlan rang the Kadens' doorbell, while Scumaci set the stage in the lobby.

Cindy Kaden opened the door. Thigh-high, Mitchie's head poked out from behind his mom's dress. He was wearing Batman pajamas. "You're certain this will be safe?" she asked. Quinlan understood her concern and alleviated her fears.

"Mitchie, those are great pajamas. I'm thinking of getting a pair myself," Quinlan joked.

Mitchie laughed. "I'm pretty sure these are just for kids."

"What I want to do," Quinlan explained, "is go down to the mailboxes and take a peek into the lobby. Like the other night, when you saw Miss Cornblatt and the man with the watermelon. Can we do that, Batman?"

"Sure, but I'm not really Batman, ya know. I'm just wearing his pajamas."

Before heading down, Quinlan handed Mitchie a paper bag containing two raspberry jelly donuts. Mitchie's eyes lit up like fireflies.

"Thanks, Chief Quinlan. Look Mom, jelly donuts."

"I see, Mitchie. Perhaps after dinner you can have one."

"Or, maybe two, if I'm real good at helping the policemen?" Mitchie wore an impish smile.

The trio walked down the flight of stairs to the mailboxes.

"Now Mitchie, I want you to look into the lobby where you saw the people the other night. I have Officer Scumaci holding a bag of groceries, pretending to be Miss Cornblatt, and someone else pretending to be the man helping her. He's holding a grocery bag with one arm and a watermelon with the other. Does that look like what you saw the other night?"

Scumaci had positioned Ryan so he'd be facing Mitchie. In Ryan's right hand was a watermelon which he tossed up and down. With his left arm he awkwardly secured a grocery bag.

"Yup, that's what I saw," Mitchie said. "But the man needs to turn around."

Quinlan motioned Scumaci to make the change. "Is that better? Is that what you saw?"

"Yup, 'cept the watermelon should be in the other hand."

"You're sure Mitchie? This is really important."

"I'm sure. Are you going to make the bad man change hands?"

"He can't, Mitchie. And, I'm pretty sure he's not our bad man."

As Mrs. Kaden and Mitchie started back up the steps, Mitchie stopped. "Wait a minute, Mom."

Quinlan turned, thinking maybe Mitchie had remembered something else. Then, Mitchie ran up to the officers, opened his paper bag, rolled his big eyes, and handed Scumaci one of his jelly donuts. "Here you go, Mr. Policeman Skoomaki. For after dinner." Quinlan smiled.

God, I love this kid.

CHAPTER 109
August 19, 1968; evening

ONCE MITCHIE KADEN confirmed what Quinlan already knew to be the truth, Ryan Cain was released and allowed to go home with the police department's sincerest apologies.

"There's no need to apologize. I'm in your debt. Things looked really bad for a while. I wasn't sure myself whether I'd committed these crimes or not. Has anyone contacted my mom to let her know I'm okay?"

"I think she'd rather hear that from you, son. Why don't you head on home and put her mind at ease? I'm sure she's worried sick. One last thing. I'd like you to attend the follow-up at the precinct tomorrow at two. Your input could prove helpful."

"I'll be there." Ryan shook hands with both Quinlan and Scumaci, feeling freer than ever before.

Regine broke into tears at the sight of her son. She hugged Ryan so hard he could barely breathe.

"You must be starving, I'll fix you something to eat," she insisted, already on her way to the refrigerator. "What did they feed you in that terrible place?"

Ryan smiled for the second time in one day. It felt good.

Following the emotional reunion, Ryan kissed his mom goodnight and headed to his room. He had a lot to think about.

Ryan lay awake replaying the occurrences of the past few months. *Let your mind go, like you do with word anagrams. Relax, let the pieces move around.*

A fly buzzed overhead, coming to rest on the wall facing Ryan. They stared at each other as though adversaries trying to understand one another. *If I were like you, I'd fly around, eavesdropping on conversations. In time, the Assassin would come to me. Son-of-a-bitch. That's it. The answer's been right in front of me the whole time.*

The pieces fell into place. There was only one viable solution—*Gunther Heber must be involved. He's been in and out of our apartment a hundred times. He could easily have taken my stuff. And, he lives next door. He can probably hear everything I say through the paper-thin walls. Gunther Heber has been "a fly on my wall" since the very beginning.*

Now, I need to prove it. Heber had means and opportunity, but what's his motive? Ryan would share his suspicions at the two o'clock meeting. Perhaps together they could come up with the *why.*

CHAPTER 110
The Writings of Isok
"Family Matters"

·

You may wonder why no one ever mentions Willow as having been afflicted by our father's rage. Willow was Daddy's little girl and in his eyes she could do no wrong. "My little princess," he called her. He was as calm and genteel a soul as you'd ever meet when he was with her.

I can't lie, Willow was a sweetheart. No one could ever say anything bad about her. And now, she's dead. I miss her every day and hate myself for not being there to save her. It was my fault, all my fault. I am a self-loathing coward. When my time came to do something important, I did nothing.

Somewhere between the moments when we come into this life and exit it, each and every one of us is meant to do something. For most of us, we never get to know what that something is. In 1964, I was certain I had found my purpose. Willow had confided to her brother that she was pregnant. Her body quivered as she spoke the words. "Derek Vespers raped me. He's the father of my baby."

She made her brother swear not to tell anyone. She needed time to work things out in her mind. Then, she'd find a way to tell her mom.

It was the Loner who could no longer stand by and do nothing. He confronted Vespers. Needless to say, that didn't go well.

Vespers laughed. He denied everything. He told the Loner to tell Willow to keep her mouth shut and his name out of it. It was her problem, not his.

A fight ensued and Vespers had the Loner on the ground. It had been four years since my encounter with the bully, Flint, in the schoolyard, but I remember the moment with great clarity. Once again it was me on the ground. It was me with fire burning in my heart, and me who swung a two by four, giving Vespers the scar on his face.

I got up and stood over that worthless piece of human garbage. Raising the lumber over my head, I readied myself to strike the finishing blow. My mind kept saying, "He has to pay for what he's done. He has to die." I could hear my father's words.

Is ok! You can do it. But in the end, I couldn't. I had been created to protect at all costs, and when it mattered most, I couldn't do it. At that moment, I hated myself. Then I was back in my cell.

CHAPTER 111
August 20, 1968; 2:00 pm

EVERYONE IN THE room shared a newfound enthusiasm. After Ryan disclosed his suspicions regarding Gunther Heber's possible involvement in the crimes, Harvey Cohen was the first to jump up and offer additional input. "If you recall, before Mr. Cain became our primary suspect, I began looking into unsolved crimes which might tie into this case. I read over three hundred dead-files. The name Sussman rang a bell, so I backtracked, and discovered that Otto Sussman was a witness to an assault on one Abraham Lerner back in October 1946. The report states he saw several youths hitting and then running away from the victim. Sussman was listed as living on 163rd Street and Amsterdam Avenue. With his cousin."

"I've seen Abraham Lerner," Abdo interjected, "while visiting Ryan at the Affiliated Jewish Hospice Care Center. He's been in a vegetative state for the last twenty-two years."

"Does this cousin of Sussman's have a name?" Quinlan asked.

"You're gonna love this, Boss. Gunther Heber is Otto Sussman's cousin."

"I'll be damned," Quinlan exclaimed.

Cohen continued presenting his findings. "Yesterday, when Ms. Aubrey mentioned the holocaust identification tattoo on Otto Sussman's arm and the discrepancy over the year he said he received it, I recalled another file. I pulled this one because of the reference to tattoos. It dates all the way back to 1946.

"In November 1946, we have an unsolved homicide of one Raymond Velasquez. The victim was found dead on the floor in the back room of his storefront tattoo parlor located on 168th Street and St. Nicholas Avenue. Cause of death was internal bleeding sustained from a beating. Before he died, Velasquez wrote this on the floor beside him in his own blood."

Cohen showed the group an enlargement of the crime scene photo. As described, written in blood, next to the body, appeared *102247X2*. "No one ever figured out what the numbers meant. The case remains unsolved."

It was Scoop's turn to chime in. "I've seen that number, or almost that number. That's the number tattooed on Otto Sussman's arm. I mean the first six digits, not the X2."

Quinlan looked puzzled. "Are you sure? How can you remember a six digit number you saw for only a few moments?"

"Because that number happens to be my birth date, October 22, 1947; 102247." Scoop wore the look of a novice chess player who had just outfoxed the master.

Quinlan was reminded of a Sherlock Holmes quote. "Once you eliminate the impossible, whatever remains, no matter how improbable, must be the truth."

CHAPTER 112

October 1946
New York City

THE AIR WAS brisk, the sky powder blue. Neighborhood locals scurried the sidewalks as Abraham Lerner stood perched atop the entryway staircase of his Lexington Avenue brownstone viewing the little people with contempt. Today, he'd visit Washington Heights. He'd heard of the beautiful flower gardens overlooking the Hudson River at Fort Tryon Park.

For sixteen months Abraham Lerner avoided the public's eye. Four hundred and eighty days had passed since he'd abandoned the face of Reich Chancellor of Germany for his new identity as a complacent, filthy-rich immigrant. Soon he would summon Eva to join him.

It was a month earlier when he first ventured out onto the streets. Now, as he walked toward the park's entrance, he thought about the lost parchment and how things might have been. *Stop obsessing.* Lerner's mind shifted to more pleasant thoughts. He smiled at the Jews walking the sidewalks, picturing them burning in his ovens.

Nearing the park, Lerner came to a sudden halt. He rubbed his eyes and looked again. There in the distance stood the Schtroeber brothers. They looked different, but he recognized them. His blood boiled with the thought of revenge. He moved toward them. "Hans! Gerhardt!"

They reacted like threatened cats. Before Lerner could get another word out of his mouth, the brothers darted into an alley, away from the view of onlookers. With Hitler sporting a new face, the brothers didn't recognize the oncoming stranger. To them, it was their worst fear come true... some Jew bastard had recognized them. The deep shadows of the tall buildings offered a strategic point of attack.

The brothers separated. Hans grabbed a piece of pipe that lay on the ground and stood in the dark hollow of a doorway, while Gerhardt awaited the approaching stranger. As Lerner rushed toward Gerhardt, Hans came up from behind, striking the head of the perceived threat to their identities, hard and often. The echoes of impatient horns and street traffic muffled Lerner's groans.

Sneering at the beaten body of the man they regarded as a pathetic Jew, they continued to kick and spit on his bloodied head. It was Hans who came up with the idea of carving a Star of David onto the man's forehead with his pocket knife. *No one would ever suspect another holocaust survivor of doing such a thing.*

The next day, the shaken brothers ventured out of their immediate neighborhood. They sought a local business owner who could tattoo a prisoner identification number onto each of their left forearms. They promised him money and paid him with death. They could leave no witness to their ploy.

CHAPTER 113

August 20, 1968; evening

RYAN CLUTCHED THE envelope containing the parchment. He heard his father's voice; *you only get to lose once when playing the game of life and death. Eventually, everyone who plays loses.* Ryan hoped that would be the case for Heber and Sussman.

Ryan made a point of bumping into Gunther Heber following his release. Later that night, he would use the parchment as the perfect lure to expose the real Shadow Assassins.

At eleven p.m. Ryan performed for Heber's benefit. The meeting of the Quad came to order.

"Can you believe those fucking idiots?" the Watcher chuckled. "They forgot to Mirandize us. All I can say is, God bless stupid cops."

"I wouldn't be so cocky if I were you," the Writer admonished. "This isn't a game. We got lucky. If we can all agree that none of us committed these murders, it can mean only one thing. Someone out there is killing people and leaving clues to make us appear guilty. You can be certain the next time a crime is committed the police won't forget to read us our rights."

"I'm afraid," the Loner admitted, directing his comments to the Watcher, a quiver in his voice. "You said your father told you, 'when the time is right, open the envelope containing the parchment.' Maybe the time is now? Maybe there's something written on it that can help us? Why don't we vote on it?"

"The parchment is mine," the Watcher snapped. "He gave it to me, but okay, we'll send Ryan to get it tomorrow."

"Do you guys know what the police were talking about?" the Optimist asked. "They said something about a guy at the Hospice Care Center regaining consciousness. They said he'd be ready to talk sometime tomorrow? What can he possibly have to do with the murders? The guy's name is Lerner. The police know something we don't. We'd better rest up. Tomorrow's gonna to be a busy day."

In turn, each declared, "Vengeance is ours."

CHAPTER 114

The Parchment
March 25, 1933

"THE FATE OF CAIN & ABEL"
Quatrain I
Lazarus shall again
Rise from the dead,
Spared by the goodness
Of righteous persons.
Abel, once slain by a sinful son,
Shall be spared by an enlightened son.

Quatrain II
It will be a cold day in hell
Before the downfall of "the evil one."
Millions will die as the "Devil's son"
Outlives the Holocaust survivors,
And dwells in the Land of Nod as able-bodied

And clear in mind and thought,
Only to pray for the mercy of death
Which will not come.

Quatrain III
Brothers in arms shall fall, but not side by side.
One shall pay for his sins in both heart and mind
In the underbelly of his own personal hell.
The other shall lie in wait by the view gardens,
And flee the ultimate heights, only to wilt
In the Garden of Eden, beside a rose,
While the flag of freedom flies above
In all its glory.

Quatrain IV
A Christian born shall save a Jew.
The dead will rise to claim their due.
An act of kindness will save a life,
As a once lost soul,
Will meet his wife.

Quatrain V
The journey of life has only begun,
As the many he was, retreats to one.
The answers he seeks no longer seem odd.
The empathetic son
Shall be graced an audience with God.

Quatrain VI
When all is said and done,
Aryan son will stand victorious
Over the deathbed
Of a threat to all of humanity.

CHAPTER 115

August 22, 1968

OTTO SUSSMAN STARED out his window pondering the situation. *That little bitch with all her fucking questions. First the tool bin, then the tattoo. Who the fuck asked her to come poking around with that cute little ass and her head full of shit that ain't none of her business? If she pieces things together, she'll be a problem.*

So long as we're doing away with the Cain kid, and Abraham Lerner, we may as well take care of Scoop Aubrey too. I'll have Gunther make an anonymous call. She might recognize my voice. He'll set up a meeting to provide her with information about the Assassin, and I'll be waiting. When she shows, I'll finish off her career with one final headline. Then, I'll pay a visit to that asshole, Lerner.

This is gonna be one great fuckin' day.

CHAPTER 116

August 22, 1968

IT WAS MID-MORNING when he made the call.

"You don't know me Ms. Aubrey, but I've been following your articles. You write good. I have information to share with you, but not over the phone. It has to do with Otto Sussman, the superintendent of the building where Derek Vespers was murdered. I think you'll find it interesting. Meet me by the flag-pole in Bennett Park at three o'clock. When I see you, I'll make contact." Gunther Heber read the words exactly as his brother had written them.

He hung up before Scoop could ask questions.

CHAPTER 117

August 22, 1968; early afternoon

FROM BEHIND THE boiler a voice called out, "Over here." Gunther Heber emerged into the dim light of the musty basement. He'd been there, in wait, since early morning. With his right hand, he pointed an SS issue Luger at Ryan's chest.

Ryan jerked backward, then froze. Throughout the night he'd anticipated this moment. How would he react? Would he be a good enough actor to fake astonishment? The gun pointed at his chest eliminated the need for pretense. His heart pounded against his ribcage. His legs trembled.

Ryan stared at Heber's face. He'd never taken a long, hard look at the man before. Gunther was a fixture of the building, like cracks in the plaster, or a mouse that scurried along a baseboard. You knew they were there, but you couldn't describe them in detail. Now, Ryan studied his adversary from head to toe, every nuance, and every action which might provide him a weakness to exploit. Heber's sweat-stained undershirt fell inches short of his waistline. His exposed belly hung over the belt loops of his khaki trousers. Matted hairs spewed wildly from his underarms and chest. Flaky grit adhered to the heavy stubble on his face.

"Gunther, what's going on? Why do you have a gun?"

Heber leaned forward, his mouth contorted to a sinister smile. "I've been looking forward to this for a very long time."

The stench of Heber's breath was a weapon all its own.

"What are you talking about, Gunther? Please, put down the gun."

"Shut up. Call me Gunther one more time and I'll kill you now... to hell with the parchment?"

"Kill me? Why would you kill me? How do you know about the parchment?"

This time Heber shouted. "Shut up, asshole."

Ryan took a step back. Heber's aggressive manner intimidated him. *This isn't going well. I need to gain control, throw him off-balance, and keep him talking.*

"Why shouldn't I call you Gunther? That's your name, isn't it?

"Gerhardt. Gerhardt Schtroeber. That's my name."

"Then, who's Gunther Heber?"

Heber's body quivered with frustration. "I said, shut up. I'm not going to tell you again."

"If I shut up, how can I tell you where the parchment is?"

Gerhardt wasn't good at verbal confrontation, especially in English. He became jittery, confused. "Don't play games with me. Tell me, where is it, where did you hide it?"

Ryan could see a change. *He's lost some of the edge in his voice.*

"If you tell me what the hell's going on, I'll tell you where to find the parchment. You won't find it without me. I've hidden it very well. I'm sure you've tried. If you're going to kill me anyway, what harm could it possibly do to tell me why?"

"What good would it do you to know?" Schtroeber asked.

"It'll satisfy my curiosity, and keep me alive for as long as it takes you to tell."

Schtroeber fidgeted with the gun. He'd have preferred to simply put a bullet in the little shit's brain and be done with him, but his brother would be angry if he didn't return with the damn parchment. "Whattaya wanna know?"

"Everything. From the beginning."

Schtroeber covered as much back history as he was privy to, about the search, imprisonment and torture of Sandor Cain, a.k.a. No. 19. His broken English became more disjointed than usual with a few German words thrown in. Ryan had often noticed that many German immigrants, including his mom, did the same thing when they became flustered or frustrated.

"In 1953," Schtroeber continued, "my brother got job as super across street from Fort Tryon Park. One day, in 1955, he see you father on the street. Hans shit his pants. He think you father might see him too. I don't believe him. I tell him, he crazy, seeing things. You father die in Germany. I know. We kill him. Or, so we think. You father. He destroy our lives. He why I end up here, a super in this shithole. From that day on, we watch for him, and when we see him again, we follow him home."

"How did my father destroy your lives? Why do you hate him so much?"

"We try to make him give us parchment many years ago, in Berlin. But No. 19, he too stubborn. We would have been heroes in der Führer's eyes. Instead, we forced to run and live here."

"So, you hate him for being more of a man than you'll ever be?" Ryan said, proud to be his father's son.

Schtroeber ignored Ryan's comment, he was on a roll. "You father already dying when we spot him here. Why do favor and kill him fast? We let him die painful death. Then, when he dead, we decide to take revenge on his family. We arrange for super in you building to have accident. I think, was 1956. Clumsy man fall on a steam pipe. That's when I take over job as super of this dump."

Schtroeber paused. "*Das ist alles.* Now where is parchment?"

"You're not telling me everything," Ryan said. "You're holding back. I can see it in your face. The deal was, you tell me everything, and then I tell you where to find the parchment."

Schtroeber's mouth formed a crooked smile. He stared into Ryan's eyes as if to say, okay, you asked for it. "You remember finding you sister in the basement? Of course, you do."

Heber, once again, became more animated. He was enjoying the thought of what was to come.

"My sister?" Ryan wasn't prepared for that. "What about my sister? Did you do something to her?" Ryan shouted, out of control. The anger in his eyes radiated hatred. He'd planned on containing his emotions to secure a confession, but this was raw, unchartered territory. He took a step toward Schtroeber. *Control your emotions. Keep it together. Hold back. You need to accomplish your plan.*

"Be still." Schtroeber commanded, cocking the hammer of his weapon. "You wouldn't want I should kill your before the end of my story, would you?" He paused to cough up some phlegm and spit it in Ryan's direction. "I tell you sister, her mama wants her to pick up laundry from basement. When she come down, she get surprise of her life, or should I say death?" Gunther forced a laugh, eager to get a rise from his helpless captive.

"I lock basement door behind us, just like I do after you come in. I want time to enjoy. After writing suicide letter, I stand her on chair. Then, I put rope around her neck. She tell me she pregnant. Wunderbar, I say. I throw other end of rope over pipe. Then, she understand. There no going to be baby. She cry till the end. If I close mein eyes and listen, I still hear Willow weeping. Good one, yes—Willow weeping, weeping willow?" He chuckled at his own brilliant play on words. "After so many years, I feel alive again. Then, I kick chair from under her. She a very good dancer."

Ryan would have been willing to rot in hell for the opportunity to get his hands around Gunther's neck. The urge to attack Heber overwhelmed him. Then, he remembered his father's words, "Think things through. Never act in anger." After years of self-inflicted guilt, the truth had now been exposed. *It wasn't my fault. It wasn't Vespers who killed Willow. I need Gunther to continue. He has to keep talking. He still hasn't cleared me of the murders.*

"Helpless women and children, is that your specialty?" Ryan egged him on. "Did you feel like a big man, killing a help-less little girl who was crying in the dark? And now, like the coward you are, you'll kill me, while I stand here defenseless. You're pathetic, Gunther. You wouldn't stand a chance against someone who could fight back."

"Shut up. You know nothing. I kill more people than you can count. Men. Real men, not like you and you father." Schtroeber was clearly agitated. He moved his story along at a faster pace. Schtroeber was now anxious to kill this young son-of-a-bitch who questioned his manhood.

"When you come out of coma, you make more opportu-nity for us to get even. "Do you know you talk in sleep? At first, I think you have friends with you, but I figure it out. Everyone at party is you. I listen at wall, while you go on and on. You and you make-believe friends, so busy making plots against enemies. You talk good game, but that all you do—talk. I enjoy 'Vengeance Is Ours.' So much, I leave it for police.

"Setting you up is easy. For years, you call me into you home to fix things. I take what I need, and put back bloody sneakers after I kill Vespers. You pick victims for us. Then, we put clues. We even call police about seeing you on night of mur-der. We take turns killing, so we have alibi. Police not suspect us. It like old days, during war. Kill whoever you want, when-ever you want, with no consequences. When police investigate, we have no motive for killings. But you have motive for all. You and police easily fooled.

"So, du bist ready to die, Jew? You ready to join you sister and father? Don't worry about you mama; I take care of her for you. Now, I'll take the parchment."

"I don't think so, asshole," called out a voice from Heber's left.

Startled, Gunther turned, his gun moving toward the sound of the voice.

"I wouldn't do that if I were you," warned another voice on Heber's right.

By the time Heber, a.k.a. Gerhardt Schtroeber, understood what was happening, it was too late. He made a quick motion to redirect his weapon toward Ryan when two shots rang out, one from Quinlan's gun, the other from Scumaci's. Heber was down—one bullet to the chest and one through his left temple. As he landed on the cold concrete floor his cocked gun discharged.

Ryan flew backward grabbing at his chest.

"Chief, the kid's been hit."

CHAPTER 118

August 22, 1968

AT THE SOUND of the shots, Abdo, who had been restricted to waiting in the lobby, ran to the basement door and kicked it in. He spotted one man face down in a pool of blood and another being cradled in the arms of Chief Quinlan. Abdo stood frozen with fear.

Scumaci ran to the entry, weapon drawn and pointed. "He's okay, Doc. He's wearing a vest."

One brother down, one to go.

The recorded confession of Gerhardt Schtroeber implicated both himself, and his brother Hans, in no less than seven murders. Quinlan gave Cohen and Tomlinson the go ahead to arrest Sussman on sight. It was no longer necessary to catch him *in the act* of attempting to kill Abraham Lerner.

Cohen and Tomlinson stood in position. They'd arranged for the front desk to direct all inquiries regarding Abraham Lerner to a designated room away from other patients. Cohen remained hidden in the cubicle's closet while Tomlinson positioned himself at the end of the hallway. Walkie-talkies in hand, they waited.

Under the blanket of Lerner's bed rested pillows, giving the appearance of a sleeping occupant. Everything was perfect. All that was missing was Sussman.

Quinlan paced. *Three fifteen, and still no word from Cohen or Tomlinson. Something's wrong, Sussman should have made an appearance by now.*

Quinlan called the stationhouse to check for messages from his officers.

"Nothing, Chief," the desk sergeant said. "But, there was a call from Scoop Aubrey."

Quinlan's voice couldn't hide the dread in his heart. "When did it come in? What did she say?"

The sergeant flipped through his call slips.

"The message came in at two thirty-two, this afternoon. Says she wants you to know she's following up on a lead from a caller. He told her he has proof of Otto Sussman's involvement. Says she'll get back to you after her meeting at three o'clock."

Quinlan prayed for the right answers to his next questions. "Did she say who she was meeting? Where she was meeting him? Please, say yes."

"Sorry, Chief. What I read to you, is all there is."

"Shit, that girl's gonna get herself killed. Scumaci, I want patrol cars posted at every entrance to Fort Tryon Park and another at Sussman's residence. Place two officers in the hallway outside his door. Nobody goes in till we get there, unless it's life or death. Get on it."

CHAPTER 119

August 22, 1968

RYAN WAS GRASPING at straws; he had nowhere else to go. Removing the envelope containing the parchment, which Abdo had given him at the time of his arrest, he skimmed the document looking for a specific quatrain.

"Here it is, Abdo. Gunther alluded to Otto Sussman as his brother. I need you to hypnotize me and summon the Watcher. He knows every inch of this neighborhood. Read him this reference, and see if he can identify its whereabouts.

"My father didn't believe in prophecies, but even he, before his death, succumbed to moments of uncertainty. Predictions made in this document have occurred. It's all we've got to work with. I can't let anything happen to Scoop Aubrey. I wasn't able to save Willow, and I live with that pain every day. But right now, I've got to do something. Please help me."

Abdo took Ryan to the quietest corner of the basement. The setting and circumstances were not conducive to hypnotherapy, but after several attempts the Watcher took center stage.

"We need your help." After an abbreviated summation, Abdo read the third quatrain.

Quatrain III
Brothers in arms shall fall, but not side by side.
One shall pay for his sins in both heart and mind
In the underbelly of his own personal hell.
The other shall lie in wait by the view gardens,
And flee the ultimate heights, only to wilt
In the Garden of Eden, beside a rose,
While the flag of freedom flies above
In all its glory.

Abdo awaited a response. Minutes felt like hours.

"I take from what you've told me the brothers are the superintendents, Heber and Sussman. And, I also assume the first portion of the quatrain refers to Gunther Heber being shot in both the heart and head in the basement of his apartment building."

"Precisely. Do you have any idea what the second half of the quatrain means?" Abdo asked. "Ryan is certain these words are significant. He believes *you* can make sense of the riddle, and I agree with Ryan's assessment. You've confided on earlier occasions that you've walked every inch of this neighborhood a hundred times. Please, think. A life is at stake."

The Watcher shut his eyes trying to visualize what he willed himself to remember.

"First of all, there are only two flagpoles whose flags are always raised. One is in Fort Tryon Park and the other is in Bennett Park. The one in Bennett Park is easier to find, as the park itself is only a couple of square blocks in size. The one in Fort Tryon Park is at a secluded area overlooking the Inwood section of Upper Manhattan and the Bronx. I can draw a map of the quickest way to get there if you'd like.

"As for *gardens*, there are no gardens in Bennett Park; and Fort Tryon Park is blooming with flower gardens, covering several square miles of grounds. Off-hand, I can't remember seeing or hearing of a 'Garden of Eden' in Washington Heights. I don't know what else I can tell you that might help."

Abdo ended the session on a somber note. "I don't know if there's anything we can do. It's already past three o'clock. I fear we may already be too late."

CHAPTER 120

August 22, 1968

THE THOUGHT OF peoples' lives teetering on the interpretation of a thirty-year-old prophecy was unsettling. However, neither Ryan nor Abdo could deny the accuracy of the first half of the quatrain. Both had hoped for more insight from the Watcher. The rest would be up to Ryan.

> "The other shall lie in wait by the view gardens,
> And then flee the ultimate heights, only to wilt
> In the Garden of Eden, beside a rose,
> While the flag of freedom flies above,
> In all its glory."

Ryan repeated the words, over and over. 'Lie in wait by the view gardens, and then flee the ultimate heights.' Deep down, he knew the words made sense. Then, it came to him. He understood.

"Abdo, tell the police to get to the flagpole in Bennett Park. 'Lie in wait by the view gardens,' could mean Sussman is somewhere in Hudson View Gardens, the apartment development across the street from the flagpole. And, 'flee the ultimate heights,' if I'm not mistaken, refers to a plaque at the base of the flagpole designating the spot as the highest point in Manhattan. I pray we're not too late."

CHAPTER 121
August 22, 1968

THE "A" TRAIN stood immobile between the 172nd Street and 181st Street stations, a mere hundred feet from Scoop's destination.

"Hey baby, wanna make out? It'll make the time go faster."

Scoop graciously declined the generous offer of the wino slumped on the seat next to hers. *Please God, not today. This could be my big break. A few more feet. I've got to get to this meeting. Damn subways.*

Twenty minutes later, the overhead fan blades rattled their cages as they struggled to circulate air. The emergency backup light flickered and the fluorescent bulbs came to life. People wiped perspiration from their brows and flung droplets to the floor.

A garbled voice exploded from the crackling fry pan they called an intercom. "Ladies and gentlemen, this is your conductor. Due to unforeseen circumstances, our next stop will be the

190th Street Station. Upon arrival, we ask that everyone exit the train. We apologize for the inconvenience."

190th Street? You've got to be kidding.

Scoop walked at a brisk pace. She rounded the corner of 187th Street and Fort Washington Avenue, heading west toward Pinehurst Avenue. Lined with storefronts on both sides of the street, the short city block bustled. Scoop passed the neighborhood pharmacy, *Gideon's Bakery, Ben's Kosher Deli, Tony's Pizza Place* and *Al's Barber Shop.*

Scurrying along, a huge sign in the *Singer Sewing Center* window caught her eye. "Clearance Sale, Two Days Only!" She made a mental note to return to the store before the sale ended. She loved a good deal, and knew just what she wanted. Right now though, she was late for her meeting and prayed that her informant was a patient man.

CHAPTER 122

August 22, 1968

"SHE'S LATE. Where is the stupid bitch?" Sussman mumbled, hidden behind the dense shrubbery lining the southernmost stairwell. *We told her three o'clock. I don't have time for this shit. I still have to get to Lerner. She's ruining everything.*

Hudson View Gardens boasted the prestige of being one of Manhattan's earliest cooperative apartment developments. Ivy adorned the craggy outer walls, while irregular paths and stairwells created the feel of a medieval town. It encompassed four acres of choice property located between Pinehurst Avenue and Cabrini Boulevard, running from 183rd to 185th Street. The back side of the property culminated in a steep slope angling downwards toward the Hudson River.

One stairwell, leading to a narrow, seldom-used alleyway, remained deserted. Its primary function served as an out-of-the-way route for deliveries and trash disposal for a sublevel grocery. Monday was the one day of the week when the small store was closed. Sussman anticipated no interruptions. He wondered if his brother had completed *his* mission... kill Ryan Cain, and secure the parchment. *Fucking parchment. What can be so important about one crappy piece of paper?*

Police cars screeched into place and barricaded the park's entrances. Officers ran toward the flagpole. Sussman became nervous. *Did that bitch call the police? I better leave. No more risks today. By now Cain should be dead. The others will have to wait. With luck, Lerner won't remember anything anyway. It's been twenty-two years. How the fuck is this guy still alive?*

Sussman retreated to the cobblestone path, weaving his way through the Hudson View development. The rough street surface made his flight to safety slow going. After fifteen minutes, Sussman found himself a mere two blocks from where he'd started. *Fuck!* The circling pathway landed him right back on Pinehurst Avenue, at the other end of the park. He could still see the police, which meant they could still see him.

To his left, Sussman spotted a narrow walkway. At the path's end, he descended the cobblestone stairs leading to Cabrini Boulevard. His calves ached. His breathing heavy, he needed time to gather his thoughts. *Maybe the cops aren't looking for me at all. Maybe, they're in the park for a different reason.* He couldn't risk going home. He knew of a secluded spot where he could rest and think. *If I can make it there, I can plan our next move.*

CHAPTER 123
August 22, 1968

QUINLAN, SCUMACI, RYAN and Abdo stood by the flag-pole in Bennett Park. Three o'clock seemed an eternity ago. The police had scoured the area with no sign of Scoop or Sussman. Their worried faces reflected the grim thoughts none of them dared speak. *Could Ryan have been wrong? Is Scoop Aubrey dead? Why did we waste so much precious time on this ridiculous prophecy?*

Ryan sat on a bench. Filled with self-contempt for being so stupid, he lowered his sweat-drenched forehead to his fingertips.

Scumaci pointed to the north end of the park. "Over there. Isn't that Scoop Aubrey?"

The four men took off in a sprint toward the redhead.

Without thinking, Ryan gave Scoop a big hug, which he quickly released, embarrassed by his show of emotion. "I'm sorry."

Scoop peered into Ryan's tearful eyes. "No problem."

"Where have you been, young lady?" Quinlan lectured. "We received your message. Do you have any idea how much danger you're in? We've been racking our brains trying to find you. We've issued an 'all-points' on Sussman. Thank God, you're alright."

"Danger? What danger? How did you find me? I didn't say where I was going, did I? That was foolish of me."

"There's been an attempt on Ryan's life, and we suspect you're next," Quinlan responded. "You can thank Ryan for finding you, but that's a long story, and he can tell you about it later. Right now, we've got to focus on locating Sussman."

Ryan took the lead. "As strange as it may be, there's no denying the first three lines of the quatrain have been right on. The last line reads 'only to wilt in the Garden of Eden, beside a rose, while the flag of freedom flies above, in all its glory.'

"I have no idea what the reference to the Garden of Eden means, but the only flagpoles are this one, and the one at Fort Tryon Park. Unless someone has a better idea, I think we should check out the other location. Abdo, do you have the map the Watcher provided?"

Stationed at the main entrance of Fort Tryon Park, Tomlinson talked into his hand-set. "Hold on, the Chief just arrived.

"Chief, I'm on with one of the officers stationed at the other end of the park. He thinks they spotted Sussman cutting into the woods. He wants to know how to proceed. What should I tell him?"

"Tell him to follow, but do not apprehend, unless there's imminent danger. Tell him we're on our way. Now, where's this flagpole? I want the entire area staked out before he gets there."

Sussman elected to take the long route to his thinking spot. It would be the path less traveled. He forged through the dense, wooded terrain, stopping often to catch his breath. Nearing the Cloisters, he climbed the forty-foot mound of jagged rocks, which placed him within a hundred yards of his desired location. The remainder of the trek would be less arduous. The aging Nazi, on the brink of collapse, stumbled forward.

The pursuing officers kept their distance, as instructed. Upon reaching the flagpole, Sussman dropped to his knees, near a small flower garden. "I'll be damned," Quinlan whispered, relieved.

"Otto Sussman, or whatever your name is, this is the police," Quinlan yelled in an authoritative tone. "We have you surrounded. You're under arrest. Lie face-down on the ground and place your hands on top of your head."

Sussman didn't have the strength to put up resistance. He'd been on the other end of the hunt many times. He knew when the chase was over, and did as he was told.

With Sussman removed, Quinlan, Scumaci, Ryan and Abdo gathered by the flagpole.

"I've got to hand it to you, son," Quinlan said to Ryan. "This has been the most bizarre case I've ever worked." Looking up at the American flag, Quinlan shook his head in amazement and conceded the quatrain's accuracy. "Ninety percent is pretty damn good. The only thing your quatrain got wrong is the rose, and Garden of Eden reference. There are no roses in this garden."

Scumaci held his hand to his mouth as he coughed out his words. "Uh, Chief, you might wanna come here for a second?" On the ground, by the garden adjacent to the spot where Sussman had 'wilted,' was a memorial plaque inscribed with the words, "Dedicated to the memory of Rose Eden."

CHAPTER 124

August 23, 1968

AFTER THE DUST of the previous day settled, the full entourage of persons involved in the case met for one last time. All that was left to do was wrap up loose ends, and send the Shadow Assassin to "their" final resting place.

Scoop's fingers tingled as she readied herself to take notes. As promised, she was the only reporter present. *I'll have my exclusive hot off the press before the news world knows what's happening. Local publication editors will throw fits.* Scoop smiled.

"I'd like to know how you came up with this plan." Harvey Cohen directed his comment to Ryan. "And how the hell did you get the Chief to go along with it? It was awful risky."

Ryan explained, "I knew, once I returned home from Bellevue, Gunther Heber would be back in his apartment listening at our adjoining wall. He'd wait to see if the Quad would provide more potential victims.

"I'd listened to the tapes of my alter egos for hours. I practiced their speech patterns, personalities, and attitudes until I had them down pat. It was important that Heber believe he was hearing a genuine meeting.

"The plan was a simple one. Divide and conquer. Make 'the Assassin' be in two different places at the same time. It seemed a certainty that Heber and Sussman were the ones to whom my father was referring when he said, 'They're here, they're coming to get you.' And, if in fact they were my father's Nazi interrogators, they would be unable to resist the temptation of discovering the contents of the lost parchment.

"I knew it would be risky, but sooner or later they'd make a move on me anyway. I'd rather set the stage in a controlled environment than be surprised at a time and place of their choosing. I decided to have the Quad members make mention of sending *me* to retrieve the 'parchment' from a hiding place in the basement. In reality, the Quad members didn't know of my existence. They had never made reference to me before. It was a flaw in the plan, but I didn't think Heber was sharp enough to catch on.

"That night, I could literally feel Heber on the other side of the wall—listening. I knew he'd be waiting in the basement the next day, all day if necessary, ready to make his move.

"The plan was to record Heber's confession. Positioning Heber would be easy. He needed to follow me to where he believed I'd hidden 'the parchment.' Chief Quinlan and Officer Scumaci would be lying in wait to make the arrest.

"The Chief nearly blew a gasket when I told him my plan, but I didn't really leave him much choice. I insisted, saying I'd do it with or without backup. He couldn't risk that I was bluffing. Sorry Chief, but things did work out."

Ryan paused and offered an apologetic look in the Chief's direction.

The Chief raised an eyebrow of disapproval. His lips pursed to say something but he restrained himself. *What if that stray bullet from Heber's gun had struck your head instead of your chest?* "Yeah, things worked out," the Chief acknowledged.

Ryan continued. "I decided on Abraham Lerner as the other lure. I provided Heber with false information, saying Lerner had miraculously awoken. The possibility of Lerner talking to the police would force them to make a move. They couldn't afford to have him identify his assailants.

"By not providing Heber with a specific time for my visit to the basement, I was assured Sussman would have to act on his own in pursuit of Lerner. I knew it would be dangerous, but it seemed the best way to catch them in the act, and at the same time get a confession.

"Chief Quinlan hated my idea, but conceded to its logic. Thank God, he insisted I wear a bulletproof vest. I've got a couple of bruised ribs, but I'm still alive.

"Heber responded as planned. I've never been more frightened in my life. I'd never looked down the barrel of a gun before. When Sussman changed plans mid-stream, chaos ensued. You all know the rest. Thanks again, Chief, for that vest. It saved my life."

Quinlan nodded.

The momentary silence afforded Cohen the opportunity to share what he had discovered. "I'd like to offer kudos to Ms. Aubrey. We checked out the tats on the brothers' arms. They did indeed match the numbers shown on the floor in the crime scene photo of the murdered tattooist. Number 102247.

"I suspect the tattooist knew the brothers were going to kill him once he'd completed his task, so he gave them the same number. In his final moments, he left the cryptic message on the floor beside his dying body. The X2 was intended to tell the police he'd etched the same number on two different people."

Cohen moved on to Sussman's story of how he and his brother ended up in Washington Heights, beginning with the first time they'd encountered Sandor Cain, a.k.a. No. 19.

"Also, Ms. Aubrey," Cohen continued, "you get a gold star for picking up on Mrs. Sussman's life insurance status. Sussman's wife died in 1954, less than a year after their marriage, and a month after the conversion of beneficiaries from her daughters to her new husband. She fell down a flight of stairs and broke her neck.

"After receiving a hefty check for fifty thousand dollars from the insurance company, Sussman shipped the girls off to live with distant relatives. They're lucky he didn't kill them too."

Tomlinson took over. "At first, Sussman tried denying everything. Said it was all a misunderstanding. But, after we played him the recording of his brother's confession we couldn't shut him up. He copped to the four 'Shadow Assassin' killings, as well as the murders of Willow Cain, and the previous superintendent of the Cains' building. In June 1966, after the attack on Ryan, the Schtroebers decided it would be advantageous to reside in the apartment next door to the Cains. The residents occupying the apartment at the time were elderly. 'They had lived long enough.' Those are his exact words. A week later they died in an accident, and Heber moved in. When Ryan came out of his coma, his alter ego's conversations inspired the creation of the Shadow Assasin.

"He bragged about his meticulous planning of Derek Vespers' murder. He'd set aside a plastic bag containing clean-up items, and a complete change of clothes. He had them stashed in the dumbwaiter.

"After cracking open Vespers' head, he undressed, wiped his feet and swapped out his soiled clothes for the clean ones. He used the dumbwaiter to send the clothes up to his apartment, where he retrieved them later. The next day, he disposed of the plastic bag with the rest of the garbage awaiting city pick-up.

"He copped to the tattooist, too. Called him a son of a bitch for giving them both the same numbers. Abraham Lerner, he said, gave them no choice. He'd recognized them on the street. Sussman said, and I quote, 'The fucking Jew bastard got what he deserved.'

"In his crazy mind, Sussman thinks he's done nothing wrong. We've got a total of nine dead and one worse than dead that we can account for. Who knows how many other victims there are that we don't know about.

"On a final note, Ms. Aubrey really pissed Sussman off when she maneuvered him into making a mistake. He knew that insisting he always kept the tool bin locked was going to come back to bite him in the ass. You played a dangerous game with a very dangerous man."

Ryan again spoke up. "I've got to ask. Scoop, what kept you from your meeting at the flagpole in Bennett Park? It must have been important to keep you from what appeared to be your big chance at obtaining damaging information on Otto Sussman."

"It was beyond my control," Scoop said. "I went to Columbia University to register for my fall classes, leaving myself plenty of time to get back for the meeting. Right before getting to my station, the train stopped. It seemed like we sat there, motionless, forever. Then, the train skipped my stop all together. I don't know why, but I'm thankful it did. That probably saved my life."

"I can fill you in on that point," the Chief said. "Once Ryan determined that your meet was going to be at Bennett Park, I contacted the Transit Authority and had them shut down the 181st Street station. No trains in or out. I didn't want to leave Heber an alternate escape route that could endanger innocent bystanders."

As the meeting came to an end the officers filtered out, offering their condolences to Ryan on the loss of his sister. After all of the officers had moved on, Scoop walked over and placed her hand on Ryan's.

The look on Ryan's face as Scoop's hand touched his reminded Abdo of something a colleague had once told him. "All any man can hope for, is a hand to hold and a heart to care."

CHAPTER 125

August 24, 1968

ABDO SAT ACROSS from Ryan, both relieved to have survived their harrowing adventure. They shared a bond beyond words.

Abdo began, "We've accomplished so much in a short period of time. I hope you will continue to come and see me. While you're cleared of all charges, there are still issues for us to deal with."

"I understand, but can we break for a couple of weeks?" Ryan pleaded. "I'm drained."

"I think that would be a good thing," Abdo acknowledged, "for both of us. However, if you don't mind, I'd like to place one more thought in your head before we break."

"Do I want to hear this?"

"I think it will help give you clarity, and something to reflect on over the next two weeks. Given your analytical mind, I want you to consider this before we meet again."

Abdo had skillfully piqued Ryan's interest. He couldn't refuse the challenge.

"Do you remember telling me you didn't cry when your father died?" Abdo asked. "Your mom says you haven't cried since you turned five years old. Are you aware of that?"

Ryan paused, trying to remember back in time. "Men don't cry, they carry their feelings on the inside."

"Where did you get that notion?" Abdo asked. He already knew the answer.

"My father told me," Ryan said. "I can still hear his words."

"So, you *are* beginning to remember things about your father. I need to explain something to you. At the time of your birth, your father was not the man he had once been. He had formed a skewed perspective on life. His experiences left him damaged, both physically and emotionally. It is a tribute to his willpower and perseverance that he overcame his staggering obstacles. He was a brilliant man who wanted nothing more than to care for his family.

"But, I've got to tell you, when your father said men don't cry, he was wrong. We all cry—men, women, and children—because we as humans feel pain and emotions, and those emotions need a release. Without release, we become human time bombs, ready to self-destruct at any moment."

Then, Abdo got to the point. "I want to talk about your sister, Willow."

Ryan looked uncomfortable. His demeanor changed. A raw nerve had been touched.

"There. Do you see what you just did?" Abdo questioned. "You pushed away, distancing yourself from my comment. And now, you're avoiding eye contact and biting your inner cheek, which tells me you're annoyed. I want you to relax. I'm not going to ask *you* to comment until we meet again, but I would like to tell you a few things."

Abdo related Regine's stories of her own childhood with her mother, among the weeping willow trees in Austria. "There's nothing your mom treasures more than the moments she spent with you and Willow in Fort Tryon Park beneath the park's solitary willow tree. Willows, both consciously and subconsciously, have played a significant role in your family's lives.

"If you still think that you are responsible for Willow's death, I'm here to tell you, you're not. It was an unreasonable burden your father placed on you as a child to protect your mother and sister. No one could have foreseen or prevented what happened."

Ryan interrupted. "It was my responsibility to make sure she was all right. She was my sister, and I wasn't there for her. I failed my father's dying request. Anyway, I don't see the relevance of my sister's death in regard to my alter egos."

"I have to disagree," Abdo said. "You've lost yourself in your guilt, and are trying to keep Willow alive through your alter egos. You cannot change what is already done. It's time to move on, for both yourself and Willow."

Ryan had no idea what Abdo was talking about, but remained silent and allowed him to continue.

"There's one more thing. And again, I'd like you to consider this on your own time, after we break. You possess a brilliant mind, and your ease with word puzzles is staggering. So, don't you think it curious that you've never noticed this?"

Abdo retrieved a piece of paper from his desk drawer and handed it to Ryan. Printed on it, were the names of Ryan's alter egos.

Watcher

Isok

Lazarus

Loner

Optimist

Writer

Ryan stared at the paper with the same intensity he'd given the parchment. After agonizing moments of containment he began to cry.

Abdo now realized with certainty, there was no longer any question as to cause and effect. Ryan's relationship with his father initiated the birth of his alter egos. And then, the inconsolable guilt of having failed to protect his sister, and his self-inflicted responsibility for her death, threw Ryan over the psychological edge. Willow's death, whether suicide or at the hands of Derek Vespers as Ryan suspected, ignited Ryan's alter egos to full-time-status. In the end, neither scenario proved true.

Watching Ryan weep, Abdo acknowledged the breakthrough. Years of suppressed guilt and emotions were rushing to the forefront of Ryan's mind. His guilt over Willow's death could now begin to heal.

PART IV
NEW BEGINNINGS

"Meeting you was fate, becoming your friend was a choice,
But falling in love with you I had no control over."
—Unknown—

CHAPTER 126

August 24, 1968

THE DOORBELL RANG, waking both Rosa and Lucinda Sane. Rosa looked at her alarm clock wondering who could be at her door so early in the morning. She threw on a robe, trying to clear her head. As she looked through the peep-hole, the young man on the other side called out, "Delivery."

"You must have the wrong apartment," Rosa replied. "I'm not expecting any deliveries."

"Are you Lucinda Sane?"

"Lucinda is my daughter, but she's not expecting anything either."

Rosa opened the door with the chain latch still on.

By this time, Lucinda had joined her mother. "What store is this from?" Rosa asked.

Rosa could tell from Lucinda's expression she had no idea what was going on.

Although hesitant, Rosa unlatched the door and signed for the package. It appeared heavy as the delivery man hoisted the box onto the kitchen table.

As the young man began to leave, Lucinda said, "Mama," looking back and forth between the man and the box. Rosa got the message. "Of course, wait a minute, young man, let me get my handbag."

After giving the man a dollar, Rosa and Lucinda stood in silence, staring at the package. Money had been so tight, for so long, they hadn't had anything delivered in years.

"Open it, Mama. Let's see what it is," Lucinda said with a childlike smile on her face.

"You open it my angel. It's addressed to you," Rosa said, her heart experiencing a rare moment of joy.

Lucinda gingerly removed the gift wrapping, wanting to savor the moment. Her heart raced as the store name, *Singer*, was exposed and the picture on the box revealed its contents.

"Look Mama, it's a sewing machine. Who would send me such a wonderful present?" In bold letters, on the box, it read FINAL SALE, NO RETURNS!

"Wait, there's a card."

When Lucinda looked back toward her mother, she saw her sitting on the sofa with tears streaming down her cheeks. "What's wrong, Mama? Don't cry."

Rosa was overwhelmed. This was the first time in a very long while she'd seen her daughter so happy.

"Read the card," Rosa begged, dying to know who had done such a wonderful thing.

Lucinda opened the small envelope. The message read, "Don't give up on your dreams."

There was no signature.

CHAPTER 127

The Writings of Isok
"The Voice Within"

Our father would always say, "There is one important thing you must always remember." Yet, each of us retains a different recollection of what the one thing is.

For the Loner, it is that there is no mind greater than your own. Nurture it at all costs. Mistakes are not acceptable. One single mistake can destroy your life forever.

For the Watcher, it's that you must distinguish your friends from your enemies and never let your enemies out of your sight.

For the Writer, everything has a reason. Record the events of history so that society can learn from its mistakes. We cannot let history repeat itself. From evil, good may yet be derived.

For the Optimist, we never know when something we do may alter the path of another person's life, or the course of history. Something which seems wrong at a given moment may bring a better life to someone's future. Everything has a reason, even though we may never know what the reason is.

For Lazarus, there is nothing more important than family. There are good people in our lives, and bad. It is all of them who make us who we are.

And for me, Isok, well, it's taken all these years, locked in my self-constructed cell, to work my way through the demons I carried. Clarity of thought overtook me. I felt the weight of my guilt, fears and animosity dragging me to my ultimate demise. It appeared there would be no redemption for me.

And then, just as I acknowledged that I had been misguided for so many years, and resolved myself to the fact I would be alone till the very end, there came a voice. I now believe this will be the last entry to my journal.

Isok heard the voice loud and clear. It sounded much like his own, only not angry.

"Isok, do you know who I am? I've waited so very long for you to come to the understanding of your destiny. It has been a long journey, but it is once again time for *us* to be reunited."

"Is that you, Lazarus? It has been a long time, hasn't it?"

THE CRIES OF INNOCENTS

Through the door of torrid emotions which imprisoned Isok, Lazarus approached, arms opened wide.

As they embraced, Isok realized he had never experienced anything so wonderful in all of his existence. He felt replenished with a new life source.

"Come, Isok. You have sacrificed and endured loneliness for too long. We have, unbeknownst to us, passed each other moving in-and-out of isolation many times. We've never truly been apart. We have shared this cell, unaware of each other's presence. We have much to talk about. The others have been awaiting us for what, to them, must seem an eternity. We'll talk on the way."

"Are you angry with me?" Isok asked.

"How can I be angry with you? By now you've realized that you and I are one, neither complete without the other. We must assimilate to again be whole, just as Ryan Cain must assimilate his alter egos, to once again be in harmony and peace with his life. I've missed you, brother. I have listened to your thoughts, but been unable to communicate until now."

"You've been privy to my thoughts and still wish to reconnect?" Isok questioned.

"You are not the evil monster you make yourself out to be. You are too hard on yourself. You had no choice. None of us did. Don't you remember—everything has a purpose. We are those emotions of '*Ryan's being*' created by the circumstances of his life. We are merely players in *his* story. You've played an instrumental role in his and our survival.

"You were created to protect your family, and that's what you did. It was you who formulated Ryan's 'Rules of Engagement' while he was in a coma. None of us would be here today if you hadn't done that. We each served a purpose.

"Dr. Betaré was right when he said, 'you cannot compel a person to do what is not in his nature.' You could no more have killed anyone, than I could have. Emotion without control is chaos. You need to let go of your guilt over Willow's death. Her death was not your fault, or mine, or Ryan's. We all share the pain, but we cannot bring her back. Forgive yourself and join us.

"We must perish from Ryan's real life, so he can once again be whole. I think you will enjoy the resting place he has chosen for us to occupy in his mind. Come Isok. Come with me... is ok!"

Before Lazarus could utter another word, he and Isok became one.

CHAPTER 128

August 26, 1968

ONE QUICK SIREN burst and the squad car pulled up along-side Scoop.

"Hey, aren't you the famous reporter, Scoop Aubrey?"

Scoop bent down to look in the window. "Hey there, Officer Scumaci, are you officially on the Height's beat now?" An opened package of chocolate cupcakes sat on the passenger seat.

"Please, call me Vinnie. And, yes, my permanent transfer papers came in yesterday."

"Congratulations. I feel safer already," Scoop said. They both laughed.

Vinnie tipped his cap. "And congrats to you, on your well-received Shadow Assassin article. I hear you've become quite the celebrity. Word is, just about every paper in the country picked up your story, a day later. How does it feel to be famous? Are you considering any of the job offers you've received?"

"How do you know about the job offers?"

"I'm a police officer, ma'am. It would be unprofessional for me to reveal my sources." They both laughed again.

"If you're not busy this weekend, maybe we could get together," Vinnie suggested. "I could share some of my investigative secrets with you over dinner. It makes for fascinating conversation."

Scoop felt bad. Vinnie was a nice guy, but she graciously declined his offer. "Sorry, I'm seeing someone. I want to see how that works out."

Vinnie looked disappointed. "Anyone I know?"

CHAPTER 129

February 19, 1972

FOR REASONS BEYOND his own understanding, Abdo felt compelled to visit Abraham Lerner each year, on the date of Ryan's awakening. Perhaps, it was his way of appreciating how fortunate Ryan had been.

This year, on the fourth anniversary of his miraculous recovery, Ryan accompanied Abdo. They had developed a fondness for each other, reaching beyond friendship or respect. Perhaps it was inevitable. Abdo had learned everything there was to know about Ryan. In turn, he'd shared a great deal of his own history. Abdo had become the male figure Ryan could look up to, the surrogate father he so desperately needed.

Abdo looked at the pitiful eighty-something-year-old man, wondering what kept him alive. *When will he finally be granted the mercy of death?*

Ryan didn't look upon the living corpse with the same compassion as his mentor. Ryan hadn't disclosed to Abdo everything he'd managed to derive from the quatrains. He had no desire to stir up painful emotions from the past, which would only serve to haunt Abdo's future.

As they stood by Lerner's bedside, Abdo, as he did each year, reiterated the story of the apprehension of the men who had assaulted Lerner. Abdo and Ryan discussed all that had occurred over the past four years, including the parchment with its uncanny accuracy, and their search to unravel its deeper meaning.

After a few minutes Abdo excused himself. He had another patient to visit. As Abdo disappeared from view, Ryan moved to a spot in clear view of Lerner's unblinking eyes. Removing the envelope from his pocket, he unfolded the forty-year-old parchment and held it outstretched for Lerner to see.

Unbeknownst to Ryan, the very same document, entitled 'THE FATE OF CAIN & ABEL," lay indecipherable, obliterated by Erik Jan Hanussen's blood, in the nightstand beside Abraham Lerner's hospice bed. His personal belongings had followed him from facility to facility since the day of his beating.

Lerner's eyes gave him away. Ryan heard the screams emanating from the virtual-corpse's skull. Lasers of hatred shot from the Devil's residence behind the pasty black pupils.

Ryan leaned down placing his mouth to Lerner's ear. "I know who you are, locked inside this shriveled body, and that you can hear me. I am Ryan Lazarus Cain, son of Sandor Cain, also known to you as No. 19."

In Abdo's absence, Ryan read the quatrains to Hitler. As he read, he explained that references to Abel were, in fact, Abe L. (Abraham Lerner) and, in Hebrew, Abel is Hevel, which translates to "nothingness," which is what Hitler exemplified, lying in bed, able to do nothing but listen.

Ryan knew Quatrain II would hold the most interest to the sociopath lying helpless before him, so he read with slow and clear precision. "'It will be a cold day in hell before the downfall of 'the evil one.' This shouldn't be mistaken to mean your downfall would never come. Rather, it refers to the freezing temperatures in Russia which caused your troops to be defeated, and war is hell.

"'Millions will die as 'the Devil's son' outlives the Holocaust survivors.' I think that speaks for itself. Are you enjoying your long life?

"'And dwells in the Land of Nod as able-bodied and clear in mind and thought.' It took me quite a while to figure that one out. *The Land of Nod* is a pun for the biblical purgatory to which Cain was exiled to wander for the remainder of his life after killing his brother Abel. And, of course, *able-bodied*, refers to Abe L.-bodied; and we both know you are clear in mind and thought.

"'Only to pray for the mercy of death which will not come?' Again, I have to assume, you damn well know what that means.

"And finally, Quatrain VI which says, 'When all is said and done, Aryan son will stand victorious over the deathbed of a threat to all of humanity.' Had you been able to read this quatrain, you would have gained confidence believing it referred to you, an Aryan son, standing over the mass graves of the millions of Jews you slaughtered. In actuality, it reads, *A Ryan son, me,* 'will stand over the deathbed of a threat to all of humanity,' *you.*"

Countless emotions ran through Ryan's head as he let all that he had explained sink into Hitler's mind. Then, he proceeded. "If you had read this back when it was written, you might have waited and invaded Russia in the springtime instead of the freezing cold of winter. You might have won the war. Thank God you never had access."

Abdo returned forty-five minutes later to find Ryan sitting in a chair reading a newspaper.

"Hey, Abdo, I don't see anything in the paper about murders or hate crimes today. Do you think, maybe, for one day, all evil in the world has come to a standstill?"

"I doubt it, Ryan. Mankind hasn't reached a stage of evolution where it is capable of a world without evil. But on a brighter note, I bumped into the executor of Mr. Lerner's estate, and I can confirm there are good things on the horizon. After a long battle, the Jewish Federation has been appointed legal guardian of Mr. Lerner's estate. They've been given complete control of his funds, to disperse as they feel necessary, and upon his death, to use as they deem he would have seen fit. I can't imagine anything would make him happier."

Ryan smiled at Abraham Lerner, and turned back to Abdo. "That's great news, I'm sure you're right."

Abdo continued, "The gentleman assured me, Mr. Lerner's money, which totals hundreds of millions of dollars, will be directed to organizations such as the Anti-Defamation League, the Jewish Children's Hospital, and Holocaust awareness programs. His monies will do more for the Jewish community than he ever could have imagined."

After exiting the room, Ryan stopped. "I'll be right back."

Ryan reentered Lerner's room, bent down, and again whispered in Hitler's ear, "Think about it old man. When you die, you'll go down in history as the single greatest contributor ever, of monies designated toward the reaffirmation of the Jewish faith. I wonder if given the choice, you would now choose to live or die."

CHAPTER 130

1975

THE DOORBELL RANG.

"I'll get it, hon," Scoop called out, as she raced to respond. "It's here."

Every year, on August 23rd, a new designer outfit, size 5, arrived at Scoop's doorstep. This year was no exception. The package, like its predecessors, bore no return address. The words on the box read: FINAL SALE, NO RETURNS, written within a heart. Scoop knew exactly where they came from, and each year, she couldn't help but get teary-eyed as she opened her new treasure.

"Look, it's gorgeous. I'll wear it tonight."

Later that evening . . .

"Scoop, come quick." She hurried to her husband's side, on the sofa. "Isn't that...?

"*Shhh*, I want to listen."

There, on the TV screen, was Lucinda Sane, about to be interviewed by a popular fashion magazine reporter.

"Ms. Sane, I'm so delighted you've agreed to join us. For those of our viewers who are not familiar with our guest's clothing designs—you soon will be. This young and modest genius to my right, through the brands of well-known multinational distributors, has been creating clothing worn by fashion conscious girls and women for the past several years. Today, our young entrepreneur is here to announce the formation of her own newly formed company, *Lusane Creations.* Let's have a big round of applause for our guest."

Lucinda blushed. She appeared uncomfortable with the praise.

"She's still the same sweet, unassuming girl I met years ago," Scoop said.

"Sweet and unassuming, yes. The same? I don't think so. You've altered her life, you made a difference." Scoop gave her man a kiss, and turned back to the show.

"Ms. Sane, would you please tell our audience how you got started in the business. I'm certain our viewers would love to know your story."

"My life changed course seven years ago, to the day," Lucinda began, "with a random act of kindness from a total stranger." For a brief moment she remained silent, thinking back on the memory of the sewing machine being delivered. "One person's goodness . . ."

Scoop wiped a tear from her eye as she snuggled closer to her soul mate. "Speaking of life changing events . . ." She gently placed Ryan's hand on her belly. ". . . I've got something wonderful to tell you."

April 19, 1976
Beach Street

INVISIBLE AS THE air they breathe.

And that's just the way they like it, savoring their anonymity. The foursome had matured in many ways. In others, not so much.

"Did you feel that? Something wonderful just happened." the Optimist called out.

"What?" The Loner jumped with excitement. "Let me guess. We're getting new baseball gloves. If I could wish for something that's what it would be. Is that what's happening? Are we getting new gloves? What would you guys wish for?"

Perhaps, a good book, and some peace and quiet, thought the Writer.

"I'd wish for amnesia," said the Watcher.

"Did you just make a joke?" the Writer asked, stunned by the out-of-character event.

"Who'd have thought you'd develop a sense of humor? This is one for the books, and I mean that literally. I've got to write this down."

The Watcher gave the Writer a noogie on top of his head.

"Ouch, cut that out, you doofus."

Bellied over with laughter, the Quad members rolled on the pristine sand.

"Stop fooling around," the Optimist admonished. "Listen. A heartbeat. A new life has begun. I can't believe you guys don't feel it. It's like a whoosh of fresh air sweeping over us. If we're going to wish for something, let's wish for our brother's safe return, so that he too can relish in this miracle thrust upon us."

"Okay, I'm changing my wish," said the Loner. "I wish Lazarus was here."

What a great ending that would make to my story, thought the Writer. "I'm in. Lazarus' return, it is."

"It would bring our lives full circle, wouldn't it?" the Watcher asked with an air of sadness, having long since given up on Lazarus' return. "You don't really think we're ever going to see him again, do you?"

"I do believe the moment is upon us," said the Optimist.

***

Later that evening . . .

As he approached the tunnel's exit, Lazarus stood alone on the tall dune overlooking the frolicking family below. On the sandy beach of Ryan Cain's mind, nestled beneath the silent willows giving way to the soothing sounds of the splashing blue-green waves, the Quad savored the paradise which had become their permanent resting place.

The Loner walked barefoot on the cool shore sands, embracing the sunset's evening breeze. He experienced an internal peace he had never before known as he kept a watchful eye out for any sign of Lazarus' return. The Watcher sipped a cool drink as he relished viewing the lives of his happy brethren. The Writer proofread the final chapter of his emotional novel about man's unending will to survive.

"He's coming, he's coming," shouted the Loner from a distance.

"I'll be damned," conceded the Watcher in disbelief.

"I thought this stuff only happened in story books," said the Writer, laying down his pad and pencil.

The Optimist said nothing. The well-deserved, *I-knew-everything-would-work-out* smile on his face said it all.

Lazarus wiped a tear from his eye as he emerged from the darkness and took his first step, down the dune, toward the Beach Street he once knew and loved. It brought back memories of days long past.

As his brothers raced to embrace him, Lazarus relished the wonder of the moment.

I am Lazarus, and I am finally home.

AUTHOR'S NOTE

Thank you for choosing to read my novel. I hope you enjoyed it.

In today's ever-expanding world of eBooks, referrals and reviews serve as an invaluable asset and, indeed, a necessity to achieving success and recognition. Without these reader-generated tools it is unlikely that a book will ever be exposed to a large audience.

If you have the time, and would be kind enough to post a review: good, bad, or indifferent, on Amazon's site, I would be eternally grateful.

Please feel free to email me directly at: WhytheFly@outlook.com. I would love to hear from you.

Sincerely,

Steven Allen Fleischmann

9529464R00240

Made in the USA
San Bernardino, CA
19 March 2014